Hot British Boyfriend

KRISTY BOYCE

An Imprint of HarperCollins*Publishers*

HarperTeen is an imprint of HarperCollins Publishers.

Hot British Boyfriend
Copyright © 2021 by Kristy Boyce

Library of Congress Control Number: 2020943932
ISBN 978-0-06-302591-2

Typography by Michelle Gengaro
20 21 22 23 24   PC/LSCH   10 9 8 7 6 5 4 3 2 1
❖
First Edition

For Mike and Liam,
my two favorite people in the world

chapter
1

By the end of tonight, I will be Andy Keating's girlfriend.
It's all I can think about as I leap over piles of my dirty clothes
and shimmy past the fairy gardens that fill my window ledge as
"Take on Me" plays for the hundredth time. I land on a discarded
dress—the third I tried on tonight—and go sliding across the lam-
inate wood floor. I'm glad Andy can't see me now . . . but I still do
one more spin as the lead singer from a-ha hits the last high note.
Usually I don't listen to eighties music, but this isn't just another
song. This is *our* song.

Crystal will be here any minute to pick me up. I need to finish my makeup, but it's hard to think of anything but Andy and
me dancing to this song at the smoothie shop. He pulled me
out from behind the counter and spun me across the rainbow-
colored tiles until we had to cling to each other so we didn't
collapse from laughing so hard. That was the moment I knew he
was falling for me. And tonight, at his end-of-summer birthday
party, I know he's going to ask me to be his girlfriend. I'm so
beyond myself with joy and nerves I have to reapply my eyeliner

three times because my hands keep shaking.

Five minutes later I clomp down the stairs in wedge heels. They're higher than what I usually wear, but I'll take the pinched toes. Andy is a basketball god and I'm going to need the extra inches for the first time he kisses me. Shivers go through me and I clutch the banister so I don't somersault into the living room.

"Wow, you look beautiful," Mom says as I appear. She's curled in her favorite chair with a cup of Earl Grey, watching a BBC miniseries.

"Thanks." I smooth my dress. I know this is a backyard party, but there's no way in hell I'm dancing under the stars with Andy in *shorts*.

"You're growing into such an amazing young woman. I hope you have a wonderful time tonight." Her eyes are shining a little too brightly and she looks ready to wrap me in a teary hug.

The doorbell rings and I leap to get it. I find Crystal in the doorway, a panicked look on her face.

"Hey! Are you okay? "

"Ellie, omigod, I need your help."

She steps into our cramped duplex and I take in the living room from her perspective, seeing the dingy wallpaper and stains on the carpet. This is the first time anyone from my new high school has been here. It's not that I'm ashamed. I know how hard Mom has to work to afford this school district. Her promotion and move from Virginia to DC came with a big pay raise, but money goes fast here and we were lucky to find a decent apartment in this area. We've done our best with the space, but all the framed art and houseplants in the world can't disguise the fact that this is nothing like the huge houses my classmates live in.

Crystal grabs my arm and pulls me farther into the living room, then points to her shoes. "They're disintegrating."

"What?"

"*Disintegrating!*"

She lifts her foot so I can see her platform heels. Sure enough, there's a huge chunk missing from the sole.

"These are my favorite shoes! I've had them since the summer before junior year—I thought they were so nice. But they're made of freaking foam! Can you believe it? Foam! I didn't notice until I saw the pieces covering the floor mat of my car." She flicks the shoe and another piece flies off and sails across the living room. It's only then that Crystal sees my mom.

"Oh, uh, sorry about that, Mrs. Nichols." She hobbles across the floor to pick up the chunk.

"No problem," Mom replies with a smirk.

"Come into the kitchen," I say. "Maybe we can, I don't know, glue them back together?"

We sit down at the kitchen table and Crystal kicks off her shoes. I take a look, but she's right: there's no saving them. Bits of foam fall off wherever I touch them.

"Why didn't you go back to your house when you noticed?"

"Traffic was horrible and I knew you were waiting for me. I didn't want us to be late." She shakes her head. "But I can't walk into Andy's wearing these! This is going to be my last party before I leave for my study abroad trip. Do you have any heels I can borrow?"

Ugh, her trip. I hate the reminder that soon she'll be living in another country. She's the only real friend I've made since moving here at the end of my junior year, and I'm not sure what I'll do without her. But then, if I'm dating Andy, I won't need to worry about that. He's friends with everyone.

"No, I'm sorry." I point down at my feet. "These are the only ones I have. Unless you want some silver strappy ones?"

She curls her lip. "No thanks. That sounds like a little much for a backyard party." She eyes my shoes. "Damn, I was really hoping you'd have more like that. Those are *so* cute."

She looks at my shoes the way I look at my mom's famous chocolate cheesecake. I can almost see the drool sliding down her chin. Usually I'd hand them over without hesitation, but I chose these shoes with a specific purpose in mind. I bite my lip. On the other hand, they would look adorable with her romper. And she was really nice when I first arrived at school, inviting me to sit with her at lunch and showing me around. She even helped me get my summer job with her at the smoothie shop.

"Um, I guess you could take mine? I'm only wearing them because"—I lower my voice—"they might give me a few extra inches if Andy and I . . ." My cheeks flush and I stop talking.

Crystal's eyes widen. "Wait, are you telling me you chose those shoes on the off chance that Andy wants to make out with you tonight?" She waggles her eyebrows. "Sounds like you've been having some fun daydreams lately."

I grin. "They're not just daydreams."

She laughs good-naturedly, but I can tell she thinks this is all in my head. And I get that. We haven't worked many shifts together lately, so she doesn't know how much Andy has been coming in. Early on, he'd just get his usual Strawberry Sunrise, give Crystal and me a wink, and leave. But these last few weeks have been different. He's been staying longer and longer at the shop, telling me about his soccer practices and pickup basketball games, teasing me for lip-synching to the loop of eighties songs that play on repeat.

I take a deep breath and tell her about last week, how he pulled me into the middle of the empty shop to dance like we were main characters in a movie montage.

"It was the most romantic thing that's ever happened to me."

She smiles. "That sounds really fun, Ellie."

But it wasn't *fun*. I mean, it was, but it was also swoony and she's not getting it. I think about going on, telling her more about Andy's latest visits, but then I hesitate. I don't want to jinx anything. And it's going to be so entertaining to see her reaction when Andy and I get together.

I bring down a collection of shoes for her and she falls for a pair of pink ballet flats immediately. Crisis averted. I give Mom a peck on the cheek and grab my key from the hook. "I'll see you later."

"Be safe! And tell me everything tomorrow over breakfast."

We hurry out to Crystal's car.

"Are you excited?" she asks as she pulls away from the curb.

"So excited!"

"You better be. Andy's parties are always epic. Just you wait."

She does a little shimmy dance and I do the same, a wave of adrenaline coursing through me. Epic is exactly what I'm hoping for.

A quick glance at Andy's street tells me that this is the biggest party I've ever been to. If kids had parties like this back in Virginia, then I was never invited. Cars line both sides of the road, and we have to park blocks away and hoof it to his house. I'm starting to wish I'd traded my heels after all.

I quicken my pace to compensate for the nerves shooting through my limbs. Small groups of people meander down the sidewalk with us. I recognize most of the others from the end-of-season pep rallies, since a lot of Andy's friends are athletes and cheerleaders, but I don't really know them. Waterford Valley is so ridiculously big that it's hard to keep people straight, especially transferring in at the end of the year. I'm so grateful to have Crystal next to me.

A few guys I recognize from Andy's basketball team wave. "Hey, Crystal!"

She blows them a kiss. Crystal might not be the most popular girl at school—she doesn't do sports or cheer or anything like that—but she's in student government and in a *ton* of clubs, so everyone seems to know her. I'm hoping to follow her lead and get involved this year.

"Omigod, *everyone* is here," I whisper as we walk through Andy's front yard and into the palatial backyard.

This isn't some little shindig with hot dogs and coolers full of melting ice and soft drinks. This is *fancy*. I knew he was rich, but his parents have gone overboard with birthday decorations and elaborate balloon creations throughout the manicured lawn. There are long tables covered in catered food along the patio and a cake that's large enough to feed a hundred people.

I rub my sweaty palms down my dress and pray my queasiness doesn't become full-out sickness. Accessorizing this outfit with puke is *not* the look I'm going for.

"Ooh!" Crystal squeals. "There's Sara!" She waves and rushes over, leaving me alone in the middle of the lawn.

My stomach squeezes and I check my phone for nonexistent texts to give myself something to do. I'd imagined that Crystal would be my guide here—at least until I found Andy—but I don't want to be a complete dork trailing after her all night. Instead, I head toward the drinks table. As I grab a water, a hand falls lightly on my shoulder.

"I see the party's arrived now."

Tingles race up my spine at his voice. Andy. And is it my imagination, or is he standing extra close to me? My heart tugs in my chest as I look up into his gorgeous blue eyes. Every time I see him, he's cuter than the last time. I can't believe I'll be calling him my boyfriend by the end of the night.

Of course he hasn't said anything specific yet—that would ruin the surprise—but I overheard him talking about it at the shop a few days ago. I was in the back, getting more blueberries, when my middle-aged shift manager tried to wait on him.

"Can I help you?"

"Oh, no thanks." Just hearing his voice made me smile. "I don't think I could drink another smoothie this week."

"Um . . . okay. Are you wanting to apply for a job, then? I don't have openings now, but I might next month if you want to take an application."

"No, sorry. I'm just"—he cleared his throat—"uh, waiting for a girl. One of your employees."

She sighed. "I should have known. You're the boyfriend?"

"Not yet. But hopefully soon."

She chuckled softly. "Ah, I remember those days. Just make sure you aren't distracting her while she's on the clock."

"Yes, ma'am."

My cheeks heated and I leaned against the supply shelf to steady myself. Andy wanted to be my *boyfriend*? I couldn't believe it. Sure, I'd thought about it before—probably every straight girl at Waterford Valley had at some point—but I'd never believed it possible until that day. It was all I could think about after that, particularly when I read his text the next evening.

I need you. The party won't be the same without you. And just wait until you see what I have planned. 😉

This had to be the night he told me how he felt.

"Happy birthday." I gesture around us. "This is amazing."

"Thanks. Mom loves doing this kind of stuff, but at least she and Dad are cool about giving us space. They usually only come out when it's time to cut the cake." He nods toward the huge house where his parents must be hiding out.

I smile and swallow hard. It was so much easier to talk to him when I didn't think he liked me. "Thanks for inviting me."

He laughs. "How could I not invite you? You make the best smoothies in a five-state radius. And I'd know—I've done a lot of traveling for basketball."

He smiles and lowers his head so his mouth is only a hair's breadth from my ear. For a second, I'm sure he's going to kiss me right here, in front of all these people. I tilt my head toward him, swaying slightly with the anticipation of it. Then a booming voice calls *"Andy!"* and he pulls away.

He jerks a thumb in the direction of the voice. "I better go or

TJ will just keep yelling at me. So glad you could make it!" He smiles apologetically and jogs away. I take a shaky breath. Whatever Andy's planning to do tonight, he better do it soon. I'm not sure how much more anticipation I can take.

Despite my best efforts, I don't get a chance to talk to him again for the next hour. I stand with Crystal while she and Sara trade details about their family vacations and nibble on the catered spread. I know I should try more to join in, but it's hard. No one else in Crystal's circle has been particularly welcoming. A group of us sat together at lunch, but mostly we talked to Crystal, not each other. It doesn't help that they've all been friends for ages and are in the same clubs and classes. But hopefully senior year will be different. With Andy on my arm and the right extracurriculars, I'll finally fit in.

Instead of talking, I watch Andy. He's constantly surrounded by friends—many of them girls. Jealousy pools in the pit of my stomach as they fawn over him. But when he steps away, his eyes lock on mine and he winks. Immediately I feel better. He sees me. He hasn't forgotten.

"Hey!" Andy yells over the crowd. "People!" Some of us quiet down, but most people aren't paying attention.

"*Shut it!*" TJ bellows.

The yard goes silent and every person turns to look at Andy. I take a step toward him, my nerves ramping up to nuclear levels.

"Remind me to never give TJ a bullhorn," Andy says, and a few people chuckle. "So anyway, thanks, everyone, for coming out to help me celebrate. I promise, the fun is just starting, but there's something I've gotta do first." He turns in my direction. "Something I've been dying to do all night."

Electricity flies through my body, jolting me like a live wire. Oh god. Oh god, oh god, oh *god*.

"I'm happy that everyone turned up for this, but there's one person that I'm especially pumped to have here. She's the most beautiful girl I've ever seen. And she also happens to make the best smoothies in the world."

A few people titter and ohhh. My entire body flares with heat and my hands fly to my mouth.

"I've been wanting to ask her out for a few weeks now, but I knew to get a girl like her I'd have to up my game. I'm probably too late, but I can't imagine her leaving—not when I'm just now realizing how awesome she is. So . . ."

I squint at his comment about me leaving—the only trip I have planned is a long weekend away to my aunt's—but then "Take on Me" comes on and I forget about everything else. Tears prick in the corners of my eyes. He's such a romantic to play our song right now.

I laugh and run to him, burying my head in his chest and wrapping my arms around his waist. He smells *so* good, like lavender laundry detergent. And he feels even better. Damn, I could get used to this.

"Of course I'll go out with you!"

His body tenses and stills. Mine does the same. My ears buzz as I lift my head from where it lies against his heart. His expression is a mixture of shock, confusion . . . and amusement. It's the last one that buries a knife in my chest.

"Uh . . ." He puts his hands on my shoulders and pushes me away from him. "Sorry, I wasn't talking about you."

I can only stare. Obviously he was talking about me. He just said I made the best smoothies in the world. He played our song.

Then realization dawns on me—thick, hot, burning—and I swivel to Crystal. She was standing just behind me when Andy started his speech. She makes smoothies. She knows that song from the shop. She's about to leave for a semester abroad in England.

And she's grinning at him like he just told her she was named prom queen.

Oh. My. God.

I catch her eye just long enough for her to tilt her head and give a shrug—as if she's helpless to resist—before she sprints to him. That's when I notice multiple people have cameras trained on me. Laughter surrounds me. And I run.

"Don't leave now, I'll still take you! At least for tonight!" TJ yells behind me as I push through the crowds toward the backyard gate. His booming voice echoes through the neighborhood.

I sprint faster, urged on by the giggles and pointed fingers. I race through the gate and trip on a stepping stone. I go sprawling in their front yard. My palms and knees burn but there's no time to clean myself up. I stand, kick off my stupid shoes, and run down the sidewalk toward the car. When I see it in the distance, I skid to a halt. *Crystal's* car! Holy hell, how much worse can this night get?

chapter

2

When I wake the next morning, my face is still red and swollen from crying. I can hardly believe last night happened. It's like the worst stress dream—the kind you have the week before the new school year or right before a big test—but I know this isn't a dream. My new dress is crumpled on the floor where I dropped it last night after Mom drove me home. My makeup is still on, if you count the trails of mascara my tears left on my cheeks.

I force myself to sit up and find a glass of ice water on my bedside table. Mom must have already snuck in here this morning. I won't be able to put her questions off forever. But how can I possibly explain why I threw myself at Andy in front of the entire freaking school?

My phone dings and I cringe. I really don't want to see what people are texting me, but I can't *not* know. I grab my phone and find a series of texts from Crystal, starting last night.

You okay?

Where are you? Are you wandering around the neighborhood right now?

I'm leaving. I hope someone was able to give you a ride.

You're clearly pissed, but I didn't know Andy was going to do that. And if the roles were reversed, I'm sure you would say yes. Obviously.

Fresh tears well up and I drop the phone on my bed.

She's not sorry.

Something cracks inside me at the realization. Even after I ran out of the party, even when I buried myself under pillows last night, I thought she'd care about hurting me. I half expected to find an apology text or email or, I don't know, maybe even an apology coffee and doughnut this morning when she returned my shoes. Hadn't we become friends over the past few months? Maybe we weren't the closest friends in the world, but we also weren't at the *make out with my crush while the entire school laughs and points* stage.

I guess I was only her friend as long as I wasn't a roadblock to what she really wanted. And that, clearly, was Andy.

I'm about to bury myself in the blankets again when another text from Crystal dings.

Sorry about the memes and gifs and stuff. People can be assholes.

Dread spreads through my limbs like poison. Oh, please no. With shaking hands, I switch to Instagram.

And there I am, in all my toe-curling, vomit-inducing humiliation. I scroll through my feed and see the video of my social demise at least four times. And the hashtags . . .

#Humiliation
#GladImNotHer
#LetHimFinish
#AsIf

I throw the phone across my bed like it's radioactive. Omigod, it's everywhere. The most embarrassing moment of my life is literally looping in my mind *and* on the internet.

I grab the closest pillow and scream into it.

Any sane person would push their phone down the garbage disposal after that, but I can't help myself. I only make it thirty minutes before I open Snapchat and Twitter and find my face there as well, the posts already raking up tons more likes and comments than any picture I've ever posted. I'm never going to be able to show my face at Waterford again now that I'm Internet Famous. When I flip back to Instagram, there's a new post from Crystal. It's a photo of her and Andy at the party, arms wrapped around each other, wide grins plastered on their faces.

@andy_baller15 really DOES throw the best parties.

I just about puke on my unicorn sheets.

A knock sounds at the door and I shove my phone under my blankets.

"I thought I heard you moving around up here." Mom slips through the door and sits on the corner of my bed. "How are you feeling? I was getting worried."

I self-consciously wipe under my eyes and scramble to sit up. Mom's tilted head and soft voice tell me that she knows exactly the state I'm in.

"Um, you know, tired."

She tilts her head farther. "You were pretty upset last night. Do you want to tell me what happened now?"

Oh, not much, Mom. Just a nuclear bomb destroying any chance I had of being accepted at my new school. It was a normal Saturday.

"Just some high school drama."

She purses her lips. "With Crystal? Is that why she didn't bring you home?"

I play with the blanket to avoid her gaze. "I don't really want to talk about Crystal."

"Okay." She pats my leg. "Whatever happened, I'm sure it'll blow over soon. A new school year always brings new drama."

She slips back out the door and I sink lower into the pillows. I can't even *think* about school. How can I go back? I can already imagine it—people playing the video as I walk down the halls or catcalling me like TJ or reenacting the whole scene for laughs. Senior year is already over and it hasn't even begun.

I don't have the courage to get back online until the next evening. I skim Instagram, hoping that everyone has moved on, but it's just as bad as it was yesterday. Maybe worse since total strangers are making fun of me now. But one post from Crystal catches my eye. It's a selfie of her kissing Andy. My immediate reaction is to stab the photo with something sharp—phone be damned—but then I see the description below the photo.

> Who needs to live in England when I can be at Waterford with @andy_baller15?!

I read it a second time.

Does . . . that mean she's not going on the trip now? Is it possible for her to drop out so close to the beginning of the school year? If Crystal is staying at Waterford, then I'm going to have to see her every day. Her studying abroad was my one solace yesterday—that she'd be gone for the entire semester. What the hell am I going to do now? Another horrifying thought wallops me—I won't just be seeing Crystal in the halls. I'll be seeing her *with* Andy, in their stupid giggling, kissing, honeymoon phase of dating. Pure torture. I squeeze my eyes shut.

Except . . .

My heart jumps in my chest. Wait. That means there's an open spot the study abroad trip. The trip I've been lusting over ever since Crystal told me about it. Granted, it's supposed to be for honors students—and I am *really* not an honors student—but maybe there's still a chance.

A spark of hope lights inside me.

If I can get on this trip, if I can avoid Crystal and Andy and everyone else for a few months, maybe my life won't be a living hell. I can start fresh. And in *England* of all places.

I launch off my bed, where I've been since the party, and sprint down the stairs. "Mom!" I hold my phone up to her.

"What's happening now?"

"I think there might be an opening on that study abroad trip I told you about."

Her eyes widen in delight. No one is a bigger anglophile than my mom. She practically came out of the womb obsessing about Princess Diana and Jane Austen.

"The one Crystal's going on? But it must be too late to join. It's in just a few weeks."

"I'm not sure. It might be, but if there's a possibility . . ."

She nods. "Right. It's definitely worth looking into." She picks up her phone, then puts it back down. Her eyebrows knit together. "Ellie, even if I'm able to get you onto the trip . . ." She heaves a sigh. "It doesn't give me enough time to save for the expense."

My shoulders slump. Of course she can't afford to send me on a trip like this. I was so caught up in the idea that I didn't think about how much it must cost. "Um . . ." I consider for a moment. "What if I threw in my savings?"

"Your car savings?"

A wave of nausea hits me, but I nod. I've had a savings account since I was twelve, but it's only been in the last few years that it really started adding up. With my last paycheck from the summer, I should be close to 2K. I'm not sure that will cover the trip, but it's something. I say as much to Mom.

"Wow. Are you really serious enough about this that you'd give up the possibility of a car? I thought you were dying for your own car."

"If you let me, I'm all in."

She nods slowly before smiling and jumping to her feet.

"All right. Tell me who to call."

My mom is a miracle worker. She's been a flurry of activity over the last three weeks, making phone calls and booking plane tickets. She even persuaded my dad to help cover the extra expenses we weren't able to, despite the fact that they've been divorced since I was two and I haven't seen him in years. I might not have won the friend lottery, but I'm definitely the Mega Millions winner of moms.

And thank god for that because the rest of August has been pure torture. I haven't spoken to a soul from school. Crystal hasn't texted since the morning after the party, and without her it's clear just how alone I am here. It didn't seem that way before because everyone likes Crystal and so I was always surrounded by people. But without her, no one has any interest in hanging out with me.

I might be willing to get over the whole thing if Crystal would apologize, but she clearly has no intention of doing that. It isn't just that she's dating Andy; it's that she forgot about me as soon as he looked at her. . . . She didn't even *try* to stand up to the others. She just let me run away while they laughed.

We worked exactly two shifts together in deathly silence before our manager got the message and scheduled us for different days. But I still had to see Andy both times when he picked her up after those shifts. The first time he didn't look at me. The second time he nodded and said, "What up?"

Like he barely knew me. Like he'd never flirted with me in this very store. Asshole.

But none of that matters now. All that's left is to spend my last night in America with Mom, drinking Earl Grey tea, eating too much of her *Great British Bake Off* galette, and watching *Emma* (the 2009 miniseries, which was still the adaptation of her heart).

"Maybe we should have done a hamburger night?" I say as I sip my second cup of tea. "Or something a bit more American?"

"You've got the rest of your life to eat burgers and barbecue— now is the time to celebrate all things British. Which reminds me, you *are* going to visit Buckingham Palace, aren't you? You never know when the queen might poke her head out."

I roll my eyes and chuckle. "Yes, I added it to my list. But first priority in London is Big Ben."

"Obviously."

"And what I really want is to see the countryside and manor houses. I hope it feels like I'm being transported into one of these movies." I nod at the screen, which makes Mom look as well.

"Oh, this part always makes me cry!" she exclaims as Mr. Knightley confesses his feelings to Emma. "There's nothing better than the look on someone's face when they realize you love them as much as they love you." She puts her hand on her heart and sighs. "Are you sure I can't go to high school in England for a few months? I think I've aged pretty well. And I've been doing lots of yoga."

"Mom." I stand and walk into the kitchen.

"Can't an old lady be jealous? Oh, these men and their *accents*. I'd do a lot of stuff if a man asked me with that voice."

"*Mom!*" I cover my face with my hands. "Is there vodka in your teacup or something?"

She giggles and I focus on adding another few sugar cubes to my tea. She's not completely wrong. It would be hard to resist a British accent. I take a sip and imagine the British boys I might meet on my trip. The thought *is* intriguing. I've been too caught up with Crystal, Andy, and anyone from Waterford posting memes about me to think about boys . . . but what if I could find a British boyfriend while I'm studying abroad? Someone *way* better than Andy. The possibilities spin out in front of me. Dates to romantic castles. Walking through the streets of London hand in hand. Kissing someone who calls me *love*. It could be the thing that redeems me after that horrific party. It could be what makes this semester truly epic.

Forget Andy. I want a hot British boyfriend.

chapter

3

After a seven-hour flight next to a *very* loud snorer and a horrendous immigration line in Heathrow, I've finally made it to my new home away from home. Or, at least, to the driveway.

Far in the distance stands Emberton Manor, looking like something plucked out of a Regency novel and dropped into the real world. I can make out spindles and arches and flying buttresses and way more chimneys than any castle needs. An uncontrollable smile spreads across my face. Mom and I studied photos of this place online, but it's more glorious than any picture we could find. And, somehow, I get to live here for the next four months.

I can't sit still. My legs twitch, my toes tap, and I squeeze my hands into balls. I'm actually *here*. Living in a different country. This. Is. Happening.

"We're almost there, miss," the driver the school sent says in his exquisite British accent.

I leap out of the car as soon as we park in the circular driveway. I follow him through the massive wooden doors and spin in a slow circle, trying to get my bearings. The ceiling high above is painted blue with tiny cherubs lounging on clouds. I'm surrounded by dark wood walls and tapestries of elegantly dressed women sitting next to small white unicorns. Unicorns! It's like a sign from heaven that I'm about to live my best life here. None of it feels real. Maybe I stepped onto a movie set . . . or back into a different time? But when I pull my attention from the surroundings, the driver is still there, waiting patiently.

"It's unfortunate you weren't able to arrive with the rest of your school group earlier today. The staff arranged a welcome breakfast and helped everyone get settled. It was rather grand."

A knot of nerves lodges under my ribs at the reminder that the other students have already arrived. I wish I could have flown over with them, but I was lucky to get a ticket at all. By now they're probably bonding over their class schedules and finding all the secret passageways in the manor. I'm twitchy to get upstairs and meet my roommate in particular. I squeeze my eyes shut. *Please* don't let her be another Crystal. I need someone I can trust. Someone as ready for a new start as I am so we can dive into this adventure together.

The driver walks around the massive foyer as if looking for someone. "Usually Henry is on duty to see to students, but he must be on break. Not sure how long he'll be gone, but if you need help with your bags, we can wait. . . ." He scratches the back of his neck.

"Oh, don't worry about it." He's clearly restless to leave and I don't want to wait around either. "I should be able to handle it. If you can just tell me where to go?"

"Yes, miss." He hands me a key from a gilded table. "Your room is 426. And remember that Mr. Odell will be welcoming all the students in the Long Gallery in about an hour." He tips his hat. "Good luck."

He steps out the door and I'm alone. That irrepressible smile from the car spreads across my face again. I look behind me to make sure no one's watching, drop my bags, and break out into a dance like I'm one of the kids from the Charlie Brown Christmas special.

I'm here. I'm *actually* here!

When I'm out of breath from dancing, I inspect my room key. It's as long as my hand and as heavy as a hardbound book. Room 426. Wait . . . does that mean I'm staying on the *fourth* floor? One look at the staircase tells me I shouldn't have done those high kicks just now.

I search around for the elevator, but it turns out to be as small as a broom closet and actually sways when I step inside. No thank you. Next I try pulling all three bags up the stairs at once to speed up the process, but they might as well be boulders. Soon my legs are shaking and I'm sweating and I haven't even reached the second floor yet.

"*Excuse* me."

I turn to find a guy on the step below me, disorientingly close and clearly annoyed. I've seen him a few times around the halls at Waterford. Light brown skin, thick brows, dark hair and eyes. Dev . . . I think? We weren't in any classes together last year.

"Ellie?" he says, his irritated tone fading when he sees my face. "I didn't know you were on this trip."

I try to hide my surprise that he knows me. Oh, please, let him know me from something other than the video. Or the memes. Or the GIFs.

"I'm the last-minute addition," I mumble.

"*You're* replacing Crystal?" He gives a half laugh. "Huh. I was wondering who it would be."

I cringe at her name, grab the handles of two of my bags, and start pulling. I'm abandoning the third one until I have caffeine and a hell of a lot more sleep.

"Jesus, what do you have in here?" Dev makes a big show of heaving the third bag up one stair, like it's filled with concrete instead of sweaters. "You know they give us the textbooks, right?"

I roll my eyes. "Don't feel obligated to help."

"And leave you to block the entire staircase?"

"I didn't bring *that* much stuff. We are living here for four months, you know."

"That doesn't mean you needed to pack the entire mall." He jerks the bag up more steps, and I flinch as the wheels bang on the wooden stairs. "Good luck fitting this into your dresser upstairs."

I shoot him a glare. I call tell he's amused by this whole luggage ordeal, but I'm too exhausted to see any humor.

"For what it's worth," he continues, "I think you got the better end of the deal on this one. Only an idiot would give up a semester abroad just to make out with her boyfriend."

The memory of the party hits me again. Crystal's beaming smile as she stared at Andy. His hands pushing me away. Everyone's laughter filling my ears so loudly that my eardrums might pop.

I freeze on the top step and Dev slams into my back.

"Oof!"

He knocks me off balance and I fall forward onto the second-floor landing. He collapses in a heap beside me. We both sit up just as one of my bags tips over and tumbles down the stairs, the racket shattering the quiet space. The bag pops open and half my stuff falls out, including Pinky, the unicorn Pillow Pet I've slept with since I was in elementary school.

My cheeks flame at Dev's muffled chuckles and I race down the stairs. "Shut up!"

"I didn't say anything."

"Your laughter is worse." I glare over my shoulder.

"So I *should* say something?"

I shove everything back into the bag and whip around. "Unless the words are *'Can I help you carry that?'* I think silence would be preferable."

He nods and grins so wide he looks like the freaking Grinch.

I jerk the bag up another stair.

chapter
4

After more heaving and hauling, we manage to get all three of my bags up to the third floor. Dev insists on going first this time.

"Huan!" Dev yells down the hall. A boy turns and waves. His black hair is short and spiked and he's wearing a shirt with the letters *KRNFX* on it. No clue what that means, but I'm thrilled to see his welcoming expression.

"Where've you been?" Huan asks, coming toward him. "I thought you got lost."

"Ellie decided to block the stairs with her freighter-sized bags, so I helped her out."

Huan blinks at me before the shine of recognition sparks in his eyes. "Oh, hey."

He cuts a glance at Dev and it's clear Huan has seen the infamous video too. My stomach clenches.

"Uh, how's it going?" he asks as he takes one of my bags and continues up the next set of stairs. "Did you have a good flight?"

I hesitate, but he smiles encouragingly at me and I feel slightly better. Just because people saw what happened at Andy's party doesn't mean they're all going to have a snarky comment.

"I'm so jet-lagged," I reply. "I stayed up watching movies."

Huan nods at Dev. "We did too. Didn't sleep at all. I know we have the same ones at home but it was still awesome. I don't know the last time I watched movies nonstop like that." He chuckles. "But I'm dying now."

"Worth it. We had to live it up while we could," Dev chimes in.

I notice he's perfectly capable of lifting my bag up the steps now. He must have been struggling before just to goad me.

"*That's* your definition of living it up?" I ask.

He shrugs. "Yep. I don't think we're going to have another seven-hour stretch here that doesn't include studying or sleep."

"Huh."

There's a reason why I never talked to Dev or Huan or anyone else on this trip at Waterford. These are the kids vying for a tenth of a point advantage in their GPA and deciding if they want to apply to both Harvard and Yale. I wasn't close to meeting the academic criteria to come here—3.75 GPA minimum and honor roll for the last year—but it turns out that the program director was willing to take an underprepared student as long as it meant more tuition money.

"We better have some free time around here," Huan says to Dev. "If I don't practice every day then I'm never going to get better."

"Practice what?" We finally make it to the fourth floor and I'm so worn out I have to force myself not to lie down on the floral carpet.

"Huan's a part-time rapper," Dev replies with the same Cheshire grin from before.

"I don't *rap*." Huan shoves Dev good-naturedly. "I beatbox."

"What's that?"

Dev groans. "*Annnd* that's all it takes . . ."

Huan loudly clears his throat. Then he starts making music with his mouth. He's not singing—it's more like the beats in the background of a rap song. Some students in the hallway turn, a few smiling like they were expecting it, and he waves and keeps going. My mouth drops into an O. It's the coolest freaking thing I've ever heard.

"Whoa! How do you do that?"

"Practice," Dev explains when Huan doesn't stop. "All. The. Time. It's like walking around with your own unwelcome soundtrack blaring."

Huan stops and someone down the hall claps. "I started when I was young. It helped my anxiety to have something to focus on."

"Well, it's awesome."

"Thanks. So, what room are you in?"

I pull my key from my pocket. "426."

"Do you remember who else was assigned to that room?" Huan asks Dev.

"Sage," he replies immediately. Huan raises his eyebrows.

I don't recognize her name from school, but hopefully she's as excited to be in England as I am. Maybe we can travel around the country together . . . look for British boys . . . It would be terrific to have a wingwoman.

"Thanks for the help," I tell them both. And I swing the door open.

chapter 5

Sage doesn't look over when I walk in. Her back is to me and she's unpacking on the lower bunk . . . that she's already claimed for herself.

"Hello?"

"Oh, hello." She regards me. No smile. I look over my shoulder for help from the boys, but they've already retreated down the hallway.

"So . . . it's Sage, right?"

She nods and focuses on carefully folding her shirts. "Nice to meet you, Ellie."

I stand in the doorway for another moment, nervous to come inside and surprised that she already knows my name. Plus, I'm disappointed because the room looks like . . . a dorm room. There are cheap beds, whitewashed walls, and small desks that probably came from IKEA. Not exactly the castle-like interior found in the common rooms. The only redeeming feature is a large window with a carved window seat.

I drop into the plastic desk chair that's closest to me and watch

Sage as she efficiently pulls out her clothes and hangs them in the closet nearest to her. Weirdly, all her clothes are the same—black or gray, simple, no frills or logos. Even weirder, she's perfectly put together after her long flight. I can't find a wrinkle in her clothes or a crease of shadow on her eyelids. I must look like a disaster in comparison, with my hair pulled back in a messy ponytail and my face oily and sweaty.

"Wow, good job organizing," I tell her, trying for a light tone. "I don't think I'll have the energy to unpack for at least a few days."

"I hope that's not true. I don't like having clutter around me."

Okay.

I try again. "How was your flight? I was talking to some other people and they said they didn't sleep at all. But how could any of us sleep when we knew we'd be here soon!"

"I took a sleeping pill and got a full seven hours." Her eyes narrow like she's sizing me up.

Omigod, this is the person I'm living with for the next four months? In this tiny box of a room? I won't survive. I've never lived in the same room as someone else before. I'm an only child so the closest I got was an occasional sleepover or a few days at camp. And I'm not an orderly person. I'm a why-put-stuff-away-just-to-get-it-out-again kind of person. Piles instead of drawers. My dream of happy roommate bonding fizzles around the edges.

Sage finishes with her clothes and starts on another bag . . . filled entirely with books and notebooks. But not fun books. Not my kind of books. There isn't a travel guide or dog-eared novel in the mix. Instead, she pulls out one thick tome after another. *Cell*

Biology. Principles of Oncology. Advanced Concepts in Population Genetics.

My eyes grow wide. "Are—are those books for our classes?"

That makes her laugh. "No. This is for my research."

"Your research?"

She rolls her shoulders back like she's preparing for a long explanation. "I'm not here for this program. It's fine, but my real interest is in working with Dr. Reese at the University of London. We've been corresponding for the last year about her research, and this program allows me to live in England, continue high school, get college credits, and have time to volunteer in her lab." She shrugs. "It's a perfect fit."

Who the hell *is* this girl? Doesn't she know she's on a fun study abroad trip and not trying to get her PhD? At least she's probably too busy planning out the next four years of her life to pay attention to the latest viral videos.

"What about you?" she asks, much to my chagrin. "What's your interest here?"

Hot British guys with amazing accents? Escaping from high school hell? Finding all the hidey-holes in the manor where fairies could be secretly living?

"Um . . . I liked the idea of getting high school and college credit at the same time."

She raises an eyebrow. "So you're not trying to put an ocean between you and Andy, then?"

I drop my head into my hands. "You've seen that damn video too?"

"Hard to avoid it."

"I guess this'll be my fresh start." I try again for a cheerful tone but my throat tightens and I can barely get the words out. How the hell is this going to be my escape from Waterford and the party when everyone—including *Population Genetics* girl—knows what a fool I made of myself? Suddenly, my jet lag is overwhelming.

I climb up the ladder and flop onto my bunk. I have no sheets, no pillow, and no hope of outrunning my past. I drop my head onto the bare mattress, too tired to care if it's dirty.

chapter

6

Minutes later—or at least it feels like only minutes—Sage shakes me.

"It's time to go downstairs. Mandatory orientation."

My brain is thick from sleep, but I force myself out of bed. I follow her to the Long Gallery, which is an insanely ornate gathering space with crystal chandeliers as wide as a king-size bed and gargoyles staring down at us. I'm surrounded by students from school—there are forty of us here in the high school program—and a few of them are already side-eyeing me. It's probably only a matter of time until they start playing the video here too.

I pretend to study one of the gargoyles rather than make eye contact with anyone. Luckily, the conversations die down once an older man wearing an impeccable tweed suit walks into the room. He climbs a small stage erected in front of the mammoth stone fireplace and claps his hands once.

"Good evening, students. Welcome to Emberton Manor. On behalf of all the faculty and staff members here, let me be the first to say how happy we are to have you."

The man's posh British accent makes it clear he's a *gentleman*. I rub a hand over my oily hair. Maybe I should have taken a shower instead of crumpling onto my bed.

"My name is Mr. Odell. I am the headmaster of Emberton Manor."

I miss the next few sentences because I'm fangirling that there's an actual *headmaster* at the school.

"For the last ten years, Hillsboro University in Virginia has endeavored to make Emberton Manor into one of the finest establishments for study abroad in England. We have restored this historical landmark back to its original grandeur and have brought in world-renowned faculty members. We are so pleased to have fifty of our students from the university here with us for the semester." There's a smattering of applause. "We have also recently expanded our admissions to Waterford Valley High School in order to provide this unique opportunity to the *most* gifted students in that senior class. You should all feel very proud of being accepted into this program."

The faculty who line either side of the stage politely clap for us. Mr. Odell eyes the crowd expectantly and I cringe. More like paid-out-the-nose-to-get-me-here student.

"In addition to your academics," Mr. Odell continues, "you will have the opportunity to attend talks on current issues in the UK, participate in extracurriculars, and experience the delightful traditions England has to offer. We hope that you will take advantage of all this. My suggestion for this weekend is to explore the manor and grounds before classes begin Monday. As you can see, it is a grand estate and there is much to discover. The closest town to the manor is Northampton. During the semester, we will have a van that drives to town during the evenings and weekends. However, let me suggest that you spend most of your time here at the manor focusing on your studies."

Someone nods in my peripheral vision and I turn to find Sage. My shoulders sag.

"I hope everyone has a wonderful semester," Mr. Odell continues. "Next we will have a few words from each of our faculty members. Then I invite everyone to stay for hors d'oeuvres and a chance to chat."

The students get increasingly restless as each teacher introduces themselves. By the time the speeches are done and the platters of appetizers come out, it's like a stampede of mad cows racing for the buffet line. I elbow through to fill my plate, then get out of the way. Everyone's voices echo around the room, creating a cacophony of sound and giving me a headache.

Two girls step in front of me. Again, I don't know their names, though I think I recognize them. The girl with the straight black hair tilts her head and studies me. I grip my plate harder.

"Um, hi?" I say.

She grimaces. "Dammit."

The other girl does a little dance. "Ha-ha, I told you that was her! You owe me twenty pounds."

"You said twenty dollars! Twenty pounds is way more!"

The girl smirks. "You shouldn't take bets you're going to lose."

My stomach drops and I almost let my cherry tomatoes roll onto the tiled floor. They're making bets about me? The noise of the room surges in my ears. I have to get out of here. I take a step back, but the first girl puts her hand out to stop me.

"Wait a minute. Can we get a selfie with you? You'll be my first photo with a celebrity!"

My eyes pop wide and I take another step back. I bump into someone and this time my tomatoes do tumble onto the ground.

"Oh god, I'm sorry!" I kneel to pick them up before someone slips and I'm the star of my second viral video in a month.

"That's why I only eat flat foods at cocktail parties. Much less risk of slippage."

I straighten at the voice. Sage nibbles delicately on a rectangular cracker and cheese. She's perfectly at ease, her short bob of dark hair framing her pale face and accentuating her chandelier earrings.

"Right. Good tip for the future," I mumble.

I look behind me, but the girls are gone. I take a deep breath in relief.

Sage pulls out a folded piece of paper from her pocket. "My class schedule."

"Oh. Uh, cool."

"I have my first class in the Wells room."

"The Wells room?"

I study her schedule more closely. It's handwritten using five different ink colors. Of course.

"For H. G. Wells," Sage replies. "Each of the classrooms is named after a famous British author from the nineteenth century." She pauses. ". . . Because Emberton was built in the nineteenth century. And the original owner dabbled in poetry himself. Didn't you read any of the info in the packet they sent us?"

"I did, yeah . . . I just didn't memorize which classrooms I'd be in."

Sage cocks her head at me as if I've just spoken in Welsh instead of English.

"Did I hear you say Wells?" We turn to find Dev and Huan walking toward us. "Are you talking about anatomy?"

"Yeah." Sage smiles approvingly and Dev's face lights up. "You're taking it too?"

"I am! Er, I mean, we both are," Dev says, gesturing to Huan. "We have British lit after, then chemistry. What about you?"

"Well, we all have British lit since it's required." Sage points down to her perfectly written schedule. "And we'll be in chem together too. Are you both in advanced calculus at the end of the day?"

"I took art history," Dev replies.

"But I have calc." Huan grins. "Looks like we've got identical schedules again this semester, Sage. Let the competition begin."

"I think you've forgotten—there *is* no competition." Sage's face is serene as she says this, but there's a glint in her eye that makes Huan laugh.

I fiddle with my plate of food, feeling even more out of place. "So you're all friends, then?"

They look at each other like they're searching for confirmation.

"I mean, yeah," Huan replies. "We've been in most of the same honors math and science courses since freshman year."

"And we worked together on that biology project last year," Dev says.

"Right. Dev and I are always together, but Sage . . ." He raises his eyebrows at her. "You're too busy for us."

She shrugs. "It's nothing personal. I'm too busy for everyone." She nods at me. "How about you, Ellie? Are you in our classes too?"

I can barely suppress a sarcastic bark of laughter. Uh, no. I did *not* sign up for premed classes. Only one science class means I have an "easy" schedule, but easy will be plenty hard for me.

"It sounds like we'll all be in chemistry and British literature together, but no anatomy or calculus for me. I have social psych in the morning and art history in the afternoon."

"Mm," Sage replies. "Well . . . I'm sure that'll be good too."

I look at the gargoyles again. Maybe they were placed here to give people something to study during awkward conversations.

"I have good news for you." Huan gently elbows me. "Looks like psych is in the Brontë room. Should be very dark and foreboding. A good atmosphere to study the human thought process." He winks and I smile back, grateful.

"Why don't we go explore and find our classrooms?" Dev's gaze lingers on Sage.

I jump at the excuse to get out of this room before more people start asking me for selfies.

Once we're away from the crowds, my mood improves. The rooms are so extravagant that I'm surprised they aren't sectioned off with velvet ropes. There are marble pillars wide enough that I can't get my arms around them and fireplaces I can walk inside and enough sculptures and paintings to fill a museum. Mom would be falling over herself at the decor. I take as many pictures as I can for her.

We end up touring all the classrooms at Sage's insistence, plus we peek at the massive library and an ornate dining room. On the other side of the manor we find a garden conservatory. As soon as I walk in, I relax. It's warmer here and the pleasant smell of freshly dug dirt wafts over me. The last rays of sunlight glow through the glass walls. I feel at home surrounded by plants. We don't have a backyard at our new duplex, but I've filled our patio with ferns and small palm trees. Plus, I have lots of miniature plants and materials on my desk for making fairy gardens.

I wander farther into the conservatory. In the middle of the floor is a sunken pond with a fountain. A few massive koi fish swim in slow circles around the lily pads. I crouch down and stare into the water.

Scuffed shoes walk next to me. I glance up to find Dev.

"This place is pretty crazy, huh?" I gesture to the mini fuchsia trees that line the wall behind him. "I can't believe someone had the money to build this in their private home."

"Actually, it was added in the 1970s as a part of the renovations when they sold the manor to Hillsboro University."

I roll my eyes.

"What?"

"Nothing, I just forget I'm surrounded by people who know the answers to everything."

He shoves his hands into his pockets. I expect him to leave then, but he stares into the palm trees.

I stand up. "Everything okay?"

"Hm? Yeah, sorry, just trying to wrap my head around the fact that I live here now."

"It's a good thing, right?"

"Sure. I mean, it's beautiful."

"*But?*"

"It's a little much." He gestures back toward the rest of the manor. "Like you said, one family used to live in all this space. And own all this stuff. I almost wish they'd give all the art and antiques to a museum so more people could experience them. Think of everyone who will go their whole lives and never see what they've collected here. It doesn't seem fair."

I blink, taken aback by the seriousness of his answer. "Well, if you start feeling too guilty, then remember the alternative. Slugging down the linoleum floors at Waterford. Staring at pee-yellow walls and posters for student government. We're living in a castle. You might as well enjoy it."

"True. All right, I'm going to bed before I fall headfirst into this pond from sleep deprivation. But Huan and I are taking the van to Northampton tomorrow if you want to come."

It takes a second to register that he's inviting me to join them. I hesitate, wondering what it'll be like to spend an entire day with this group. We don't seem to have much in common. But on the other hand, I don't want to explore a foreign city on my own, and at least they aren't teasing me about Andy's party. I smile, my earlier negativity forgotten. Tomorrow I'm going out to explore England!

"And, uh, maybe you could bring Sage?" he adds.

I nod, though I'm curious about how timid he sounds asking that. Could Dev have a crush on Sage? I did notice a few of his lingering glances in her direction. I bet that's the real reason for my invite, but I don't mind. This might be exactly what Sage needs to loosen up while she's here. Things are looking better already.

chapter

7

I can't get my eyes open wide enough as the van takes us into Northampton the next day. As beautiful as the manor is, this is why I came to England. Real British stores! And food! And *boys*! Oh, hell yes.

The van rolls by green fields dotted with white sheep and old stone cottages, before leaving the countryside behind and heading into civilization. The narrow road widens and I have the disorienting feeling of seeing a flipped version of America. So much of it is the same. Asphalt roads, traffic circles, roadside litter. But everything is also the opposite. When we get to the first traffic circle, I almost scream when the van turns left rather than right. I catch Huan's eye and he chuckles.

The outskirts of Northampton only hold touches of the England from my dreams. Mostly it's brick buildings and concrete, but every once in a while there's something charming like a Gothic stone church next to a run-down electronics store. As we drive deeper into the city, the buildings creep higher and turn from brick to honey-colored stone similar to Emberton Manor.

I jump out as soon as the van stops and swing around to take everything in. Even Sage is wide-eyed. We cross the street and find a huge open square surrounded by buildings on all sides. They're squashed together, and none of them have the same roofline or color or windows. It's so wonderfully European.

"What's that?" A girl from Emberton points to rows and rows of stands with red-and-white-striped awnings.

"The Sunday flea market," Sage replies like it's obvious.

"Awesome."

I turn to Sage, Huan, and Dev. "Do you want to go look around?"

"We need fish and chips first." Dev points to a shop with a blindingly yellow door and windows.

We each get a greasy brown bag full of fried fish and fries (er, chips) and my stomach churns with hunger.

"Vinegar and HP Sauce are around the side," the cashier says.

Huan sticks out his tongue in disgust. Dev, however, is already grabbing a bottle. "Best to eat like the locals," he says before dousing everything. I eye the thick brown sauce. No thank you. Brits might have the right idea about tea and scones, but I'll stick to my ketchup any day.

We all squeeze onto a bench and the others start shoveling food into their mouths, but I hesitate. There's no way I can eat this without getting grease all over my hands, my face, maybe even my clothes. I'd never have eaten something like this in front of Andy or Crystal. She always rolled her eyes when I took more than one smoothie sample during a shift. But god, does it smell good.

"If you're not eating that, then I'm taking it." Huan grabs for my bag.

"No." I jerk it back. "I'm eating it. I was just . . . smelling it first."

Dev and Sage launch into a conversation about the city and I take the opportunity to bite into my fish without everyone watching me. Grease and salt and heat burst in my mouth and I forget what I might look like. This is a thousand times better than any fish I've had before.

I hear giggling close by and turn to find the two "selfie" girls from the reception standing on the sidewalk to the right of us. They're pointing at something on their phones. The fish curdles in my stomach. Did they see my greasy face? Omigod, what if they're posting some gross photo of me right now and I find a million new snide comments about me next time I get online?

I hastily wipe my mouth and chin and turn to the others. "Did you see what those girls were doing? They didn't, um, take my picture or anything, did they?"

Dev's eyebrows shoot up. "No. Why would they? You know, one meme doesn't actually make you famous or anything."

I duck my head in embarrassment. "I know that. I don't *want* people taking pictures of me. But last night . . ." I trail off, feeling dumb even explaining it.

"Nicole and Heather are harmless," Huan says. "Though they're a little silly for my taste. Always caught up with whatever the new thing is." He smirks. "Are you the 'new thing'?"

I curl my lip. "I hope not."

"So . . . what happened at that party? I'm sure there's more to that story."

"You all know exactly what happened. Don't pretend you didn't watch the video and laugh at me just like everyone else." I don't know what else to say. I don't want to go over every miserable moment of that party again.

Dev and Huan exchange glances, but Sage only sniffs. "I saw it but I didn't laugh. I was too horrified that Crystal was giving up this trip for that idiot."

"Absolutely. I don't get what everyone sees in the guy," Huan replies. "Yeah, he's good at basketball, but that's because he doesn't care about anything else. He's the most boring kid at our school."

"You don't have to explain it to me," Dev says between mouthfuls. "I can't imagine anyone would throw themselves at him that way unless he gave them a reason to do it. He probably got a high from it. I've known the kid since elementary and he's always been a hemorrhoidal asshole."

I burst out laughing. Huan and Sage join in and we all double over. I've never heard a better descriptor for Andy.

Huan shakes his head and slaps Dev on the back. "Now *that's* a phrase that's meme-worthy."

This flea market alone is worth the ticket price to England. Everywhere the four of us turn, there's some new thing to look at. Locally made goat cheese, every fruit and vegetable grown in England, old CDs and vinyl records, vintage books, perfumed soaps and candles. We've only been up and down the first three rows and I already have a mental list ten items deep of stuff I want to go back and buy.

When we walk past a booth dedicated to Cicely Mary Barker, I almost pee myself with excitement. I'm practically trembling as I touch one of the collectible books. She created these flower fairy drawings that were everything my ten-year-old—okay, fine—my seventeen-year-old self ever wanted. How can you not love adorable girls with wings and petal dresses, sitting inside flowers?

"Did you want to stop?" Dev asks me.

I linger by the notebooks, then shake my head. No need to announce my dorky interests to all of Emberton by parading into classes with school supplies covered in fairies.

Next we stop at a stall where all the merchandise is plastered with the Union Jack flag. I flip through the shirts and Sage and Dev browse the mug collection. Dev's Cheshire grin is back and I can't tell if it's because of the cheap prices or the fact that he and Sage are talking.

I hold up a shirt—*I like my men the way I like my tea. Hot and British.*—to show the group when something in my peripheral vision catches my attention. To my abject horror, two extremely cute guys are staring at me.

Nope, not at me. At the shirt I'm holding.

I hurl the shirt back on the table like it's a flaming pile of poop. My heart beats out of my chest. Oh god, they're making fun of me right now, I know it. *Don't look up*, I tell myself. *Don't do it, idiot.*

I do it.

chapter

8

Okay, they *are* chuckling. But not in a mean way. And then the guy with sand-colored hair—the one who looks like he's stepped off the set of a BBC drama—smiles at me. My heart stops. A drop-dead gorgeous guy *smiled* at me. Now that's something to tell the grandkids about. Wait, could they be *our* grandkids? I shake my head. I'm getting ahead of myself.

I turn before they somehow realize the insane thoughts running through my head. When I glance back up, they've already disappeared into the crowd. My shoulders slump. Maybe if I hadn't been holding that stupid shirt they'd have come over and introduced themselves. Probably not, but it's a nice thought.

Huan follows my gaze. "Do you think they go to our school?"

I jump. I didn't know anyone else had seen them. "They aren't American," I say in a quiet voice.

I wasn't close enough to hear them speak, but I can tell. There's just something about them. A level of sophistication that leaves me feeling like a fanny-pack-wearing, white-tennis-shoe-sporting American. Definitely not in their league.

The rest of the group is still engrossed in their shopping, so I take the opportunity to head back over to the fairy booth for a few minutes. It's even better than I thought originally. They have books, posters, calendars, art prints—and I want it all. I flip through the prints before spotting a table of small fairy figurines. I scurry over and reach for one as another hand snakes out for the same box. Our hands touch and I pull back, looking up.

"Excuse me."

Oh. My. God. It's him. It's gorgeous sandy-haired British boy. And his accent is so beautiful that I can't move.

He cocks his head at me. "I know you. You're the girl who likes her . . . *tea* hot, isn't it?"

My cheeks flare with heat. "I . . . no. I mean, I do like my tea hot, but I don't like—I mean . . ." I shake my head. "It was just a stupid shirt."

He throws his head back and laughs, and I find myself laughing with him.

"It's not stupid. I quite like that shirt." He lifts the box he's still holding. "I didn't mean to steal this from you. Did you want this one?"

"No, it's okay. I was only looking."

Eek, is this really happening? This feels like a dream. I pick up another box at random to calm myself, but peek at him out of the corner of my eye. Is it possible that I found a ridiculously handsome British guy who also knows about Cicely Mary Barker? Can life be that perfect?

He turns the box over, inspecting it. "You're sure? My little sister would probably love this."

My stomach drops. Okay, so not *quite* that perfect.

"Or is this one better?" he asks, picking up a second box. "I think I may need some assistance. You see, I wouldn't want to choose the wrong flower. My sister is terribly picky."

He has a teasing smile that I can't help but return. I take the fairy dressed in white petals and holding the daisy. "This one is clearly superior."

He chuckles. "Clearly."

In the walkway, two young girls squeal and race into the stall. "Mummy, hurry, look at these!"

"They certainly know who they're marketing to," the guy comments with a slight eye roll. "Who are you buying for? Do you have an excitable little sister too?"

I fidget with the box still in my hands. "Oh no . . . definitely not. I'm an only child. I was browsing. You know, taking in the sights."

"Yes. As am I." He steps closer and my heart flutters. "I'm Will."

What's my name again?

"I'm, uh, El—" My throat closes and I have to swallow before I can speak.

"Elle?" He says it slowly, like he's turning it around in his mouth. "That's a pretty name."

"Oh, um, thank you," I say, blushing. Technically my name *is* Elle, but no one's ever called me that. I've been trying to get people to call me Elle forever, but it's always been Ellie—which sounds like I'm still wearing diapers—or Eleanor—which sounds like I need an adult diaper. Elle sounds so sophisticated when he says it.

Like I'm not a little girl anymore.

The other guy from before walks up and Will gestures to him. "This is my best mate, Frank."

Frank has on tight red jeans and a loose T-shirt with an open neck that shows his collarbones. His blond hair is curly and flips in weird ways on the top of his head.

"Are you from around here, Elle?" Will asks, but the upturn at the corner of his mouth tells me that he already knows the answer.

"Um, Emberton Manor. I mean, I'm a student there. I'm from America."

"Naturally. Well, it's very nice to meet you. How are you liking England?"

"I'm liking it a lot right now," I blurt. And immediately want to crawl under the table.

"Have you had a chance to walk around much?" he asks, seemingly oblivious to my embarrassment. "I'd be happy to show you if you'd like. You know, give you the local touch."

I nod way too enthusiastically. Will quickly pays for the fairy and follows me to the stall where my group lingers. They stare at us.

"Hey, guys," I say. "This is Will and Frank. They're going to show me around the market. I'll meet up with you in a bit, okay?"

"But you haven't introduced us to your friends yet," Frank interrupts. "I'd love to meet them."

"Oh, right. Sorry. This is Sage, Dev, and Huan," I say, pointing to each in turn. Frank winks when I point to Huan and Huan's cheeks go as red as mine must be. Realization dawns on me. It looks like I'm not the only one who likes my British men as hot as my tea.

I'm floating as I walk away at Will's side. Whose life is this? Not mine. Then I remember I have to somehow hold a conversation with him and drop back to the ground.

"Will, I wasn't finished at the Barn," Frank says.

"You never are."

"The Barn?" I ask.

"The Vinyl Barn." Will points to the booth catty-corner to us. "Frank is trying to buy every vinyl record in existence. He thinks he's *very* cool."

"I am very cool," he replies with a laugh.

Will studies me. "What kind of music do you listen to, Elle?"

The intensity of his gaze tells me this isn't just a casual question. There's a "right" answer—but I have no idea what it is. I grasp for a band he might like, but nothing comes to mind. I mostly listen to oldies and pop music and I doubt Selena Gomez is at the top of his list. Oh Lord. I blurt something out.

"The Beatles."

Will and Frank exchange a look. *Dammit*. My stomach sinks.

"Mmm," Will replies. "Yeah, I don't mind some of their later stuff. The druggy stuff."

Not exactly a ringing endorsement. But then I remember a band Crystal liked and blurt it out. "And The 1975."

Will nods and I exhale. I passed the test.

"Me too," he says. "They can be melancholy, but in a meta kind of way, you know?"

"Mmm." I have no idea what he means. "Definitely."

The moment we get to the booth, they both start flipping

through racks of records. I take the chance to study Will. God, he's beautiful. Maybe he's an athlete? He's very tan and fit. It's easy to tell because of the way his navy pants cling to him. I could spend all day staring at him.

"So, what subject are you studying at university?" Will says without looking up from the records.

My eyes go wide. He thinks I'm a college student. Of course he does. Emberton is owned by an American university and these guys are clearly not in high school. I think of correcting him, but once again I leave it. I might as well be considered a college student while I'm in England—I'm taking classes with college students and professors. And I don't want them exchanging more knowing looks. Or walking away.

"Psychology," I say, thinking of my first scheduled class. "But, uh, I've just started so I don't know much about it yet."

"Brilliant. You can psychoanalyze me."

Yes, please. "Are you in school around here?"

His expression darkens. "No. I'm working right now."

I want to ask more but think better of it. Instead, I flip through records with them. Do people actually listen to these things nowadays? Wouldn't the sound quality suck? Whatever, it doesn't matter. I've only been in the country for two days and I've managed to befriend gorgeous British boys. I'll worry about everything else later.

While they browse, I try to memorize band names in case Will asks me more questions. Frank keeps holding up records like they're trophies and high-fiving Will. I honestly don't even recognize these bands. The Stone Roses? The Fratellis? But I do notice that Frank seems partial to rap. Maybe he likes beatboxing too?

My group catches my eye as they stroll by. Huan waggles his eyebrows at me and Sage watches Will disapprovingly. Dev mouths, *Having fun?* I nod and Will notices.

"Did you want to go back to your friends?"

"No."

"Good, because I'm not ready to let you go yet." He turns to Frank. "We'll meet up with you." Frank waves us off.

People turn as we walk past. Vendors tip their hats in Will's direction. Girls actively glare at me, which is awesome. I was completely invisible when I walked into this market—just another shopper—but now I'm *someone*. I've been so busy hiding from everyone since the party, and it's a welcome change to want to be seen again.

The only problem is that I'm going to have to make words with my mouth if I want to keep his interest. "So, um, how long have you lived here?"

"Oh, I don't live here." He laughs. "I live in London. I'm only in Northampton until my father sorts himself and lets me back home."

"You two . . . fought?" I'm not sure I have a good enough grasp on British lingo to follow his meaning.

"He was upset about my A levels. He wanted me to attend Oxford and my scores weren't up for it." He kicks a rock. "He's more worried about impressing everyone else than about what I want to do with my life."

"So why does he want you to live in Northampton?"

"I'm working at his estate agents' office here until I can *prove my maturity*. He says the job will wake me up to life, but really he just wants me out of London. Too many distractions."

I'm surprised by his bitter tone. Northampton seems like an ideal place to live, but what do I know? I'm sure London must be way more glamorous in comparison. I search around for a better conversation topic, despite the fact that he's even cuter when he's grumpy.

"Well, at least you have friends here. Frank seems really nice. Do you work together?"

"No, he doesn't give a toss about being an estate agent. He's taking a gap year to be a production apprentice with the BBC down in London. He wants to work in radio."

"Whoa, that's cool."

His shoulders release. "He's the *best*. Most of my London mates would never come out here, but he says he likes the calmer pace."

"I think it's amazing here."

He inspects me, smiling. "So, you're a real, red-blooded American? How many cowboy hats do you own? Do you have an American flag hanging in every room of your house?" I start to argue, but he interrupts me. "No, more importantly—do you take the flags with you when you eat your daily McDonald's?"

I laugh. "What?! You must not have met very many Americans before."

"Certainly none as beautiful as you."

Oh wow, he's too charming for his own good.

We continue walking—or soaring, in my case—through the

stalls. Will tells me about one of the houses he's helping to sell and I tell him all about Emberton. He's heard of the manor, but never been inside, so I give him the full rundown of its grandeur. We browse as we talk, picking up items and looking through racks of clothing.

"Are you all right for a moment?" he asks when I pause at a booth to smell their homemade candles. "There's something I need to go get."

I put down the candle. "I can go with you."

"No, take your time."

He hurries away before I can stop him. I squint at his back, wondering why he didn't want me to come. Did I say something dumb without realizing? Was I boring him? I hope this isn't an excuse to get away from me.

I turn back to the candles and pretend to inspect each one, nerves making my palms sweat as I wait. A few minutes later something white waves in my peripheral vision. I turn to see Will with a bouquet of white daisies wrapped in brown paper. He holds them out.

"For you." He closes the distance between us. "I wanted to surprise you. I thought you deserved them since you found that daisy fairy for me. I hope you like them."

"Oh!" I squeeze them so tight I might accidentally snap the stems. "Wow, I love them. That's so sweet of you."

We keep walking and I can't stop thinking of Mom and how thrilled she'll be to hear about this entire day. She'll want to know everything about the city, the flea market, and Will. Plus, after boycotting Instagram and every other app for the last few weeks, it would be pretty amazing to have something good to post. So I suck up all the courage I have and ask him, "Could we get a photo together? You're the first British friend I've made here."

"You consider me a friend, then?" he asks, smiling. "Good. I need more friends." He leans close so that our faces are only inches apart. "Smile!"

Ah, sweet, sweet redemption. I'm plastering this sucker all *over* the internet.

"Oi!" We turn to find Frank coming toward us. "I'm bored."

Will purses his lips. I try to act natural and not like my heart is sinking at the idea of him leaving. "It's fine," I say. "I should find my friends anyway."

"I could drive you back to Emberton if you're ready."

My pulse quickens. "Do you mind?"

"Certainly not. What kind of gentleman would I be if I abandoned you here?" His hand grazes my arm and my skin tingles where he touched me.

We find Sage and Huan at a used-book booth. Sage is so engrossed she doesn't notice us, while Huan is busy on his phone. Dev is nowhere to be seen.

"Hey, guys," I say.

"Finally!" Huan exclaims without looking up. "It's impossible to get Sage to leave and I don't know where Dev went to. Have you seen him?"

"Right here." Dev walks into the booth, quickly shoving a paper into his pocket.

"So . . ." I'm suddenly nervous. "I think I'm going to head back to Emberton now."

"Weren't you listening before?" Dev asks. "The van doesn't come until four p.m. We still have time to see the guildhall before we go back."

"Oh, well . . ." I glance at Will. "Um, Will's going to drive me back."

They snap to attention at that.

"I don't think that's a good idea," Sage says.

"She'll be perfectly safe," Will replies. "I don't have room for everyone, but I have enough space for one more. Maybe you'd like to accompany us?" He smiles mischievously at Sage. I might be jealous if it weren't for her palpable disinterest.

"I'll go," Dev blurts.

I take a step closer to him. "That's *really* not necessary."

His gaze shifts between Sage and Will, looking wary. "Sure it is. That way, you know, Sage has more time here to look around."

"Then you stay with Sage," I whisper. "I'll be fine."

He rolls his eyes. "Having a British accent doesn't preclude someone from being an ax murderer. Didn't you ever watch *Luther*?"

He strides over to Will and Frank, and I'm pretty sure they heard that last comment, judging by their concerned glances. I huff in annoyance and follow along.

We leave the market square and walk another few blocks to get to the parking lot. Around us are European cars with weird yellow license plates. They all look pretty normal except for the one Will is walking toward. I don't know crap about cars, but even I know the car in front of us is *nice*.

Dev does a stutter step when he sees the Jaguar figurine on the hood.

"Ready?" Will asks me.

I've never been more ready for anything in my life.

The drive is incredible. Warm air whips at my face and hair through the open window. Every time another car zooms past on the wrong side I freak out and lean toward Will, then crazy-laugh once it's passed. Spending my car fund on this trip is already *well* worth it.

Dev leans forward between the two front seats. "Looks like you're having a good time up there, Ellie."

"Ellie?" Will looks over at me. "Do you go by Ellie?"

"No. It's Elle. It's what I prefer. He's being dumb." I stare at Dev, willing him not to rat me out.

Dev's mouth quirks up in a smile. "Yep. That's me. Always being dumb."

"You know," Frank says from the back, "Will doesn't care for his given name either."

"Oh, sod off, Frank."

"What is it?"

"His mother insisted on naming him Willoughby." Frank tries to muffle a chuckle.

"After the character in *Sense and Sensibility*?" I ask.

Will glares at the car in front of us. "I hate that woman's bloody books. My whole life people won't stop talking to me about them."

Good to know. I guess I won't be convincing him to take me on any of the Jane Austen tours Mom and I researched.

Will turns onto the long dirt drive that leads back to Emberton Manor. It's good he knows his way around since I'm completely clueless. The car bounces over the bumpy road and kicks dirt into the air. Emberton looks magnificent in the distance, but I don't feel the same excitement I did when I arrived. How am I ever going to see Will again if I'm here every day?

Will must be thinking the same thing because he slows and leans toward me. "Today was fun," he whispers.

"It was." He smells divine, like lemon and thyme. A thousand times better than Andy. I want to bury my nose in his shirt.

"I'd like to see you again, Elle."

"Me too."

"I'm having some friends over to my house next weekend. They'll mostly be getting pissed, but you'll know all about that from university."

I blink, not 100 percent sure what he's saying. Behind me, Dev makes a choking sound.

"Um, you mean a party?" I ask. When he nods, I nod with him. "Yes. Wow, that would be . . . amazing."

"So you'll come?" His face brightens. "Can I pick you up around seven next Saturday?"

"Won't you have schoolwork, Elle?" Dev asks pointedly.

I glare at him. "No. I should be fine. Seven sounds perfect."

"You're welcome to come too," Will says to Dev. "And bring your friends."

Frank sits up at that.

Will rockets down the circular drive quicker than he should

and leaves a huge trail of dust in the car's wake. There are students milling around the grounds and they stop and turn. I cringe, a knee-jerk reaction, but shake it off. Today, at least, I have nothing to be embarrassed about. In fact, I bet every girl at Emberton wishes she could switch places with me right now.

I open the car door to step out and Will catches my hand. He pulls me close enough that I can smell the lemon tang of his cologne again. "I don't even know your last name."

"Nichols." I can barely speak, he's so close.

"Will Chapman."

He doesn't pull away and I'm physically incapable of doing so. We sit there until Dev pushes on the back of my seat, shattering the moment.

"Let's go, *Elle*."

I shoot another glare at Dev before exchanging phone numbers with Will and saying goodbye. When he drives away, leaving us in a cloud of dust, I wave so big that I must look like a groupie outside a celebrity's hotel. I only stop when the car is completely out of sight. Dev gapes at me like I'm the biggest idiot he's ever met.

"Well," he says, "you didn't lie about your last name. That's something at least."

chapter 9

Monday morning comes too soon. Sage is up at six a.m. *Humming.* I cover my face with Pinky and groan. All I want to do is stay in bed for another five hours, but her off-key version of Radiohead's "Creep" makes that difficult. Finally I pull out my phone. Mom wrote me back a long email with way too many "squees!!" for a forty-year-old woman. She's definitely beside herself with how handsome Will is. And she's not the only one. There are a dozen comments from girls at Waterford composed of heart-eye emojis and complaints about missing out on all the fun in England. That's a welcome change.

Every time I relive that hour with Will at the flea market, I'm filled with a thrill of joy . . . followed by a jolt of fear. He was so charming and *so* cute. How the hell am I going to hold his interest at the party this weekend when I couldn't even hold Andy's?

"Hey."

I yelp and jump back. Sage stands at my bedside, her face level with my bunk.

"You better get up now if you still plan on showering and

eating breakfast. Otherwise you won't get to class early and you'll have to sit in the back row."

I grin and lie back down. That sounds perfect to me.

After a quick breakfast croissant and Nutella (I've decided I'm eating Nutella every day in England), I slide into my seat for my first class. Unfortunately I don't know anyone else in psych. About half the class seems to be college students who have no interest in us, and the other Waterford Valley students are already chatting with friends. I'm grateful to Dev for inviting me to Northampton yesterday. I'm getting the impression that most students here aren't looking to make new friends.

Our professor walks in and the class falls quiet.

"Good morning, everyone, and welcome to Emberton Manor! Look at this beautiful room we've been given for the semester." She gestures around and the rest of us follow her hands. The room is the antithesis of Waterford Valley.

"I'm Dr. Stevenson. Let's go around for introductions and then we'll begin."

One by one, each person says their name, where they're from, whether they are in high school or college, and what they're most looking forward to experiencing in England. Since I can't exactly say *making out with a British guy*, I mention visiting Big Ben in London. Dr. Stevenson nods encouragingly and makes little jokes as the introductions go on. At least she doesn't seem like the scary college professors I was expecting.

When everyone is finished, she smiles and pulls out a stack of papers from her bag.

"Okay, I want to hit the ground running so we can move quickly through the introductory information. I'm assuming you all read chapters one and two prior to class today as instructed on the syllabus?"

Wait, what? I glance left and right, hoping to see wild eyes and confused expressions, but the other students either look resigned, bored, or anxious as they flip through . . . are those *notes*? How do they have notes? This is our first day of class!

"We'll have reading quizzes throughout the semester to assess your level of understanding. That way I can tailor our discussions to any material that was confusing."

Dr. Stevenson hands the quiz to the front row.

"Everything off your desk." She nods at me and I shove my stuff in my bag before I'm sent to the dungeon or whatever they use for detention around here. I take a quiz from the person to my left and skim the first few questions.

What are the two elements that a researcher must include in order to have a true experiment?

Which correlation shows a stronger predictive relationship between two variables: $r = -.87$ or $r = .86$?

Which of the following best illustrates the theme of "power of the situation"?

Dr. Stevenson paces through the class, pretending to be kind and normal, but I can see through her pleasant facade now. She's the devil dressed in an ill-fitting blazer.

Vocabulary, dates, and assignment details are pouring from every orifice of my body when I stagger back to my room after my last class of the day. To my surprise, Sage isn't studying. She slings a small bag over her shoulder and heads for the door.

"Where are you going?"

She pauses. "I'm heading to Northampton for the afternoon."

Hope swells in me. Sage blowing off our first afternoon of studying to hang out in the city? Maybe I was wrong about her. I drop my bag and step closer, an eager look on my face.

"Uh, did you want to come?"

"If you don't mind. I could really use the break." I grab my wallet. "Do you already have plans?" My thoughts trail to shopping, dinner . . .

"I want to buy more school supplies."

Of course she does.

Sage and I board the van and she immediately pulls out a planner as big as her lap and flips to this week. She starts jotting down due dates for each class in different-colored pens. Her cursive is perfect. Maybe she does calligraphy on the side.

Usually I'd be put off by her ignoring me, but after an entire day of lectures, I need the silence. We're almost to Northampton when she finally sits back, looking as contented as a fat cat after a bowl of milk.

"Impressive," I say.

"More like required. Between classes and my research in London, I need to organize every hour in the day or I'll go crazy." She looks me up and down. "Do you have a planner, Ellie?"

"Well . . . I was waiting to, uh, get something from England."

"Oh, I can help you pick one out!"

I laugh at her sudden enthusiasm. "You really love school, huh?"

"I don't always love it. But I take it seriously, if that's what you mean. It's the ticket to my future."

Of course school is Sage's ticket. She'll probably get into any college she wants, unlike me. I'm not sure I'm destined for college at all. It's not that I'm a horrible student. I'm not flunking out or anything. I've just never done well enough in school to really care about it. I've rarely made the merit roll over the years and I've never been on the honor roll. Plus, it's hard to be motivated when I don't have a career in mind.

"I just want to soak in every minute of England."

"I do too." Sage puts her forehead to the window. "But this trip isn't only about me. I promised my mom that big things would happen if she let me come on this trip. I can't let her down."

"That sounds like a lot of pressure."

"Well, not all of us can treat this like a vacation."

I flinch. I don't want to argue with her, but I have no interest in spending this entire semester locked inside a room studying. This is a once-in-a-lifetime chance to live in another country and *forget* about regular life, not dive deeper into it. Maybe, if I start small, I can get Sage to see that too.

The van stops and I follow her into an office supply store. She rolls her shoulders back. "Let's do this."

It turns out shopping for school supplies is actually fun with someone like Sage to show you the ropes. I already knew about the basics—yellow highlighters and sharply pointed pencils—but I had no idea such a range of products were available to help me manage my life. I find a desk organizer set covered in a pattern of ferns and pick out color-coordinating pens, notebooks, and Post-its. Sage picks out a planner for me that's so detailed I can schedule my studying down to the half hour. The thought makes me break out in a cold sweat, but then she shows me how I can give myself a rainbow sticker every time I finish one of my daily goals. I end up buying five extra sticker packs. I might not enjoy studying, but I do love crafts.

By the time we're finished shopping, we're laden down with bags and smiling. Everything here is just different enough to make the most mundane shopping trip more exciting.

"Do you want to grab a coffee before we go back?" I ask. I'm nervous Sage will say no, but she nods enthusiastically.

"*Yes.* I need more caffeine or I'm not going to make it to dinner."

We duck into an adorable little coffee shop, grab coffees and scones for good measure, then wander farther down the street. It's fun to take in the city with her. We get a kick out of how many barbershops line this section of the road—at least three—and a sketchy-looking restaurant called American Pizza & Fish Bar.

We exchange a glance.

"Could be interesting . . . ," I say, and raise my eyebrows.

She laughs. "No thanks. I'm all filled up from that scone." She pats her stomach.

I point to a garden shop next door.

"Do you mind?"

She shrugs and I push open the door. While she's distracted looking at the bouquets in the front of the store, I walk deeper into the back and find a small section dedicated to fairy gardening. Different types of moss, decorative stones, hot glue guns, and tiny wooden birdhouses dot the shelves, along with tons of fairy figurines. I can't wipe the grin off my face. It would be so fun to work on a fairy garden while I'm here, though I doubt I could find any place private enough to do that.

"What's all this?"

I jump. "Oh . . . this is stuff to make fairy gardens. I think."

She eyes me and then picks up one of the birdhouses to inspect it.

Nerves work up my spine. My fairy gardens aren't something I announce to others anymore. I learned that the hard way during my sophomore year back in Virginia. My old friend Laura and I had always done fun stuff like this growing up. We'd spent years making up stories about fairies and unicorns and gnomes that lived in the bases of trees. We'd even started our very own fairy club together, complete with delicate flower crowns, wings, and elaborate fairy gardens. Every time we got allowance money, we'd beg one of our moms to take us to the craft store so we could choose a new figurine to add to the gardens.

As we got older, we dropped the wings, but I stayed loyal to the gardens. I didn't see anything wrong with them . . . until I asked Laura and a few girls from her lacrosse team to spend the night. Their eyes went wide when they saw the gardens spread out across my bedroom.

"Are those . . . do you play with *fairies*?" one had asked.

Laura looked horrified. "You still have this stuff?"

I glanced between her and the others, who were smirking and starting to giggle. "Yeah . . ."

"Jesus, Ellie, what are you—eight or something? No wonder no one wants to date you."

That had made the girls crack up. Laura didn't hang out with me much after that. I ate lunch with some girls from my French class and never brought up my hobbies again.

"Do you like to make this kind of stuff?" Sage asks.

I immediately shake my head. "No. I mean, I used to. But it's for kids."

"This isn't a children's store," she says with a frown. "You should get some"—she points a finger at me—"as long as it doesn't make the room messy."

"Oh . . . I don't know."

"Ellie, you're not fooling anyone. I can see you pining for it."

She takes my school supply bags so I have two hands. The nerves that had been building in me fizzle away. Sage doesn't seem the least bit judgmental about this. In fact, she looks pretty intrigued. Smiling, I pick up a few supplies, including a bag of iridescent blue stones to make little streams in the gardens. I take it all up to the register, stopping twice to pick up more houseplants to use in the gardens. The woman at the cash register hands me a flyer with my purchases.

"Thought you might want to pop by for this. We've got some

products coming in for the fairy gardens and we're doing a program at the local park to demonstrate the new techniques."

I skim the advertisement. It's clearly a program created with children in mind, but all ages are welcome. And it's on a Wednesday afternoon. If I hurry after my last class, I should be able to make it to Northampton in time. I pocket the paper, grateful for something else to look forward to.

Back in the van, our purchases take up two seats. I peek into one of the garden bags, already imagining what type of fairy garden I could create for our window, while Sage rummages through the school supplies.

"Thanks for letting me tag along," I say quietly to her back. "I know this probably wasn't what you had in mind when you decided to go to Northampton today."

"No, it wasn't." She pulls out my new planner with a flourish and hands it to me. "It was much better."

Warmth tingles through my chest. "Yeah, it was."

"And we haven't even gotten started yet. Just wait until we transfer all your due dates in here. We'll get to use the entire rainbow of Sharpies!"

This morning I would have rolled my eyes at that, but now it actually sounds pretty fun.

chapter

10

"Can you stand still for two seconds?" Dev says. "You're making me jumpy and I don't even care about this party."

I roll my eyes. I can't help it if my nerves are out of control—I've been waiting all week for Will's party. This is the first one I've gone to since Andy's and I'm desperate for it to go well. Luckily, Will's arrival saves me from arguing. Like last time, he pulls into the circular driveway so quickly that gravel shoots out from under the tires like tiny bullets.

I cover my face, hoping that nothing gets on my outfit. It took me an hour to decide between something fancy—*am I trying too hard?*—and casual—*do I come across like I don't care?*—before finally settling on a skirt and cropped sweater. But one glance at Will tells me there was no point trying to fit in with him.

He's perfection incarnate. No one at Waterford could pull off the combo of a tight navy shirt and a blue linen blazer without looking like they were headed to church or homecoming, but Will makes it look totally normal. I sneak a glance at Dev and Huan, whose biggest fashion achievements are putting on clean T-shirts. No one's going to need to guess who the Americans are.

"Elle, you look wonderful. I'm so glad you could come."

I shove my hands in the pockets of my skirt to hide my shaking. Elle. *Right*, he calls me Elle.

"And good to see you blokes as well. You both look like you could use some fun." He motions them to the back seats, clearly saving the passenger seat for me.

We pile in and Will takes off down the driveway so fast I'm sure a grounds keeper will jump out of the bushes and race after the car.

"Where's your other friend? From the flea market?"

"Sage is in London," Dev replies.

"She goes there every Friday to work on a research project," Huan adds.

"Bloody hell, you all do take this seriously."

"Well, this isn't a vacation for us," Dev says. "We're here to work."

The comment reminds me of Sage. They really would be cute together.

"All of you?" Will quirks his eyebrow at me.

"Not all of us. I want to experience the culture too."

"Good! And I'd be more than happy to help you enjoy it." He reaches over and gives my hand a light squeeze. "You can worry about working when you're back in America."

"It's a plan."

Joy fills me at the idea that this might be the beginning of even more time with Will. I know everyone else is here for academics, but

I'm perfectly okay with a subpar GPA if it means more Will time.

"So you aren't in school?" Dev asks him.

Will's eyes narrow slightly. "I'm working as an estate agent for my father right now."

"I love British real estate," I blurt.

I know nothing about real estate.

Will turns onto another road lined with trees. It's only when an enormous house appears in the distance that I realize this isn't a road. It's Will's *driveway*. I'm even more intimidated when I see both the number and types of cars parked in front of the house. It's like pulling into a luxury car dealership.

Huan's eyes widen as we make our way inside, but Dev frowns as if the house has personally offended him. I love it, though, even if my mom's duplex could fit in the front hall. It's bright, airy, and perfectly coordinated in creams, blues, and greens. Will's parents clearly dropped a ton of money on an interior designer.

"Wow, this looks like a magazine spread."

"I'll have to tell Father. He's dying to get *Architectural Digest* in here. Thinks it'll be good for business." Will tosses out the words like it's no big deal.

We walk through a wood-paneled hallway and into an expansive kitchen. A girl and guy lean against the far counter, their heads inches apart, oblivious to us. Bottles of alcohol cover a massive island—so many that they blur in my vision. Will chuckles at my expression.

"It's hard to get anyone out here from London unless I can promise loads of alcohol."

I nod and smile, but I'm sweating. The extent of my drinking

experience has been a few sips of vomit-inducing light beer during a small party at Crystal's house. And before Waterford Valley,
parties I went to consisted of some sleepovers with microwave popcorn and embarrassing games of Truth or Dare. What if Will's
expecting me to get . . . *pissed* like everyone else? I suddenly regret
not correcting him when he assumed I was in college. It seemed
harmless enough at the time, but now I'm not so sure.

"Took you lot long enough!"

Frank walks through the patio doors. His hair is even more
incredible than it was at the market. Piles of frizzy blond curls sit
on his head like whipped frosting. He grins at me, but his gaze
lingers on Huan.

"Anyone a bowler?" he asks. "They're trying to get a game in
the back but everyone's too rat-arsed to get it down the pitch."

"You have bowling lanes outside?" I stand on my toes and peer
out the glass doors. "It's been a while since I went bowling, but I
wasn't too bad in middle school."

Everyone but Huan starts laughing. Loudly.

"What?"

"*This* is why I invited them," Will tells Frank, and wipes his
eyes. "I knew it'd be good fun." He turns to me. "Frank was talking about cricket."

I stare blankly.

"Only Will's favorite sport of all time," Frank says.

To my shock, Dev steps forward. "Do you need someone good?
I've played before, but not much."

"Nah, mate, everyone out there is half in the bag already. If
you're facing the right direction, you'll be fine," Will says.

"Please"—Frank motions to Dev—"get outside before he starts talking about the national team."

"Do you mind?" Dev glances from Huan to me.

I shake my head and Huan replies, "Go ahead. I'll . . . have a look around."

Frank grabs a few bottles on the counter and waves them in Huan's direction. "I make a mean gin and tonic."

Dev heads out, Huan drifts toward Frank and the alcohol, and suddenly Will and I are alone.

"It looks like your mates are sorted. Why don't we get a drink too?" He points to three spigots built into the onyx counter. "I prefer the drafts to the bottles."

I nod, dumbfounded. He has this in his *kitchen*? "That's, um, impressive."

"Thanks." He juts his thumb toward the backyard, where the cricket game has started. "None of those wankers care. You know, I was thinking of investing in a brewery. I spent my last holiday in Germany touring some there. Fascinating stuff. Just have to convince my father." He turns and smiles at me. "Sorry. You'll learn to avoid certain subjects with me or I'll never stop talking. Frank walks away when I get on a run."

"I like listening to you talk."

"The same here. Your accent is adorable."

I blush. *My* accent?

He pours two beers, one dark and one light, and passes me the lighter one, grinning excitedly. "A mild ale."

I hate beer, but I'd try sewer water if he handed it to me with such excitement. I take a big drink and have to stop myself from

73

spitting it out on his shoes. The nastiness is overpowering.

He raises his eyebrows. "I see you're not much of a beer drinker. No matter, I'll win you over eventually."

I'm suddenly liking beer a lot more. "It's only that, you know, I'm not twenty-one yet, so I haven't had many opportunities."

"I didn't take you for someone to follow the rules, Elle."

It's hard to speak when he's so close to me. "Right. Definitely not."

Someone shouts and Will peeks out the window at the cricket game. "It should be quieter on the veranda."

He takes my hand and leads me through a massive living and dining room to an enclosed patio. Enormous hydrangea bushes with melon-sized white blooms surround us. I want to spend the next hour inspecting the gardens that encircle his house—there's something particularly charming about an English garden—but I have a feeling that's not how he wants to spend time at his party.

"If my house had a patio like this, I'd never leave." In the distance, there's a whoop followed by laughter. "I guess we're being rude not joining your friends, huh?"

He waves a hand dismissively. "They won't care. They're happy as long as there's plenty of my father's liquor to drink."

I must appear confused, because he shrugs. "I still invite the group out sometimes but it isn't the same anymore. I hardly see them. They're at university and I'm working." He smiles. "That's why I'm so happy you could come. It's time I started meeting new people."

"I'm glad to be of service." I grasp for something we can talk about. "So, um, do you travel a lot? In Europe, I mean?"

"Loads." He sits down on a cushioned seat and I follow suit.

"My mum loves to travel. She still takes us on holiday every summer and winter."

"That sounds wonderful."

He takes another drink. "Cities in Europe start to blend together after a while, though. Probably my favorite trips are abroad. Like America. Where did you say you're from again?"

"Washington, DC. Well, I moved there this spring."

He smiles. "Great museums."

"Some of the best."

"I wish I'd seen more of America. Or even gone to school there. There's so much more to the world than what's around here."

"Are you kidding? You're living in a dream! This house . . . this country . . ."

"If only I saw my world like you see it."

He brushes my hair from my face and I swear I'm in a romantic comedy. I can almost hear the music swelling.

"I'm really happy I found you looking at that fairy booth at the market, Elle. You're exactly what I need right now."

He shifts his weight toward me and my heart threatens to give out. His lips are full and I want to bite them. And then take a picture of myself biting them and make that my new phone case.

"You *arse*!" The yell cuts through the evening stillness.

Will pulls back and groans. "My friends have the worst timing."

I want to grab his hands and make him stay here with me. Instead, we hurry around the outside of the house to the wide manicured yard in the back. There are at least twenty people here, including a group of guys muttering and shooting glares at someone across the lawn.

Dev.

"Oi, Will!" one of the guys calls. "Who's this tosser you got us as bowler? He threw the ball at Charlie's face."

I rush to Dev's side. "What's going on?" I whisper. "You hit that guy in the *face*?"

He scowls at me. "It's not my fault that moron missed the ball by a mile. He's probably on his fifth drink."

"That's the point!" I check if everyone's still glaring at us. "Everyone's drunk here. You couldn't just lob a softball at him?"

"That's not even how cricket works!"

I exhale and go to Will's side. He's pulled Charlie from the ground but the guy is groaning and holding his eye like it's about to fall out.

"Dev is really sorry. He didn't mean to."

Charlie mumbles something unintelligible.

Will brushes off his back and the others huddle closer, cutting me out of the circle.

I nudge my toe through the grass, which is so thick it looks fake, and spot some acorns. They're adorable—round, intact, and tiny. They would be perfect as the roof of a little fairy house. Will is still talking so I hurry over and scoop up a handful.

"Elle?"

I spin, hiding the acorns behind my back. "Hmm?"

He frowns at me. "Were you . . . picking up something from the ground? Tell me one of these wankers isn't leaving their trash everywhere?"

"Oh no!" I bite my lip and produce the acorns. "I just, um, saw these acorns and thought they were cute, so . . ."

Will's frown deepens. "Cute?"

Why couldn't I have left the damned acorns on the ground like a regular person?!

He gestures at Charlie. "He thinks he has a concussion."

"Do you want me to get some ice?"

"That would be great. Thank you."

I run into the kitchen, making sure to pocket a few acorns when I'm farther away, and find Huan and Frank still there. They're laughing at something on Huan's phone. When Huan sees me, he sobers. "Trouble? What'd Dev do this time?"

"Knocked Charlie to the ground with a cricket ball." I grab a towel and open the freezer. Forget about stuff being smaller in Europe. It's twice as large as ours at home.

"Eh, don't rush," Frank says. "Charlie's a wimp. He moaned for an hour once after he fell on the sidewalk outside a club." But even as he says this, he reaches past me for an ice pack and hands it to me.

Sure enough, Charlie is still moaning when I get back out, Huan and Frank trailing behind. I hand the pack to Will and he smiles gratefully at me. Dev is still standing apart from everyone.

A couple other people start muttering. I glance around, panicky, and catch Huan's eye. He's sensing it as well. People are drunk, bored, and getting mutinous. The party needs a distraction before they turn on Dev—and Huan and me by association.

"All right, show's over," Frank calls from the kitchen door. "What we need is some music. Will, please tell me you have something good here. I can't take any of your father's eighties rock."

"Music isn't going to heal my eye," Charlie complains. "I'm

supposed to see Tara tomorrow."

Huan takes a step forward, clears his throat loudly . . . and starts beatboxing. The yard goes silent. He begins slowly. His eyes rest on something above our heads and his cheeks blow in and out, his tongue flicking like he's spitting at us. The rhythm changes and speeds up. Shivers run through me. The sounds he's making shouldn't be possible for humans.

Frank leans back in surprise. People holler and I join in. How can he get his mouth to move so quickly or make so many different shapes? Frank must be thinking the same thing because now he's right beside Huan, staring at him with a mix of glee and adoration.

"Whoooo!" Dev screams.

Frank feigns swooning.

Aaaand tonight is officially awesome again.

When Huan finishes, he's flushed, out of breath, and completely alight with happiness. I can't hear myself think from the cheering. For a second Andy's party pops into my head and a rush of gratitude fills me to be here right now instead of back home. I'm definitely posting photos of this party.

"Let's get this chap a pint!" Frank yells, and pulls Huan back toward the kitchen. The entire crowd follows, including Charlie, who appears miffed at being forgotten so quickly.

"Leave it to Huan to save my ass again," Dev says in my ear.

"Yeah, he's basically the best part about knowing you."

"Don't I know it." He puts his hand out and produces a handful of the acorns I was admiring before. "I saw you before. I don't know why you'd want these, but to each their own." He tips them into my hand and shrugs at my surprised expression.

I stare down at them and then back at him. "I . . . um . . ."

"Sorry I almost torpedoed your big party." His eyes catch something in the distance and he nods at the nuts. "Incoming."

I shove the acorns into my skirt pocket moments before Will is at my side. When I look up, Dev is already weaving through the crowd toward Huan.

Will's fingers entwine with mine and all other thoughts leave my brain. "I didn't know you were bringing entertainment as well as beauty to the party," he whispers in my ear.

"And don't forget a little violence."

He chuckles and pulls me closer. "You are a girl of many talents."

chapter

11

"You were amazing," I tell Huan for the hundredth time. We're still talking about the party at lunch Monday afternoon.

He grins, then shakes his head modestly. He flips between looking sheepish and smug every time we bring it up.

I'm sitting next to him with Dev and Sage across from us, along with their friend Sam and his girlfriend, Kelly. Everyone leans toward Huan in anticipation, as if he might do an encore performance right now. I'm still a little in shock to have a whole table of people to sit with after only one week here. I'd come to the cafeteria alone this afternoon, but when everyone else arrived, they immediately sat down with me, as if I'd been holding the table for them. And maybe I had been, without realizing. It's such a relief to be accepted so easily by them. Not just as someone who is allowed to sit with them, like I was at Crystal's table, but as one of their own. As if I've known them for years the way they've known each other.

"Eh, I'm not as good as you all think I am," Huan replies. "You don't have enough experience to know what it means to be amazing. I'm, like, a novice at it."

"He's right," Dev replies. "I hear him practice *a lot* and it's really not as hard as it seems." Dev clicks his tongue, blows through his lips, and starts making the weirdest, grossest sounds in the world. It's like the devil's trying to speak through him.

The entire table erupts in laughter. Huan waves his hands in horror and I reach across to slap Dev on the shoulder. Even Sage laughs at his ridiculousness, which makes him do it more.

"I don't think I ever thanked you for bringing us along," Huan whispers to me.

"I'm just happy you had a good time."

"Well, I clearly wasn't the only one."

I cough to cover my embarrassment. I couldn't get Will off my mind the whole weekend. Sure, I'd been hoping to date someone over here, but now . . . I don't just want any British boy. I want *Will*. He's everything I could ask for—charming, fun, gorgeous— he's perfect. But the more I think about him, the more I realize how absurd this whole idea is. And seeing multiple posts from Andy over the weekend, talking about how amazing and beautiful Crystal is, doesn't help. How could someone like Will ever want to date me? What am I bringing to the table? I'm the weird girl hiding acorns like a squirrel. We're nothing alike.

I start when I realize Huan is still studying me. "So, um, do you think you'd be interested in seeing everyone again?" I say before he can ask what I was just thinking about.

"Frank's already texted twice about getting together. He wants to take me to London, introduce me to some industry people he knows."

"*What?* That's incredible! When are you going?"

"I'm not." He waves his hand dismissively. "Chemistry is about to bury me as it is. I don't have time for all that."

"Are you kidding me? This could be a huge break for you."

"Beatboxing is just a hobby."

"Give it up, Ellie," Dev says with his face full of crisps. (I'm really trying to get this whole British slang thing.) "Huan can be crazy stubborn."

"But—why don't you want to try?"

"I'm going to school for medicine. I've wanted that since I was eleven."

I search the table for support but no one jumps in to help me argue my case. My shoulders sag. "You're so talented, though."

"He's talented in science as well. Not as talented as me, but who is?" Sage teases.

Huan snorts.

"But . . ." I shake my head and focus on my uneaten sandwich. I've never been around people who were already this confident about what they wanted to do with their lives. Is this normal? Do all high school seniors have a twenty-year plan laid out for themselves? I wish I were that certain about what I want to do . . . or had any direction at all.

"Is everyone going to the talk on college application essays tonight?" Sam asks, leaning forward and surveying the table.

I groan inwardly. The last thing I want to do is talk about college right now. Everyone but Sage and I nod. At least I'm not the only one skipping it.

"I finished all my applications before I came here," Sage

explains. "I didn't want the distraction. Plus, I'm doing early action at Yale, so I had to work on it over the summer."

"Impressive," Sam says with a nod.

"Are you applying to colleges close to home too?" Dev asks her, his expression a little too eager.

She shrugs. "Yeah, a few. Mostly safety schools. I'd like to go out west if I don't get into Yale."

Dev slumps a bit in his seat. He's so clearly into Sage, but I can't tell if she's noticed yet.

He turns to me. "What about you, Ellie? Already have college plans?"

I clasp my hands tightly in my lap. "Um, I already finished my applications too."

It's not a lie, but it's also not something I want to brag about. I applied to a community college where I'm basically guaranteed to get in, and I only did that because Mom forced me before I left. I wish I were passionate about something sensible like medicine or business, but the idea of studying that kind of stuff makes me want to puke. I don't want to waste money to get a degree I don't care about, particularly when I'm not a fan of school to begin with. I'd rather not think about next year at all.

"Where'd you apply?" Sam asks me. There's a judgmental tone underlying his words and I'm suddenly wishing he'd chosen to sit somewhere else.

"Um . . ." My knee is bouncing so fast it's shaking my chair. Dev sees it.

"No place you could get into, I'm sure," Dev says to him. "Speaking of overachievers, how's your research position going, Sage?"

The conversation shifts and I blow out a breath. Did anyone but Dev notice my hesitation? I appreciate him changing the subject, but I also hate that he had to do that. One week in and it's already clear that one of these things is not like the others.

My phone buzzes the next evening, jerking me out of a stupor. I fold down the page in *Beowulf* and read the text from Will. There's a picture of a gorgeous stone cottage.

Know any buyers? 😉 Wish I were with you instead.

He hasn't forgotten about me! Before I can respond, he sends another text.

What are you doing this Saturday? Have you been to
Bath?

No, not yet. I'd love to visit though.

I have to type the words twice because my hands tremble and I keep hitting the wrong keys.

Good, then it's decided. We'll spend the day there. Now I
have something to look forward to.

I squeeze my phone to my chest like it's Pinky. A trip with Will! Just the two of us, going to a beautiful city in England! I'm shaky at the possibility of it. This is my chance to get to know him better. To convince him to keep seeing me. I just need to figure out how to do that, particularly when the sight of him makes words disintegrate in my mouth.

"Liking *Beowulf*?" Sage asks over her shoulder.

I squint in confusion before I realize I must have squealed when I got the text from Will. "No, I'm finding *Beowulf* a bit dry. But Will just invited me to Bath this Saturday."

She smirks. "Sounds educational."

"My favorite kind of education," I say, rubbing my hands together.

I try rereading the same page in *Beowulf* two more times before deciding I need a break. I push my books to the side and gingerly pull out my bag of fairy garden supplies I bought with Sage, along with the acorns from Will's party. I've been dying to try a technique where you attach them to wire to make tiny acorn lanterns for the garden. It's still strange to be making things like that around others, though.

Click. Click. Click.

I turn at the odd noise. "Whoa. You knit?" I ask.

Sage messes with the big ball of violet yarn that's sitting on her lap. "It's relaxing once you get the hang of it. The trick is to do simple projects so you don't have to count stitches."

I watch her work, a small smile on my lips. All she needs is a rocking chair and a crackling fireplace. Come to think of it, I bet we could find both of those somewhere in Emberton . . . that would make the *cutest* picture if I could get her to pose for it.

I hold up my bag. "I love doing crafty stuff, but knitting looks too complicated to be relaxing. I'd rather stick stuff together with a hot glue gun."

"Like your fingers?"

"Ha-ha, no." Well, not lately. "I thought I'd start working on the fairy garden for our room."

"That sounds like an excuse to stop reading *Beowulf*."

Ugh, she already knows me too well. I wave at the yarn to distract her. "So what are you making?"

"A baby blanket. I've got to finish it before Christmas."

My eyes flick to the wall above her desk, where she's tacked a few pictures. There's one of a baby asleep in someone's arms.

Sage follows my gaze and nods. "That's Maddie. She's three months old."

"She's cute. Is she your cousin?"

"My niece."

"Aww! Is it fun being an aunt?"

"I guess." Sage's focus is glued to her knitting. "Mostly weird. My sister, Wren, just turned eighteen, so . . ."

"Oh. Right." I try to search for something to say that won't be rude or prying. Luckily, I'm saved from replying by a knock on the door. I put *Beowulf* over my acorns before opening the door to find Dev.

"How's it going?" He walks in and immediately sees the book. "You haven't finished reading that yet?"

"You and Sage need to stop ganging up on me. I'm trying."

Sage eyes him over her knitting. "She's *not* trying."

Dev holds out a mug to her. "I was in the kitchen getting tea and thought you might like one. Irish breakfast. I remembered it's your favorite."

"Oh, thanks. I could use the caffeine."

"Nothing for me?" Not that I really expected it. It's clear Dev isn't here for me.

"Sorry, didn't know if you'd even be here. I thought UK Ken might have come to take you out again."

I laugh. UK Ken—yeah, Will bears some resemblance to a Ken doll, if by that I mean perfectly sculpted.

"Not tonight. But he just invited me to go to Bath with him this Saturday. I still can't believe how perfect he is."

Dev pretends to puke.

"What's your problem with Will?"

"Willoughby is fine. I just don't get why you're so obsessed with him."

"Um, did you see him? He's the most gorgeous guy I've ever met. And that *accent* . . ."

He shakes his head. "And people say it's men who only care about looks."

"Sage, help me out!" I gesture at her. "I know you haven't spent much time with him, but come on—he's at least a fifteen on a ten-point scale, right?"

She puts her knitting down. "If the top score on the hotness scale is ten, then he can't be a fifteen. That would be mathematically impossible."

I groan.

"But . . . putting that detail aside . . . I'd say he's at least a twelve." She grins at me and Dev throws up his hands in disgust.

"See!" I exclaim. "There you have it—verified by the smartest person any of us know!"

"You're both the worst," Dev says, but his eyes are twinkling. "And I guess you don't care that he doesn't know the first thing about you?"

"That's why I need to spend more time with him."

"Sure. So you can tell him your name is Elle and you love real estate."

"Your boyfriend doesn't know your real name?" Sage asks.

"Elle *is* my real name! Technically, at least. And he's not my boyfriend . . . yet." I glare at Dev. "We're getting to know each other slowly."

"Maybe you should tell him your father owns Jaguar. Or that you're the heiress to Heineken. I bet that'll pique his interest."

I kick out at him and he laughs.

"So, what *do* you know about him?" he asks.

"He's working for his father's very successful real estate company. He . . . he's traveled all over Europe and has been to America twice. And he likes imported beer and cricket."

"And let me guess, you told him that you also love cricket?"

"I can learn to like it."

"I bet you don't know the first thing about it."

"That's what Wikipedia is for."

"Ellie, you can't trust those sites. Anyone can write stuff up there," Sage says. "You need primary sources."

Oh Lord, only Sage would suggest using primary sources to decide what to say to a guy.

She points at Dev. "You're on the cricket team here. You can help her."

"Oh, hell no. I don't want anything to do with this train wreck in the making."

"How do you know about cricket?" I ask.

"Just because you've never heard of it doesn't mean that no one has." He rolls his eyes. "It's a huge deal in India. My whole family is obsessed."

Huh. I cock my head.

"I'm not getting pulled into this weird little drama with UK Ken, though. If you want to learn about cricket, there are plenty of other ways. You could even join! It's a coed team."

Now I roll my eyes. "Like I have extra time to join a sport here. Maybe I can come by your room sometime if I have questions? Just one or two?"

"Fine." He turns to Sage. "How's the tea?"

"Oh . . ." She takes a small sip. "It's good. Just the right amount of sugar."

I look back and forth between them. They'd make a really adorable couple if they could get on the same page, but Sage seems oblivious to how Dev feels and I have zero faith that Dev knows what he's doing either. For all their AP classes and study strategies, it's comforting to know that they're just as clueless about some stuff in life.

chapter

12

I'm jittery as I step out of Will's car onto the streets of Bath the following Saturday. That's probably 30 percent due to the crazy-narrow roads Will barreled down on our drive here, and 70 percent sitting next to him. I can barely make eye contact with him as he comes around the car to join me. He's dressed perfectly, from his snug jeans to his scuffed boots to his double-breasted navy peacoat. Don't even get me started on that coat. The popped-up collar alone makes my heart leap.

We walk down a narrow city lane lined with upscale stores selling clothing, bath products, and lots of other things I don't need but desperately want. Something about their unfamiliar European names makes me twitchy to explore them all. Unfortunately, it's late morning and most don't look open yet.

Will points to a coffee shop. "Do you want to pop in for a drink?"

I nod enthusiastically and follow him inside. The building is quaint and toasty warm compared to the crisp September morning. I scan the menu. "What kind of tea are you getting?"

"Why do you assume I'm getting tea? Just because I'm English?" He winks. "You know, we don't all drink tea. Some of us need loads more caffeine to wake us up."

Think before speaking, Ellie!

Silence grows as we wait in line. I can't think of what to say. I rehearsed conversation starters in bed last night. *What's your favorite TV show? Do you think British comedies are as funny as Americans do? How do you get your hair to do that amazing swoopy thing?* But now the topics all sound ridiculous. And it doesn't help that I can see other people checking out Will.

"Thanks for bringing me here today," I say finally. "I've barely seen any of England yet."

"Happy to. I looked forward to it all week."

"Me too. I've been counting down the days."

Will hands me my coffee and we sit at a tiny bistro table by the door. "So, tell me about yourself."

I blink. I've got nothing. "Um, I don't know. There's not much to tell. My life is much more boring than yours."

"But you don't know my life. How do you know I'm not the most boring person in England?" His smile is wicked. "Perhaps I spend all my time working on my stamp collection. Or know every word of Elvish. Or have a room filled with porcelain dolls."

I laugh. "That doesn't sound boring—just creepy."

"Too right. I went overboard there." He leans forward. "But the point remains the same. Have you ever thought that your life might be as intriguing to me as my life is to you?"

I shake my head.

"Well, start thinking it. I don't spend my time on things that don't interest me."

My stomach flips like I've dropped from an enormous roller coaster. My mouth is glued shut, but I force myself to think of something to tell him. I can't let him realize he might be wrong about me.

"I go to—I mean, I went to Waterford Valley High in DC," I say, catching myself. "My mother processes claims for an insurance company. And, I'll admit, she really loves watching Jane Austen adaptations in her spare time."

He rolls his eyes good-naturedly. "Sounds like our mothers would get along splendidly. Like I said, she named me Willoughby for a reason. And what about your father? Is he also perpetually in love with damned Mr. Darcy?"

"Eh, I don't really see my dad. My parents divorced when I was little. He sends birthday cards and checks, that's about it."

Will cocks his head in sympathy, but I shrug. I know it's strange to talk about my father that way, but our lack of a relationship isn't something I mourn. I know Mom is happier without him and she's been all the family I need.

"I'm sorry. Though I'm a little jealous of that relationship. Only cards and money from my father would be an absolute blessing. He's entirely too involved with my life . . . or at least in trying to shape it into something he approves of. I keep waiting for him to realize I'm an adult and can make my own decisions, but—" He shrugs, his expression dark for a moment, but then he waves a hand and his face turns smooth and easy again. "What kinds of things do you like?"

"Well, um, listening to music. And fantasy novels. And scary movies as long as there isn't too much blood."

"I'm obsessed with scary movies! Especially the ones where the tension keeps building until you think you're going to burst and then—*boom!*—someone jumps out and you about fall out of your chair."

"Yes!" I laugh and he joins in. "One time a few years ago I jumped so big I literally threw my popcorn tub onto the person behind me. Great movie, but I was bummed I'd wasted all my snacks."

"We'll buy an extra tub when we go." He smiles. "There's no point in going to the cinema without popcorn."

"My thoughts exactly."

I let myself relax. Talking to him isn't as hard as I'd thought it would be. There's something warm and friendly about him. Should I tell him my more embarrassing interests too? The acorns didn't go over well at his party, but that *was* pretty odd. Maybe he won't think the other things are embarrassing—just adorable. "Another thing I really like is"—I take a deep breath—"unicorns."

"Unicorns?"

"Yeah . . ." My stomach sinks at his dumbfounded expression. *Abort!* Too soon for unicorns! Much too soon. "Never mind, I don't know. I liked their horns and stuff."

"Oh . . ." He takes a sip of coffee as if he's buying time. "You mean you liked them when you were a kid? Yeah, I liked the silliest things when I was younger too. I couldn't get enough of Paddington Bear. Books, shows—I probably had twenty of the toys. My mum would even dress me in a blue duffer coat and pack me marmalade sandwiches when we'd go to the park. She still talks about it."

Well, he's nailing the adorable vibe, but I'm sure Will doesn't still own a Paddington Bear hoodie to wear when he's feeling down. My level of cool is never going to match his.

"Do you miss America?" he asks.

"Not too much. I do miss my big bed at home. And, you know, not having to share a bathroom with anyone. But mostly I'm excited to be here. I want to make the most of it."

"And is that what you're doing right now?"

I smile shyly. "Absolutely. I can't think of anyplace else I'd rather be."

"Me neither." He holds out his hands toward me. "You're so different from the other girls I've known. There's no drama with you. I can tell you're someone who likes to have fun."

I roll back my shoulders. That's true. That's *exactly* what I want to do in England. "Yes, absolutely."

He smiles at me and squeezes my hand. My heart speeds at his touch. "Then what do you want to do first? I've been here loads of times, so today is all about you."

From all my research with Mom, I know there are a ton of sights in Bath related to Jane Austen. Some of her books were set here and it would be amazing to tour those places after watching the movies so many times. But I push it out of my mind. I'm here to spend time with Will. Anything will be good if he's by my side.

"I don't want you to be bored," I say. "We should try to find something you haven't done before."

"I haven't done *this* before." He waves his hand between us with a mischievous grin. Damn, a girl could get in so much trouble for that grin.

"Well . . . how about the Roman Baths?"

He stands decisively. "To the baths we go."

It turns out we were already close, so within a few minutes, Will has bought our tickets and I'm following him into the entrance.

"The terrace," he announces as I step out onto a stone walkway lined with statues. He walks to the edge and points down. "And the grand bath."

"Wow." Below me is a huge rectangular pool of water. I'm a bit surprised that it's exposed to the elements and more than a bit surprised that it's green. "Did people actually take baths in there? It looks kind of . . . gross."

Will chuckles. "Let's hope so or the name of this city is bollocks."

We zoom through the "museum" areas—models of the baths, historic items behind glass, plaques with important information in small print. Part of me is curious to know more about the history, but most of me only wants to be close to Will. However, as we pass some metal squares on a wall, Will stops short.

"Now this part is worth a longer look. These are the curses."

"Curses?" I lean closer.

"From the Romans. People would write out curses against others who had hurt them or stolen from them and drop the curses in the bath for a goddess. She was supposed to get revenge for them."

"Hmm." The corner of my mouth twitches up, thinking of the curses I'd write.

"Exactly," Will whispers. "I could write up a curse or two if I thought that goddess was still knocking about."

"Who would you curse?" I ask before thinking.

Will's expression closes and I know I asked too personal a question. But when he answers, his tone is light. "The constable who gave me a speeding notice on my way to get you this morning."

"You got a ticket! You didn't say anything."

He wraps a hand around my waist and pulls me toward him. "I was excited to see you. I drove a little too fast."

I breathe in the lemony tang of his cologne and forget all about curses.

Eventually we get back to the green bath we'd seen from the terrace above. I make a beeline for the water, but Will holds me back. "No one is supposed to touch the water. They say it's poisonous."

"Seriously?"

Steam rises from the water and it makes the entire place eerie and magical, like a scene in one of my fantasy novels, right before men in cloaks step out of the shadows and start foretelling the future.

"We aren't rule followers, though, are we?" Will winks and kneels in front of the water.

I follow him, grinning. "Time to live on the wild side." I put my finger in the water.

His eyes glitter and he does the same, twisting his pinkie finger around my own.

After the baths, Will and I stroll through a few touristy stores before heading to a pub. He gets into a conversation with the bartender about their selection of ales and I take the opportunity to text some photos to Mom and post a particularly good one of Will and me in front of a Roman statue. I can't resist the opportunity to show everyone back home what an amazing time I'm having, particularly since Crystal and Andy have no problem posting hourly photos together. It's satisfying, but for once Instagram can't capture just how wonderful the day has been.

Will returns with beer, which I try to drink in tiny sips. Luckily the bartender didn't question my age when Will bought our drinks, but my luck isn't going to hold up forever.

There are TVs all over the pub playing sports, and Will seems content to sit in silence and watch until our food is ready, but it's not interesting enough to keep my attention. I want to spend every second of today getting to know him better.

"What do you have going on this week? More work?"

"Always."

"So I guess you definitely don't want to take over the family business?"

He barks out a laugh. "I'd rather string myself up by the toes. I can't wait to be finished helping Dad with all this."

"It does sound like a lot. What do you want to do after? Do you already have plans?"

He glances at the TV and back at me. "I'm not sure yet. I don't like planning that far in the future."

"I'm the same," I reply, nodding. "Everyone else seems to have it all figured out, but I have no idea. I keep hoping I'll have this sudden flash of inspiration and know exactly what I want to do, but it's not coming. And it doesn't help that I'm surrounded by people already planning out their medical residencies."

"Yes, my parents are always on at me about university, but I'm not one for school. But a couple of my mates went in together to invest in a club in the West End. I was thinking of doing something like that."

"Running a nightclub?"

"Not a nightclub necessarily. More like the brewery idea I mentioned at the party."

"That sounds awesome. I bet there's so much to know about brewing beer, though."

"Probably. But I don't need to actually know how it works. I only need the capital to invest in someone who does." He raises his beer like he's about to give a toast. "To all the gain and none of the work."

I raise my beer too.

It's strange to hear someone talk like this—having so much money that they don't need to think about the work involved in starting a business. It's a whole other world from what I'm used to. But if it means he has more free time to spend with me, then I'll happily cheers to that.

Our food comes and Will turns his attention back to the TV. I squint at the screen. England vs. West Indies. Dammit, I wish I understood this game. Even after Googling it I can't keep it straight.

"What do you think of the game?" Will asks.

His expression is so eager. I remember Frank saying this was Will's favorite sport in the world. It would be so great to bond with him over this, the way Crystal did with Andy. She knew all about the NBA teams when he'd bring it up, but I never paid attention.

"It's great!" I make my voice extra cheerful. "So different from the stuff in America."

"Yeah?" His expression brightens further. "It really is the best sport. It would be wonderful to have someone who appreciated it too." He intertwines his fingers in mine and I find myself nodding.

"Yes. Absolutely."

He lifts my hand to his lips and I have to clench my jaw so I don't squeal. The heat from his kiss spreads up my arm and through my chest.

After another grateful smile, Will goes back to watching cricket and I stare down at my food. Being with him is heaven, but it's pretty obvious we don't have much in common. I know nothing about cricket or breweries or nightclubs. I don't understand British real estate and he doesn't want to talk about it anyway. I haven't traveled to any of the other countries he's been to and I don't know the TV shows he watches. Sure, we can complain about the weather here, or how much school sucks, or talk about some American movies he's seen, but how far will that take us? One more date? Two?

My throat aches. I don't want to be rejected again. Not by someone like Will. But . . . maybe rejection isn't inevitable. Just because I don't know anything about breweries or cricket doesn't mean I *can't* know about them. I just need to learn more. That's what Crystal did with Andy. She took the time to learn about all that. I can do the same.

I sit up, my new resolve pushing away my dread. Will takes my hand again and I keep ahold of him, never wanting to let go. I like the way I feel when Will looks at me. Like I'm something special. Like I'm worth his attention.

By the time we start the drive home, the sun is setting and the temperature has dropped drastically. When he turns onto the long driveway to Emberton, Will stops the car rather than speeding me back to the school.

I sit up. "Is everything okay?"

"I wanted to talk for a second without any nosy students interrupting."

Fears swirl through me. *He doesn't have time to see me anymore. I'm too boring. He just wants to be friends. He* doesn't *want to be friends.*

"I had a great time today." He reaches out and pries my hand from the seat. "When I'm with you, you remind me to be happy."

My hand trembles in his.

"Did you have a good time?"

"Of course."

"Good. Because I'd like to feel this way a whole lot more."

He brushes his fingers through my hair. I suck in a breath as he leans closer. Then our lips meet and I might melt the car with the heat that explodes through my body. I've never felt anything so wonderful in my life.

chapter 13

My epically romantic kiss with Will is far from my thoughts by the time I finish with classes on Wednesday. I got a D on my last British lit quiz . . . which is still better than the F I got on my chem homework. I drag myself down the hallway and to the van. The only bright spot today is that the fairy garden class is happening in Northampton this afternoon.

It would be one thing if everyone else was also dying in their classes. Then we could all sit around complaining about how horrible the professors are and how unfair this whole place is. But everyone else is doing fine. Well, I'm not sure if they're psychologically fine, but their grades are good and mine are *not*. Every day I think the pace of classes will slow or I'll miraculously understand more, but instead the opposite happens.

I collapse into one of the van seats and peek at Instagram. I turned my notifications off right after Andy's party so I'm surprised to see how many people have liked the photos of me and Will. Warm relief rolls through me. I know it's dumb, but it feels good to have people know I'm not depressed or pining over Andy. He and Crystal seem to be going strong and I want everyone to know I've bounced back too. I hate thinking about returning to Waterford, but at least when it happens, I want to be known for more than that party.

Twenty minutes later the driver drops me off at the edge of the Northampton park. My heart swells like an overinflated balloon as I take in my surroundings and I forget my earlier worries. I love the adorable row homes that line one side of the street, with their bright blue doors, tiny front gardens, and double chimneys. I love the squat European cars with their long yellow license plates. And most of all, I love that it's a random Wednesday evening in the middle of September and I'm *here*—in a foreign country—all on my own.

This part of the park is mostly grass with a few old soccer nets, but in the distance, I can see picnic tables pushed together with a pop-up tent covering them. Given that the tent is festooned with balloons and flowers, I think I've found my spot.

I turn out to be the only (semi)adult there who isn't either employed by the gardening store or accompanying a child. And, unfortunately, their "new techniques" end up being pretty simple. Once it's clear there's nothing new to learn, I jump in to help a little girl glue the individual scales of a pine cone onto the roof of her wooden birdhouse. It's really fun. I wish I could teach classes like this every day instead of taking classes. Or, better yet, I wish there were a college major dedicated to designing fairy gardens. Then *I'd* be the A+ student for once.

I'm not ready to go back to Emberton (and all the studying that awaits) when the class is done, so I wander around the park. It's spitting rain, but that just makes it feel more British. In the distance, there's a large group of people running around. And I think I see hoops set into the ground. Could I actually have stumbled upon a *Quidditch* game?! I've never seen one in real life. I laugh and jog toward the field.

As I get closer my grin spreads so wide I think my lip might split. I read the Harry Potter books straight through when I was young and fell in love with them. They've always been my comfort reads when I'm feeling down or lonely. Granted, the fact that the author turned out to be a bit of an Umbridge is hard to stomach, but I'm trying not to let her ruin the books for me.

I study the field. Just like in the books, there are three hoops on either end of the field, the middle one higher than the other two, though all within reach without having to fly on a broom. And—*oh my*—the players have brooms. Not movie props, but short, yellow broom handles. Every person on the field has one between their legs as they run and jump and dart.

I freeze. What . . . the . . . hell?

I take a step forward, then another. That can't possibly be . . . there's no way . . .

But I'm not making it up. *Dev* is on the field.

My mouth drops open and I march closer as if pulled by a spell. There's no doubt it's him. He's sweating, his broom sticking out behind his legs, and he's clasping a big white ball in one hand. He tosses it at someone's back, and they trip and drop their broom. My astonishment turns into full belly laughs. I can't believe I'm seeing Dev—serious, focused *Dev*—playing Quidditch!

Best. Day. Ever.

A referee calls time and the teams separate and head toward the sidelines. Someone jerks the hoops from the ground. Dev walks with another guy, animatedly talking. They must be describing something that happened in the game because they're pretending to throw balls at imaginary people. I keep laughing as I walk slowly toward them, despite the intensifying rain. It's fascinating what you can learn about someone when they don't know you're watching.

Suddenly Dev turns and our eyes meet. Dev's broom falls to the ground.

"Hey!" I call, and wave.

A few more people turn toward me, but I don't recognize anyone else from Emberton. This must be a citywide group. Dev's eyes bulge and he says something to his friend before rushing toward me.

"Ellie!" he says in a hushed voice. "How the hell did you find me here?"

"I was at a gardening class in the park." I gesture back the way I came. "I thought I saw a Quidditch game and I had to come investigate."

He looks behind me, clearly frazzled. "Is anyone with you? Did you tell Huan? Or Sage?"

"No. It's just me." I gesture to the field. "So what's all this? You're playing *Quidditch*? Have I discovered your deep dark secret?"

"Don't start with me."

I hold up my hands. "I'm not *starting*. I think this might be the best thing I've ever witnessed. It's just so"—I nod at his broom and smile again—"unexpected! I never pictured you being into this."

He shoves his hands into his pockets and stares at the ground. "It's something I've wanted to do for a while. To let off steam. When I first read the books, I always thought how cool it would be to play Quidditch. There was a team back in DC, but I couldn't get to the practices, so when I saw the flyer at the flea market for the local team . . ."

He's been keeping this a secret since our first days here? I thought I had him all figured out, but there might be more to Dev than I originally realized.

"You know, Quidditch is a really big deal now," he adds. "It's a legitimate sport. There's even a world cup."

It's raining hard enough now that my clothes are painted onto me. "Is there someplace else we can discuss this?"

He squints at me and then up at the sky, like he's only now noticing the rain. Boys.

"Yeah, come on."

He backtracks to grab his bag and gestures for me to follow him. We run under the big trees that line the park. I try to wipe the rain off me, which works about as well as trying to wipe my skin off my body.

"Are you pissed I found out?"

He sighs. "No. Though it would help if you'd stop smiling like that."

I try, but the smile widens. "I'm sorry, I'm sorry! It's just, your broomstick and the balls, and—"

He begins to chuckle. "I'm one of the beaters, though the

captain wants me to be the snitch runner."

"A snitch runner? What does that mean?"

"It's almost exactly the same as in the books." Dev smiles. "Except I'd dress in gold and run around the field with a tennis ball inside a gym sock tied to my waist."

I burst out laughing and he does the same. He pulls a gym sock out of his bag and starts swinging it around his head. I wipe tears from my eyes and wave him away. I can't breathe. We laugh until my stomach hurts and Dev is sucking in air.

"Glad I could brighten your evening." He shoves the sock in his bag and we both laugh again. "It's honestly not as ridiculous as I make it sound. It's a rough game." He points down at his bloody shins. "I think the rain has calmed down. Do you want to get something to eat before we catch the van?"

"Sure. What do you want?"

"Something *American*."

"Pizza?" I ask.

"Uh, that's Italian."

"Not when it comes from Pizza Hut."

chapter
14

The Pizza Hut looks . . . like a Pizza Hut. Probably the biggest differences are the prices (ouch) and the fact that we can order wine with our dinner. Luckily Dev and I like the same toppings, so we quickly settle on a sausage and green olive pizza and two cups of fizzy orange Tango.

"So, about those cricket questions . . . ," I say.

Dev takes a swig and sits back in the seat to regard me. "I still think this whole thing is dumb."

"It's not. When Will and I were in Bath, he was saying how much he loves cricket and how he wants to be able to talk to me about it. But then I'd watch the game and have zero idea what was going on."

"On Saturday? England vs. West Indies? That was a good game."

"See! Please, I need to *try* to understand this game. It'll be my in with him."

"He already spent the day with you in Bath. Don't you think

you're already . . . in?" His mouth pinches as if he's eaten something disgusting.

"I don't know. Maybe I am right now, but what are we going to talk about next time?"

"Hmm, that is a puzzler. Have you ever thought about bringing up something you care about?"

"I'll bring up my stuff too. But for now I need to know more about what he's interested in."

"And what happens when he wants to talk about something else?"

"Well, I'll learn more about that stuff too. I've made a list." I pull out my phone. "Cricket is obvious. I should know something about types of beers and probably a couple of breweries. And I should know about some of the other sports just in case. Soccer—or it's football here, right?—but also . . . what's the name of it? The violent one?"

"Rugby?"

"Right! Yes, that. And, I don't know? I was thinking something with music. Maybe—"

"Stop. You're making my ears bleed."

"What? I'm only trying to be prepared."

"To be a totally different person around him! Why do you even—actually, never mind." He takes another drink and shakes his head. "I don't know, Ellie. This sounds time intensive. The classes here are no joke, I've got cricket, my extracurriculars—"

"You mean Quidditch."

"*Yes*, Quidditch. And practice interviews, college application workshops. I was debating trying out for the academic triathlon too. I can explain more about cricket now, but I don't have time to tutor you on how to date a British boy. Plus, that's my *worst* subject."

"Believe me, I'd ask someone else so I could avoid all this teasing. But everyone is as clueless as me. I mean, really, am I supposed to ask Huan about cricket?"

Dev smiles.

"Or maybe Sage can tutor me with her vast cricket vocabulary?"

"Don't doubt her. She probably studied up on it before getting here."

I lean forward. Time to bring out the big guns. "Speaking of Sage . . ."

"Hmm?" His voice is normal but his eyes narrow.

"Let's stop playing. You clearly like her." Dev looks ready to deny it, but I interrupt him. "It's cool. I can see why you do."

He blinks. "Can you? No one else gets it."

"Sure. You're both serious about school. You've been in the same honors classes. You have lots in common."

"Yeah. But it's not just that." He leans in eagerly, like he's excited to finally have someone to share this with. "She's so confident in herself. She never apologizes when she outscores the rest of the class. She'd never even think to. And you can have a real conversation with her. I mean, not that she and I have had a lot of deep conversations or anything, but I bet we could."

I can't help but smile. His enthusiasm is adorable.

"I think you two would be great together. And we can make

this work for both of us. You can come by our dorm in the evenings when Sage is around. I know you're dying for a reason to anyway. Now you have an excuse that doesn't include you being creepy. You help me out with Will and I'll put in a good word with Sage about you."

"She's not going to care about your opinion."

"We're roommates. I might have some sway with her."

He raises an eyebrow.

"Either way, you'll be around her. I learned in psych that proximity is the single biggest predictor of attraction. This gives you more proximity! *And* you can make fun of me as much as you want."

"Like you could stop me." But he's smiling.

"Deal?"

"On two conditions. One, classes still come first."

"Yeah, yeah."

"And two, you can't tell anyone about Quidditch until I tell you it's okay."

"What? No way! I'm already debating whether I should announce it at lunch tomorrow or try to get ahold of a broom and act it out."

His eyes widen. "You have to promise. This is something I want to do by myself for now. If the others find out, they'll all want to come and there will be teasing. I'll never live it down."

"Fine." I look down my nose at him. "But who's trying to hide themselves now?"

He scowls, but the arrival of pizza distracts us. It's *delicious*. I don't know if they have a different recipe in Northampton or something, but I can't get the slices into my mouth quick enough.

"It's not a competition, you know," Dev says, laughing.

"Maybe not for you."

I swipe another slice for good measure and sit back, surprised by how fun it is to have dinner with him. Partially because I get to troll him mercilessly about Quidditch now, but it's not just that. All this time, I figured Dev only cared about getting straight As, but we're actually more similar than I realized. It's nice knowing someone else with a wacky interest they don't like sharing publicly. I like being in on the secret.

"You know, if you want to get to know Will better, you should ask about his family. You can learn a lot about people that way. Have you tried that?"

"Actually, we did discuss it," I say in a superior voice.

"And?"

"And . . ." I purse my lips. Hmm, I guess I don't really know much. "I know he has a bad relationship with his dad . . ." I pause. "He has a younger sister. Oh, and his mother loves to travel!"

Dev nods. "Well, that's something, I guess. Did you tell him about your family?"

"A little. There wasn't much to say. I don't really know my father, and Mom . . . well, she's more in love with Britain than I am. Before I came here, we had a two-week movie marathon of every BBC book adaptation ever created. But that's not the kind of info that's going to endear me to Will."

"Not necessarily. I think it's cool you did that. Are you guys close?"

I hesitate. I don't usually like talking about Mom in-depth—it always seems dorky to say how much I like spending time with her. Aren't teenagers supposed to hate their moms? I've just never felt like that. She annoys the crap out of me sometimes, but she's also one of my closest friends.

"Yeah," I reply slowly. "I've basically lost touch with people from my old school since we moved, so she and I are together most nights and weekends." I pick at an olive and wait for a snarky comment.

"Same," he replies without the slightest judgment. "Not about the moving stuff or movie marathons—my parents don't watch a lot of movies—but mostly I'm either at school or with my family."

"That's cool."

"Was it hard moving schools? That sounds miserable."

"I don't miss Virginia. My old friends back there . . . I guess you could say they outgrew me. I was actually relieved when mom got the job offer in DC. Then Crystal befriended me and I couldn't believe my luck." I shrug. "But we all know how that turned out."

"Eh, give it two months. You don't know Andy the way the rest of us do—he'll be onto someone new before we get back to America." He points at me. "And if you hadn't transferred to Waterford, then you'd never have gotten the chance to eat this very delicious pizza. So it all worked out."

"Very true." I make a show of taking a big bite. When I've finished chewing I ask, "So, are you liking it over here? Or do you miss your family?"

His expression softens. "Both. I can't help missing them. They won't stop emailing and calling me." He pulls out his phone. "Yup, two more emails and a couple of pictures since I checked last."

"Wow."

"It's mostly my siblings." He pulls up a photo. It's a selfie of him, a younger boy, and two little girls. "This is Anaya and Riya," he says, pointing to the two girls. They're both ridiculously cute— the youngest has her dark hair in ringlet pigtails. "And this is Sahil. He's a freshman this year. He's pretty bummed that I'm gone now that we're finally in the same building again."

"Why'd you decide to come, then? Our high school has plenty of good AP options."

I assume. I haven't really looked into those.

He pushes the pizza around his plate. "My parents and I thought this would strengthen my applications. Everyone takes AP classes nowadays, but not everyone takes college classes in a foreign country. I haven't done a lot of extracurriculars since I've been so focused on school, but between the advanced content, small class sizes, and one-on-one contact with professors here, I'm hoping this will make me stand out a little more."

"I'm sure your applications are going to stand out no matter what. You're a straight A student, aren't you?"

"Every little bit helps. And I need to get a good scholarship. A *full* scholarship. It's going to be nearly impossible for my parents to send all four of us to college without help. And as they've told me many times, they're relying on me to set the example for my brother and sisters. I can't disappoint them."

"That makes sense."

He sits back and regards me. "You know, I can't believe I'm saying this, but I'm glad you found me tonight."

I raise my Tango. "To Quidditch, cricket, and getting what we want in life."

We clink glasses.

"And to tutoring." His smile turns sly. "You know, I tutor my siblings sometimes."

"Yeah?"

"I'm *very* thorough. They hate it."

chapter

15

"Okay, what's 'leg before wicket'?"

I groan and lean back in my chair. "I don't know."

Dev sighs and exchanges a glance with Sage.

"It's not that hard, Ellie," Sage tells me. "Just use common sense."

True to his word, Dev has come to our dorm at seven p.m. sharp every night this week. In fact, I've spent more time with him since finding him on the Quidditch pitch than I had in the previous four weeks combined. At first Sage didn't seem too happy about the extra company and noise, but I think she's starting to secretly like it. In fact, Dev should be pretty damn grateful that I'm useless at this stuff because that's the only reason he and Sage have been bonding: mutual exasperation over how slowly I'm learning these terms.

"Ugh." I rub my eyes. "I guess, um, he puts his leg in front of the cricket and—"

"You have to use the right word. The wooden stumps are called the wicket, not the cricket."

"Fine. He puts his leg in front of the wicket instead of using his bat to block the ball."

Dev nods. "Okay, good enough. Now tell me what the creases are."

"We've already been over this!"

"Uh-huh. And you haven't gotten it right yet."

"Hey! That's not entirely true. I knew about the different types of cricket games! Though I still can't believe there's a type that lasts for five days. That's just insane."

"Actually, there's a fun fact about that. Did you know the longest cricket game lasted over a week?"

I groan. "Dev, you've *got* to learn the definition of fun."

"And you've got to learn the definitions of overs and innings."

I groan louder. Why does Will have to like boring things?

"Hey, have you finished your *Beowulf* paper yet?"

I turn, but Dev's actually bent over Sage's desk. Real smooth conversation starter.

"Finished it two days ago," she says.

"Cool," he replies. "Yeah. I finished it last night. So you have the night free, then? You know, people are watching the newest season of *Doctor Who* down in the common room if you want to check it out. It's a pretty awesome show."

"Thanks, but I should work. I have some articles I need to read for Dr. Reese."

Dev deflates. Ugh, Sage is not going to make this easy on him.

"How about you, Ellie? All done?" Sage asks brightly, and I

wonder if she's trying to deflect Dev's attention.

"Um, I'm getting there."

Dev's eyes widen. "It's due tomorrow."

"I know. I'll finish it."

"Can I see it?" he asks, pointing to my laptop.

Hesitantly, I pull it up, then climb up to my bed. I'm exhausted. Between classes, reading, papers, and studying up on Will's interests, sleep has fallen off the priority list.

"This isn't bad." Dev can't hide the surprise in his voice.

"Yeah?"

"You need a stronger introduction. And you should beef up your section on Tolkien's criticism. But, overall, it's strong. Solid B at least."

I squint down at the laptop to make sure he's reading the right document. Huh. I did devote extra time to it at the library since Will was with his father all day and couldn't text me. I guess it's a little easier to focus when I'm not waiting for the next chime on my phone.

My phone lights up. Speaking of which! I give Dev and Sage an apologetic look. Dev shrugs and walks back over to Sage's desk.

"Hello?"

"Elle! I was hoping to catch you. Am I interrupting?"

"No, not at all." I climb down from bed, step out of the room, and walk down the hall to a comfy chair overlooking the grounds. I curl into it, my exhaustion forgotten.

"How's Brighton?"

"Eh, it'd probably be great if I weren't here with Father," he says. "Tell me about your day. It had to be better than mine."

"Oh, I don't know about that. Just standard school stuff. Breakfast, classes, studying, more classes, more studying. I didn't know I was signing up for so much work when I decided to come here."

"Do you really have to study that much? It can't be that important."

I squeeze my eyes shut, thinking about my newest study topics with Dev. "Some of it is."

I hear him shift and imagine him stretching and leaning back in a chair. He sighs again. "I wish we could do something together. Or go away someplace. Let's pretend—what would you want to do?"

"If we went away someplace together?"

"Exactly."

"Um . . . I don't know. I'd probably be happy anywhere. As long as it wasn't a morgue or something."

His laugh sends a thrill down my spine. "Your only limitation is no morgues? You really aren't picky."

"What about you? Where would you want to go?"

"If I were with you? Anywhere."

My whole body tingles. If he were here right now I'd kiss him so hard.

A voice on Will's end calls his name and he growls. "Father again. I should probably go."

"I'm glad you called."

"Me too. And we'll see each other when I'm back?"

"Yes, absolutely. I can't wait."

I end the call and lean back in the chair, soaking in the delight of talking to him. *If I were with you? Anywhere.*

I'm too happy to work on my paper, so I scroll through my Bath photos again. Who would have thought I'd soar from the depths of high school humiliation to dating someone this perfect? Clearly no one back home. A few girls have even jumped into my DMs to accuse me of photoshopping Will into my photos! As if I know enough about computers to do that. But I'm taking it as a compliment . . . and an excuse to keep posting even more.

Eventually I make myself get up. Dev is still in the room, talking with Sage. She takes one look at me and clucks her tongue. "A good call, I see."

"Very good." I smile and sink into my chair.

"Well, you missed a very enlightening conversation on English literature," Dev tells me.

"You know," Sage says, "the British Museum has the oldest surviving copy of *Beowulf*. I was thinking of visiting it sometime."

Dev turns. "Really?"

"Visit what?"

"The original text of *Beowulf*," Sage tells me, and picks up her copy. "It's not always on display, but sometimes the public can view it. Plus, they have *Canterbury Tales*, a folio of Shakespeare's works, the original *Alice's Adventures Under Ground*. . . . It must be amazing."

Dev jumps out of his chair. "We should plan a trip!" he practically screams.

I catch his eye and put out my hand like I'm pushing a brake pedal.

Sage turns, her eyes shining. "We could split our time between the library and the British Museum—"

"Maybe St. Paul's Cathedral?" Dev adds.

"Yes!" Sage claps. "I've barely gotten to see the city on my research Fridays." She turns to me. "You haven't been to London yet, have you, Ellie?"

I shake my head in surprise.

"You should come with us."

"Um . . ." I would love to visit London, but I don't want to butt in. I glance at Dev.

"Yes, come." He nods encouragingly. "I'll ask Huan too. It would be fun to have a group go together."

"Really? It does sound fun. Maybe we could go to Harrods too?"

Dev and Sage frown at me, perplexed.

"The famous department store? They have a memorial to Princess Diana there."

"Well, sure . . . ," Sage adds. "If we have time, I guess. So you're coming?"

"I'm coming. As long as you promise to break up the museums with some fluff."

chapter
16

"It's too much to memorize." I drop my head onto the desk. Five weeks in means our first tests, and my brain is about to explode from so much studying. I spent the entire weekend focusing on chemistry and social psych, but now my brain is officially closed for business. I've been reading over my art history notes and I'm no closer to having all these artists and paintings memorized. In fact, I'm one flash card away from setting my textbooks on fire.

Sage looks up from her planner. "If you don't like memorization, then you shouldn't have taken art history. What did you think it was going to be about?"

"I don't know. I didn't really know what art history was. It sounded ea—"

"Don't even say it," she replies with a judgmental eyebrow raise.

I sigh and flip through the pages of my art history textbook. It's as heavy as a tombstone and the pages are filled with glossy color photographs of artwork. There are just way too many pieces to remember, and it doesn't help that they're all blurring together in my mind. I need a new way to study.

I squint at the pages, an idea forming. I reach for my scissors and the rainbow of Sharpies I bought with Sage, then pull up a web browser, my spirits lifting immediately.

Ten minutes later, I've printed out photos of fifty pieces of art. I fan them out for Sage. "Look! I'm going to cut each one out and write all the stuff I need to know on the back. I thought I could even color code the types of information to make it easier."

Her mouth tugs up in a smile. "I thought you hated studying?"

"Well, this doesn't count."

"As long as you actually study all this stuff after you finish making it."

I sigh again. "Yeah. That *is* the worst part."

"Oh, stop pouting. What are you even doing here still? Go do this with Dev. You know he loves that stuff."

"He loves craft projects?"

"*No*, art history." She purses her lips. "You need to be more observant."

"So, you've been 'observing' Dev, have you?" I wink suggestively.

"I shouldn't have said anything."

"No, no, I'm happy to talk about you and Dev."

"There is no me and Dev. Just me, sitting here, trying to finish my homework at a decent hour so I can go to sleep."

"You can't tell me you've never thought about it, though. You guys seem perfect for each other." I cock my head at her. "Unless you're not thinking about guys in general?"

"I like the *idea* of guys—just not the reality." She shakes her head hard enough that her dangling earrings smack her neck. "I'm too busy for all the drama."

"Too busy for a date? I know you're serious about school and research, but you have to have some fun too."

"I can have fun later. The research I'm doing here is important. Dr. Reese is studying the genetic contributions to cancer, and if she's successful, then it could really impact treatment plans. I have a chance to be a part of that, but the lab I'm working at is really competitive. I can't lose my position."

I grimace. It's hard to argue with that. My promise to help Dev with Sage is looking much tougher to fulfill than I'd imagined.

Even though I'm not convinced that Dev is going to be interested in my silly study strategy, I head to his and Huan's room on the off chance she's right. I'm expecting it to be as silent as a church in there, but music blares through their door.

"Good evening, Miss Nichols."

My head snaps up and I find Dr. Michaels in the hallway. Ugh, I didn't think about room checks. One of the faculty comes by every night at ten to make sure all the high school students are accounted for. We either need to be in our rooms or have signed in at one of the study areas in the manor or we get written up. I'm jealous of the college students who have full run of the place.

"What are you doing down on the boys' floor tonight?" His expression is neutral, but his voice can't hide his suspicion.

I pull a few of my art history cards out of my book bag. "Studying art history with Dev."

His face brightens. "Oh, very nice. I'm sure Dev would be a great study partner. Such a bright boy."

"Mm, yes." I'm *not* repeating that to him. He'll never stop quoting it back to me.

"I'll just get the room check out of the way so I don't disturb your studying." Dr. Michaels knocks.

"Come in!" Dev opens the door. "Oh, hi, Dr. Michaels."

"Evening, Dev. Just checking for you and Huan."

"Here!" Huan calls from within the room.

"Wonderful." He takes a step to the side so I'm right in front of Dev. "And Ellie is here for her tutoring session."

My eyes bulge. He thinks Dev is *tutoring* me? Well, okay, he *is*—but only in cricket. Of course he'd assume that, though. Why would we ever study together otherwise?

Dev's eyes also widen. "Oh . . . right. Hey, Ellie. Um, come in."

"Thanks." I shuffle into his room.

"I know you're only studying, but still . . ." Dr. Michaels knocks twice on the door. "Remember to keep the door open until Ellie goes back to her room."

"I will," Dev replies immediately. We stand in silence until we hear him knocking on the next door.

Dev's brows furrow. "What's going on?"

"Sage sent me up here."

His whole body lifts for a moment and I realize how that sounds. "Sorry. I mean, I was annoying her with my whining so she said I should come bother you instead. I ran into Dr. Michaels on the way."

"Oh. Right."

I'm surprisingly hurt at his downtrodden expression. I don't know what to say so I focus on their room. It's not nearly as messy as I was expecting, though there are piles of clothes scattered on the floor. Darth Vader and Darth Maul posters cover one wall.

"A big fan of the dark side?" I ask Huan with a smile.

"The biggest. The dark side is always cooler than the light."

"Particularly when it includes shirtless Kylo Ren, right?"

He winks. "I like that you get me."

I laugh and walk over to his desk. "What are you working on?"

He points at a YouTube video, which turns out to be the source of the music I heard. "Just working on some new tricks."

"Cool! I want to hear."

"Oh, don't worry about that. You wouldn't be able to stop him if you wanted to," Dev replies.

Huan makes some weird squeaking noises with his mouth that don't sound anything like music. I smile encouragingly. I listen for another minute but it's weird to watch somebody who's staring intently at a video of another person's mouth, so I turn back to Dev. Unsurprisingly, his desk is covered with books and notes. There's even a stack of index cards in the corner.

"Are you making flash cards too?"

He frowns. "You're making flash cards?"

"Well, not exactly." I pull out the art I printed and explain my idea.

"Wow, that's actually . . . ingenious." He holds up his own flash cards. "I already made these but I wrote the name of the painting on one side—I didn't think about printing out the pictures."

"Maybe I can glue the pictures onto your cards? That would save a bunch of time."

"Do you have—"

I whip out multiple glue sticks, grinning widely. He laughs and rolls his eyes.

"I see Sage already got to you."

"Nah, I've loved doing this kind of stuff forever. It's the studying part I don't like."

I get to work cutting and Dev matches the art to the right card since I'm a little fuzzy on that part. He holds up a painting of a woman breastfeeding outside while a man watches her. I know it's famous, but it's not one of my favorites.

"*La Tempesta*," he says when it's clear I don't remember the name. "Did you know that this is one of the first examples of a Renaissance painter who put people into the landscape? Giorgione was much more interested in landscapes than other painters at that time. Imagine being the *first* to do something. Is that even possible now? And think of all the paintings that were influenced by this one piece of art. Hundreds—no, thousands, maybe hundreds of thousands—of other artists have studied this work."

"Do we need to know that for the test?"

He sighs. "No. Well, maybe the first part. I just think it's fascinating. Plus, it helps me remember it."

I examine the painting again. I still don't particularly love the style, but he's right. I'll remember that one on the test.

Robotic sounds are coming from the beatboxer in the video now. They're so realistic that I wonder if he's faking the audio. Huan, however, sounds like a whiny toddler. I catch Dev's eye and we both crack up.

Huan grabs a pencil and chucks it at us. "You two can go screw yourselves."

"Maybe we should find a more . . . hospitable place to study," Dev says.

"Robots and Renaissance art don't mix. But I'm not sure there's anyplace to go at this point."

Technically we're allowed anywhere as long as we check in and stay inside Emberton at night, but they close down the library and cafeteria at ten. There are little nooks with chairs and window benches, but I think Dev is going to want a real table.

He grins and shoves his textbook into his book bag. "I've got an idea. Pack up."

We walk together in silence through the manor, past the Long Gallery and the entrance to the library. I'm not exactly sure where we're going, but I'm willing to follow along and find out. Dev continues toward the back of the manor and into one of the gilded rooms where we have class during the day. I think he's going to walk right into one of the wood-paneled walls until I see a tiny handle carved into the wood. My eyes go wide.

"Is that—"

"A secret passage." He's beaming now. "I found it one night when I went exploring. Supposedly they're all over the manor."

He pulls on the door and it gives way, revealing a dark hallway that's much simpler than the rest of the manor. The floors are rough stone and the walls are whitewashed. It's dead silent back here and I'm suddenly glad that Dev is next to me. I wouldn't be surprised if a Dementor whooshed down the hallway at any moment.

"This way." He shuts the door behind himself and strides down the corridor. "I'm pretty sure this was one of the back walkways for the servants. You know, so the owners never had to see them working." He rolls his eyes.

"Wow." How many students know about this section of the manor?

"Here's the room."

He opens a set of double doors to reveal a small parlor. There's a table and chairs, a comfortable-looking leather couch, and two armchairs sitting in front of a fireplace. A few embers remain in the fire and the tang of wood smoke scents the air. We must not be the only ones who come here. I flop into a chair and sigh deeply. This room is homey and comforting in a way the rest of the manor is not.

I close my eyes and tip my head back. "Are we allowed to be back here?"

"I'm not sure. Technically, probably not."

I sit up. "Wait, are *you* breaking a rule?"

He waves me away. "It's not a rule if there's no sign. Anyway, it's just not on the official tour because it was the servants' parlor when this was a private residence. They probably don't think it's fancy enough." He shakes his head and points to the intricately carved fireplace mantel.

"So I guess you still think the manor is too fancy?"

"Those massive rooms make me feel small. This reminds me of home."

"Well, sure, because we all have floor-to-ceiling windows like in here. In fact, the fireplace in my bedroom is only slightly larger than this one. It's pedestrian, really."

He stares at me and I swat his arm. "I'm kidding! Geez, give me some credit."

"Sorry, sorry! I just figured your family must have some money."

I blink. "Why would you say that?"

"Well, because . . . you know, because you're here."

"So are you."

"But I got in on my grades."

"And I got in on my . . . ?"

He shifts uncomfortably and pulls out his books.

Oh. My whole body floods with heat. He knows we had to pay out the nose so I could come here. Not that everyone else didn't have to pay, but my payments were more like bribes since I don't meet the requisite GPA and honor roll requirements. That must be what everyone is thinking. That I'm too stupid to be here. That I'm the idiot the teachers have to put up with so they can get their money. Screw that. I grab my book bag and stand.

Dev touches my arm. "Wait. Don't go. That was a shitty thing to bring up. I didn't mean it."

I jerk away. "Yes, you did."

"I meant . . ." He shakes his head. "I don't know, I'm an asshole. Sahil's always telling me so. I just didn't believe him."

"He and I would get along really well."

He tugs me down into a seat. "Yeah, you probably would. Now sit down so we can study, please."

I hesitate, but don't put my stuff back down.

"I don't think you're stupid," Dev says.

"Wow. Do they have a class on giving compliments? You could be the professor."

"Shit, I know I'm bad at this." He rubs his eyes with the heels of his hands and meets my gaze. "Look, I think you're smarter than you realize. Funnier too. And half the guys on my Quidditch team were asking for my 'hot friend's number' at the next practice. So you clearly have more going for you than most of the people here, including me. Okay? Can we study Raphael now?"

He turns away and flips through the flash cards. I stand there frozen. Dev thinks I'm smart. And . . . wait, his teammates think I'm *hot*? Does he think that too? I debate retorting—or asking him which guys he's talking about—but he's gripping the flash cards so tightly that they're starting to bend.

"Thanks for showing the room to me, Dev." I drop my book bag on the floor.

He shoves the flash cards into my hands. "It's your turn to match the art to the cards. And no cheating."

chapter
17

Our flash cards do the trick. I'm shocked when Dr. Lotfi hands me back the test the following week and there's an 80 percent circled in green ink. I got a B-. Sure, it might be the lowest possible B-, but it's the highest I've ever scored in art history! I've never been so proud of a grade before. I didn't think I had it in me.

Unsurprisingly, Dev got a 98 percent, along with a *Nice!* in big letters across the top margin. Dev leans over to see my grade and I have a sudden urge to rip my paper away. His eyebrows lift and for a second I'm certain he's going to make some sarcastic comment. But he only whispers, "Not bad."

When class ends, he follows me into the hallway.

"So, I have some homework for you." His eyes shine with excitement.

"Unless it's researching the best stores for our trip to London, I've got plenty already."

"You aren't really going to make us go shopping, are you? That's such a waste of time when we're only in London for the day."

"You should be begging for my shopping help." I take a step

back and give him an obvious once-over. His jeans could use some distressing and his tennis shoes scream *I'm American!* but, if I'm being honest, he already looks pretty good. He's wearing a cricket shirt that isn't nearly as baggy as what most boys from our class wear. And blue is a good color on him. I never noticed before.

"Like what you see?" He grins and does an exaggerated spin that makes a few people in the hall chuckle.

"Omigod, stop. I was just looking at your clothes."

"You were checking me out."

"I was *not*!"

I shove him to distract from the blush I know is coming. If I'm not careful then he'll never let me live this down. I'd be lying if I said Dev wasn't cute, but my attention is elsewhere.

"And we definitely need to take you shopping in London. You can't wear cricket shirts to class every day. You need something more sophisticated."

"So now you want to pick out a new wardrobe for me? I thought girls only did that for the boys they were dating. Shouldn't you be focusing on Willoughby instead?" His expression is mischievous.

"Will doesn't need a new wardrobe. There's nothing left to improve on."

He snorts. "Anyway, our intramural cricket team is holding our first scrimmage this Saturday and I thought you could come." He announces this as if he's showing me a secret door into the fairy world. "This will be perfect for you. I think the reason you've been struggling with some of the terms is because you need to see the game being played."

"You made me watch four hours of cricket on YouTube."

"And did you actually do that?"

I sigh. I made it through thirty minutes and was damn impressed with myself.

"That's what I thought. Anyway, this will be better. Not only will you be able to see the plays and the calls from the referees, but honestly"—he rubs the back of his neck—"the game is going to go way slower than the professional games you tried watching. We're not that good yet."

"That sounds promising."

"You'll come?"

"Yeah. Of course."

"Great!" He points down the crowded hallway to Sage. "I'm going to see if I can persuade her now. See you at dinner." He grins and crosses his fingers.

People push past me, hurrying toward their rooms or the library or extracurriculars. I should follow them. I might be done with the first round of tests this semester, but other assignment due dates are just around the corner. More reading, article reviews for psych, and a big group presentation in chemistry in two and half weeks. That one is especially intimidating because Sam is in my group and he's turned out to be a pretentious jerk. He loves to sneer and laugh/cough whenever I'm confused by something in class, and his favorite two words are *Well, actually.* I'd be happy if I never had to spend another minute in his presence.

If Will was back in Northampton, I'd escape on the first van into town, but unfortunately he's still away with his dad. I just need a release from the pressure for a few minutes. I hurry across the manor until I get to the conservatory. No one else is there. I breathe in the earthy scent and drop into the nearest bench.

"Hard day?"

I jerk up to see an older woman in the back of the glass room. She's pushing a huge tank with a hose attached.

"Um . . . just needed a second to relax."

"This place is perfect for that." She waters a large umbrella plant. I watch her, envying her quiet work. "It's so beautiful here."

"Are you a gardener as well?"

"I mean, I have plants back home, but only the usual stuff. Ferns, spider plants, peace lilies. And I like to make silly stuff like fairy gardens. But nothing like this." I gesture toward the wall of delicate orchids to my left.

"If you like doing something, then it's not silly."

"I guess."

"At least you have an interest in gardening. I don't think most people your age see the appeal. No one even glances in here."

Beyond the glass doors students walk past, oblivious. Most of them don't care about gardening, that's definitely true. But they like beautiful places. And quiet rooms for studying.

"Maybe if you got more comfortable seating?"

"Like some upholstered chairs?" she replies sarcastically.

"Why not? You have space here in the middle." I stand and point. "You could position them around the pond so people could look at the water while they're studying. And maybe put some tables and chairs in the corners. There should be space if you rearrange those potted ferns by the hibiscus."

"You know an awful lot about this." She studies me. "I'll think about it. And I'd like to see some of those fairy gardens you make. Bring me some pictures. I may even have a few things you could use in them."

"Oh . . . um, okay. Thanks."

She brushes some dirt off her hands onto her pants. "Feeling better now?"

"Yeah, actually."

"I've always found gardening to be a great escape. But you don't want to spend so much time alone with plants that you forget how to be around others." She nods toward the entrance. "Hopefully you have some friends to spend time with as well?"

I nod. My thoughts go first to Dev, but then an idea comes to me. What if I invited Will to Dev's cricket game this weekend? He should be back by then and it would be the perfect opportunity to see him. I still don't know all the details of the game, but I know enough now to hold a conversation. The idea of having Will by my side again feels like a cool compress on a burn.

"Absolutely. Thanks again!" I pull my phone out and go in search of more bars.

"I'm putting you to work next time," she calls after me.

chapter

18

I have to knock three times on Dev and Huan's door the Saturday of the cricket game before anyone opens it.

"Hey." Huan pulls a long-sleeved shirt down over his jeans. More shirts lie in a pile on his bed, including a few Star Wars ones, and I get the impression that he's already changed clothes multiple times today.

"Will and Frank are almost here!" I say. "We're supposed to meet them outside."

I'd called Will right away to invite him to the game this weekend. I was nervous that he'd have something better to do than watch amateur cricket, but he jumped at the idea. And, a few hours later, he texted to say that Frank wanted to come too. I'm grateful to have the whole day with him. The few times we've seen each other since Bath have felt like something out of my daydreams—walking hand in hand down quaint British streets, shy smiles over dinner, kissing under the moonlight—but since we're both burned out from work or school, our dates are short and our conversations never delve into anything too serious. Mostly we just talk about silly things like the weirdest stuff he's seen while walking through properties with clients (they once found a mannequin with one arm and a clown wig in a basement). Hopefully today we can spend the entire time bonding over cricket. I'd love to surprise him with my new knowledge.

Huan puts his hands on my shoulders. "Don't freak out. All we're doing is watching a cricket game. Dev wasn't this nervous and he's *playing* in it."

I run my sweaty hands down my pants. I wish Dev and Sage were with us, but Dev is warming up and Sage insisted she needed to spend the day catching up on her reading. Poor Dev.

My phone vibrates and I whip it out. "They're here!" I cry, making Huan jump.

"Christ, Ellie, cool it or you're going to scare him away in two seconds."

But Huan's pace matches my own as we bustle through the manor to meet the guys in the circular driveway.

"Hi!" I yell as soon as I'm out the door. Will breaks into a huge smile and reaches out to hug me. We walk through the fields that lie behind the manor toward the cricket pitch. I peek over at Huan and Frank, and they're already absorbed in conversation. I grin and tilt my head back so the sun can warm my cheeks on this cool October day. Emberton feels different with Will here—bright and shiny like it's my first day again.

"It's been too long since I saw a proper game of cricket that wasn't on the telly. I didn't even know Emberton had a team."

"Well, I'm not sure how *proper* they are. Dev warned me it could be rough."

"Is he watching with us as well?"

"He's on the team. He's the one who invited me to come. That's how I got the idea to invite you."

Will's pace slows. "He invited you to watch him play?"

Crap. That did not come out well. "No—I mean, not in that way. He—" I pause, realizing I can't tell Will the truth about why Dev invited me without revealing that I enlisted him to help me date Will. "He, um, just knows I'm interested in cricket."

"Huh. How nice of him." Will points at the few metal bleachers that line one side of the pitch. The crowd is sparse, maybe twelve others in all. "Is . . . that where we're going?"

"Yeah. I guess they don't get big crowds for the games." I laugh, but it comes out like a squeak. "But at least we'll be right up front!"

We climb the bleachers, which end up being a little rickety. I trip on one of the steps and Will's hand shoots out to steady me before I can lose my balance. *Swoon.*

"This should be an interesting day." He takes my hand and we shimmy-step down the bench.

My knee won't stop bouncing after we sit. Maybe this wasn't a good idea for a date. I mean, last Saturday Will surprised me with reservations to the fanciest Italian restaurant in Northampton. Why did I think this would be equivalent? On impulse I lean over. "I know this isn't what you're used to. Sorry I couldn't invite you to something cooler."

"No apologies." He lays his hand on my leg and shivers run up my back. "Truth be told, I'm not really here for the cricket."

"That makes two of us," Frank says.

"Don't you mean three?" Huan adds.

At that moment the two teams of Emberton students come onto the field and we clap and whistle politely. Unfortunately, Dev was right about the game. Even with my limited knowledge, I can tell it's slow and boring. On the professional teams, the bowler will throw the ball at almost a hundred miles per hour. Here it's looking like ten.

"So . . . ," Huan says slowly. "I don't get it. Is it like a weird version of baseball?"

Will huffs. "You must be putting us on."

Frank clasps his hand over Huan's mouth with wide eyes. "*Shhhh.* We mustn't question cricket in front of you know who." He jerks a thumb toward Will dramatically. "We just smile and nod as if it makes sense."

I laugh. "Have you gone to a lot of games together?" I ask Frank.

"A few." He and Will smile at each other. "You can't be mates with Will without having a little cricket in your life, but I try to wiggle out of it whenever I can. Though . . . I do make exceptions."

"I don't want to poke the bear, but what's the point of the sticks behind the batter?" Huan asks.

"That's called a wicket," I say. "The bowler from the other team tries to hit it with the ball to get the batsman out. Or, if the batsman manages to hit the ball, one of the fielders will try to catch the ball to get him out. So, I mean, I guess it's a bit like one of the bases in baseball, but I'm not sure cricket fans would agree." I sit taller, proud I remembered all that even if I still don't find it interesting.

Will stares and I expect him to argue or correct me. Instead, a surprised smile spreads across his face. "Impressive," he whispers, and kisses me behind the ear. "And I thought you couldn't be sexier."

He thinks I'm sexy? Because of *cricket*? Dear god, I'm going to have to buy Dev a Cadbury bar as big as his head to thank him.

His eyes shine. "How did you learn about cricket?"

"I just, you know, wanted to learn. So I studied up."

"Brilliant. Now we can watch all the games together."

I nod enthusiastically. I know that's *a lot* of cricket, but warmth still bubbles up in my chest. I'm so glad he wants to share one of his favorite activities with me. "I think Emberton will be doing more matches like this. You could come watch them all with me."

He laughs and gestures to the pitch. "Well, that might be a bit much even for me. And don't forget I'll be leaving for Belgium soon." He swats at the air, a sour look marring his face. "I didn't tell you—Father just backed out. Something always comes up last minute."

"Oh no."

"Actually it'll be nicer now. I can have a bit of a lie-in after all the work I've been doing." He wraps his arm around my waist and pulls me close. "I'll miss seeing you, though."

"I'll miss you too." An idea occurs to me and I shift to see his face. "Wait, isn't Belgium known for its beer?"

"Why do you think I agreed to go?"

"This could be a great opportunity, then. You've been talking about investing in a brewery—you could take this chance to tour some, talk to the owners, taste test. You could gather everything you learn and present it to your father."

"Actually, I don't think it's smart to pursue that anymore. The market is saturated with breweries and if I don't invest wisely on my first go, Father will *never* trust me. But my mates and I went to a pop-up restaurant in London a few weeks ago—the food was absolutely brill—and the chef's looking for an investor." He turns to Frank. "Wasn't that food amazing?"

"It was. But you still shouldn't invest in him."

"You don't think I should invest in anything."

"Because it's not *you* investing—it's your father's money. You'll never get away from him if you do that. You need to invest in yourself."

"He's always going on like that." Will rolls his eyes at me.

"You need to find something you're really passionate about," Frank continues.

"I don't know about that. People who do something they love end up hating it."

Frank throws his hands in the air. "That's not true!"

"People always hate their jobs. The quickest way to hate something is to start doing it for a living."

"Then what are we supposed to do with our lives?" Huan asks.

"Do something you don't care about that makes you lots of money. You can do everything you love on the side."

I bark out a laugh in surprise. Well, *that's* a new life strategy. Maybe I should go premed after all. Huan and Frank exchange a derisive glance. Frank catches my eye and shakes his head just slightly, as if to say, "Don't listen to his BS." I suppress a smile.

The game is never-ending. Huan and Frank don't notice, though—they're too caught up talking about music and the concerts Frank's been to lately. I love seeing Huan so happy and animated with Frank. It's exactly what I want with Will. Our conversations aren't quite as comfortable as Huan and Frank's yet, but we're definitely getting there.

Eventually Will pulls out his phone, a universal sign that he's bored. I look around, trying to think of anything to liven this up.

"There's not much around here in the way of concessions, but I could probably raid the Emberton kitchen," I say. "Snacks always make things better."

"That would be fantastic." He leans in to kiss me. "Hurry back."

"Whoa, look who you've brought to cricket. What a trade-up!"

I freeze, inches from Will's face, and turn at the voice. It's the girls from the welcome orientation—Nicole and Heather. Their expressions hold no malice, but my stomach tightens with worry. They look *way* too intrigued by Will. I hope they don't blurt out something crazy in front of him. All I want is for us to have a fun day here without any reminders of what happened with Andy or Crystal.

I shake my head in warning, but they pay no attention.

"Hello," Will says curiously.

The girls practically squeal. "Hiii!" Heather turns to me. "Where'd you meet?"

"Northampton." It comes out as a whisper.

Nicole's eyes widen. "Aren't you lucky."

"Nah, you've got that backwards." Will stands and reaches for my hand. "Are you girls looking to meet someone? I have loads of mates who'd be chuffed to have an American girlfriend like I do."

I inhale sharply. He thinks of me as his *girlfriend*? I didn't know we were so serious. Tendrils of electricity zip through my arms and legs and I have to stop myself from doing high kicks across the stands like Heath Ledger in *10 Things I Hate About You*.

Nicole beams and Heather steps up next to her. "Yes, please."

"Your word is my command," Will says with a laugh. "We can't send you back to university alone."

Nicole and Heather exchange confused glances and my eyes bug out. Oh no . . .

"We're not in college yet—we're here with our high school study abroad program." Nicole flutters her eyelashes at him. "But I'd be happy to never go back. I *love* it here."

Will squints. "Sorry, I must be a little slow today. Don't you all go to school together?"

I tug his arm. "I'm getting really thirsty. Why don't you come help me get drinks? I could take you around Emberton. It's really beautiful."

Will's gaze doesn't leave Nicole and Heather, but Huan comes into my peripheral vision, Frank hovering at his side.

Heather nods brightly, oblivious to everything but Will. "Yep, we're all in the same program, though Ellie joined last minute."

Will's face slowly morphs from confusion to shock. I sway backward, my joy from seconds ago buried by dread.

He turns to me. "Wait, am I understanding this right? You're still in high school?" His voice is just above a whisper.

I nod mutely.

Will is silent for a moment. Then he steps down the bleachers and says, "I could use that snack now."

chapter 19

I blink a few times and follow him. The girls wave good-bye, clearly confused by the sudden change in Will's mood. Dev catches my eye as we walk past the field. He's too far away to talk to without yelling, but his brow is furrowed. I point toward Emberton and mimic drinking. He points back to the pitch and it's clear he's almost up to bat. I look from him to Will, who is striding ahead of me. I do want to see Dev play, but this isn't the right time. And I'm sure he'll understand since he only invited me as a form of homework.

I mouth an apology and hurry to Will, who is far ahead now.

"You're in high school?" he repeats when I catch up to him. "You haven't graduated?"

I grimace at the annoyance in his voice. Will is usually so laid-back that I'd almost convinced myself he wouldn't care about my graduation status. But I was clearly wrong.

"I'll graduate soon."

"Yeah?"

"Well, um, at the end of the school year. But really, is that so long in the grand scheme of things? Spring will be here before we know it." I'm hoping for a tiny smile, but he rolls his eyes.

"Why didn't you tell me that?"

"I don't know." I drop my gaze to the ground. "I just—you and Frank had already graduated and we'd just met and I *am* taking classes with college students and . . ." My shoulders slump. "I don't know. I guess I just wanted you to . . . to like me."

"And you thought lying to me was the way to make that happen?" His eyebrows pinch together. "Frank tried to tell me something about Huan being in high school in America but I told him he must be wrong. I look like such an arse now."

He widens his stride so that I have to speed walk to keep up. "I'm sorry, Will. I really am. It was a stupid thing to say. I kind of blurted it out at the flea market and I didn't know how to correct you afterward."

Will stops abruptly in front of Emberton. I take his hands in mine. He doesn't pull away, but he doesn't grip them either.

"Why don't we go somewhere and talk?" I turn toward the manor. "We could grab drinks inside? Or we could go somewhere else. Maybe get some lunch."

He looks at the manor and then back at me. His face is still pinched. "I think I'm going to head out. I'm knackered and Mum's been on at me about packing for the trip. You understand, right?"

"I . . ." My legs are shaky and I can't get a deep breath. Oh no, what's happening? What's he thinking? "Are we okay? I wish you wouldn't go right now. Maybe you can just stay a little longer?"

"No. I think it's better if I go."

"What about Frank?" I wave back at the cricket game, desperate to find a reason to make him stay. "You can't go without him. We at least need to go back and tell him you're leaving."

He glances in the direction of the pitch but shakes his head. "No, I won't pull him away from his date. He can call a cab when he's ready." He heaves a sigh. "We'll talk after I'm back from Belgium, okay? Mum will murder me if I'm texting over the holiday."

I wander aimlessly through the manor after Will drives away, lost in my thoughts but not ready to share them with anyone else yet. The scene with Will keeps replaying in my mind. *Why* did he have to find out about Waterford? I should have pulled him off the bleachers as soon as Nicole and Heather saw him. Or grabbed him and kissed him so hard he forgot what we were talking about. Now he's upset and I don't know what to do to make things go back to the way they were.

I find myself at the conservatory. It's the only place around here where I'm not surrounded by people. In fact, I'm the only one here again. I wander around, taking stock of the plants and watching the fish swim in lazy circles. I know there's one voice that'll calm me. I pull out my phone.

"Mom?"

"Honey!" Mom's voice is loud and bright. "Oh, I'm so glad you called. I was just thinking about you."

"I miss you." My voice is thick and I close my eyes.

"Is something going on? It seems early for you to be calling me."

I look around in confusion. "It's two p.m."

Mom laughs and the sound smooths the pointy edges in my

mind. "I completely forgot about the time difference. It's nine a.m. over here."

I sit down on a bench and lay my head back. "Are you drinking tea and reading?"

"What else would I be doing on a Saturday morning?"

I smile. Brits may know their way around a teapot, but I can't wait to have a cup of Mom's English breakfast when I get back home. "Things are . . . okay, I guess. The classes are still really hard so I haven't been able to travel as much as I was hoping."

"And . . ."

I wince at her knowing tone. "And the boy I met over here—Will—he's leaving on a trip with his family so I won't see him for a while. Things are a little . . . weird between us right now."

"Did he hurt you?"

I groan. "Mom, no, of course not. We . . . I don't know, I don't want to get into it. Today just didn't go the way I was planning."

"Yeah, life has a way of doing that. What about your new friends? How are things going with them?"

"Good. Actually we're planning a trip to London next weekend. I forgot to tell you."

Mom squeals and I have to pull my phone from my ear. "Do you still have a list of all my recommendations? There's so much to see there. How much time will you have?"

"We haven't figured it out yet." I laugh at her excitement. "But I'll be sure to share your list for consideration."

"Consideration." She sniffs. "My list is *the* list. There's nothing to consider." Then her voice grows more serious. "Listen, I'm really happy you've found some new friends over there. I was getting a little worried at the end of the summer, but I feel so much better knowing you're with kids you like."

"Thanks, Mom."

She's right, and I know I shouldn't avoid them just because I'm upset about Will and me. I stand and walk back toward the cricket field, filling her in about my classwork and our London plans so far. When I get closer, I see people trailing back toward Emberton. I must have lost track of time. Sage is in the distance, walking toward me with Huan, Frank, and Dev. I say goodbye to Mom and walk over.

"Hey! What are you doing out here?" I ask her.

"I could only read for so long before I needed a break. And I've never seen a real cricket match before—only the clips you watched in our room."

"Unfortunately, you still haven't seen a real match," Dev says with a smirk.

"It was a good speed, mate," Frank says. "Any quicker and I wouldn't have been able to keep up."

"How was the rest of the game?" I ask.

"Dev scored the winning run." Huan slaps him on the back. "I screamed so loud my voice is hoarse now. I might not be able to beatbox for a few days."

"Multiple days of quiet in our room?" Dev shakes his head. "This day keeps getting better and better."

"That's amazing, Dev. I'm sorry I missed it."

"Me too." He doesn't look at me as he speaks.

Huan and Frank eye me expectantly, clearly thinking about

the way Will and I left the game, but I shake my head. I don't want to bring up what happened with Will right now. It's not cool to take over the conversation when Dev's still on a high from the game. Plus, I don't want to explain that I lied about being in college. I can only imagine the look Sage would give me.

Dev turns to the others. "Anyway, I'm heading inside. I've got to call Sahil. He'll want to hear everything."

He bounds off toward the manor and I watch him, guilt welling in the pit of my stomach. Not only is everything screwed up with Will, I was wallowing so much I didn't even see Dev's big moment. I hunch my shoulders and follow the others back to Emberton, wishing I had a redo button for today.

chapter
20

The next week crawls by. I don't hear from Will, other than a text from the airport to say he's leaving for Belgium and that we'll talk when he gets back. The only thing that pulls me from my funk are thoughts of London. When Saturday finally arrives, I don't need an alarm to wake up.

"Excited?" I ask Sage.

"Absolutely." She puts in chandelier earrings with little pewter books. The small addition accentuates her short hair and reminds me of how striking she can be. "My only worry is that we won't get to everything on the list. It's pretty jam-packed."

"Either way you'll have the whole day with Dev." I bump my hip into hers.

"I already told you that I'm not looking for a boyfriend."

"I know you aren't *looking*." I come up behind her so our faces are both reflected in the small mirror. "Let's just relax and have a fun day together. We'll explore London and you can spend time with him. He's a pretty fun guy if you get to know him."

Sage shoots me a withering gaze. "You forget I've known him since I was in fifth grade. And like I already said, I want to tell Mom and Wren about the lifesaving research I'm helping with, not which boys I dated. Plus, Wren's always been boy-crazy and look where that got her." Sage nods toward the half-finished baby blanket lying across her desk chair.

"Um, you know she had to do a little more than walk around a museum with someone to get her bundle of joy."

Sage huffs. "Oh, I'm aware. Do you know how many sex talks I got from Mom after Wren got pregnant? I couldn't walk out to get the mail without her putting a condom in my back pocket."

My jaw drops open. Sage and I have definitely gotten closer over the last seven weeks, but talk of condoms is *way* beyond our usual topics of conversation. Sage's amused smile—like she loves that she's shocked me—makes me burst out laughing.

"What did you do with all of them?" I flip through one of her genetics books. "Are you using them as bookmarks?"

"Stop!" She laughs and slams the book closed. "Actually"—her cheeks turn pink—"I sold about a dozen to the guy who had a locker next to mine last year. He was too embarrassed to go buy some and I wanted extra money." She points to her earrings. "Guess how I was able to pay for these?"

"Ack! Those are *condom* earrings?!"

I fall back onto her bed, laughing, and she follows suit. When I can get a breath, I point at her. "And you're *sure* you won't be needing any of those?"

She smirks. "I didn't say I sold them *all*. They have a long

expiration date and I might have more free time after graduation."
I squeal with laughter and she throws a sweater at me.

A knock interrupts us. I throw the sweater back at her and swing the door open. Huan is there. He's used extra gel to make his hair stand straight up and he has on a Union Jack T-shirt that says, *If I Had a British Accent, I'd Never Shut Up.*

"Nice."

"Frank gave it to me after the cricket game." He looks between us. "Sounded like you two were having a good time."

"Just talking about shopping and extracurricular activities," I say, and Sage snorts behind me.

Dev pops his head in the door. "Are you two coming?"

I turn to Sage. "Didn't you say you weren't until after graduation?"

The sweater smacks me straight in my face this time.

Thirty minutes later, I stare out the window as our train whizzes toward London, happy to eat up the view of the countryside. Beside me, Huan is texting (Frank?) and Dev and Sage sit across from us with their heads tipped toward each other, flipping through his London tour book and discussing entrance times. They're so cute it gives me a pang in my stomach. What is Will doing right now in Belgium?

We're about twenty minutes from London when my phone rings. My heart does a double beat when I see it's Will calling.

"Hello?" I say quietly. Three faces automatically turn to me.

"Hello, Elle."

Heat rolls over me at his beautiful voice.

"I wasn't expecting to hear from you until Monday." I step over Huan's and Dev's legs and walk down the center aisle of the train. I don't like having everyone staring at me. "How are you? How's Belgium?"

"Horrible. We're on our way home." His voice is grim. "The whole trip was rubbish. It never stopped raining and the hotel messed up our reservation. We had to stay in one room and we're about ready to rip each other to pieces."

I muffle a surprised laugh. "I'm sorry you had a bad time," I say, even though it doesn't seem that weird for Will and his sister to stay in the same room as his mom. From what I know of Will, I'm sure they weren't slumming it at some hole-in-the-wall hotel.

"At least now I'm back sooner so we can talk in person. I couldn't stop thinking about you in Belgium."

"You couldn't?"

"I—" He pauses. "I know I didn't leave it in the best way and I've been gutted about it. Can I pop over this afternoon so we can talk?"

I look around the train in confusion and realize he doesn't know about our trip today. I think I mentioned it once in a text, but we haven't exactly been in close contact this past week.

"Um, actually I'm not at Emberton. A couple of us are heading down to London for the day."

"You are?" He laughs. "Then we have to see each other! I'll be getting back into London in a few hours' time. One at the latest. And now I can put off that godforsaken drive back to Northampton for another day."

"Um . . ."

Will in London? Today? I'm simultaneously thrilled and horrified. I'm not sure I'm mentally prepared to have a *talk* with him today, if that's what he's hoping for. But he did say that he felt bad about how he left things. If he didn't want to date me anymore, he wouldn't have called. I glance down at my jeans and London Tube shirt. Ugh, why couldn't I have worn something that didn't scream *dorky tourist*?

Will keeps talking, undeterred by my hesitation. "This is brilliant. I really have wanted to talk to you. I'm not happy that you lied about going to university, but I get it. I used to lie about my age all the time to get into clubs with my friends. And it's not like you're that much younger than me. I'm sorry I acted like a wanker about it. Can I make it up to you?"

"I—I mean, seeing you sounds amazing. It's just . . . Well, I feel kind of bad. We made plans to see all the sights. There's, like, a color-coded itinerary and—"

"Oh. I'd forgotten about your friends. What sights? Not those bloody tourist traps, I hope."

My stomach tightens. "Well . . ."

"I understand. You weren't expecting this. Would you rather spend the day with them?"

I only hesitate a moment. "No! I'd love to spend the day with you. Text me when you get in and I'll tell you where to pick me up."

I put my phone in my pocket and peer down the train car at my friends. Huan cocks his head like he's asking if I'm okay. I give him a thumbs-up, but my stomach sinks thinking about explaining this to them. They're going to kill me, but I can't pass up the chance to see Will today. He sounded good on the phone, but I won't be able to relax about us until we're together in person.

"Was that Willoughby?" Dev asks when I return.

"Yeah."

I must have a horrible poker face because he immediately blows out a breath and leans back in his seat. "Please tell me you aren't about to tell us what I think you're about to tell us."

"That was an overly complicated sentence," Sage says.

I cringe.

"Ellie, no!" Huan looks between Dev and me. "You aren't ditching us, right? You said Will was in Belgium."

"He was—but his family is getting back early into London and—"

"You can't ditch us!" Huan repeats. "We spent forever planning this trip. We're supposed to see King's Cross station, Big Ben, St. Paul's Cathedral . . . if you aren't here, these two are going to drop the fun stuff altogether and spend the whole time in museums."

"We're still going to the Globe Theatre," Sage says. "Dr. Florence said she'll give us extra credit if we do."

Huan rolls his eyes. "You don't need extra credit."

"But I still want it."

"I'm so sorry, you guys. I had no idea this would happen. And I really was looking forward to today but . . . when he asked . . ."

Dev groans.

"What?" I ask sharply.

"You always choose him over us."

"That's not true."

Dev plays with his phone and I study him, irritation rising in me. Then realization hits me.

"Are you talking about the cricket match?"

"No," he replies in a wholly unconvincing voice.

I cross my arms over my chest. He never said a word to me about missing his game.

"I didn't think I needed to stay the whole time since it was assigned to me as homework."

"Homework you asked for."

Huan and Sage look back and forth as if they're at a tennis match.

"Right. In order to get closer to Will. Which is clearly happening since he wants to spend the day with me in London. That was the whole point, in case you've forgotten."

Dev jabs at his phone screen. "I haven't. Don't worry about that."

"Then why do you care?"

Now the middle-aged couple across the aisle is staring.

"You missed my wicket," Dev whispers. "You're the only one who even knows what that means."

"I know. I sat through those lessons," Sage adds.

"Yeah, but you came after that too." His voice morphs from bitter to sad when he speaks to her. "Never mind. I just didn't think you were someone who'd put her boyfriend in front of her friends."

I slump down into my seat.

"Hang on." Huan holds up a hand. "Don't get me wrong, I'm upset too, but we can't blame her for wanting to spend the day with her boyfriend in one of the most amazing cities in the world. Her *very* gorgeous boyfriend, I don't have to remind you." He turns to me. "Not that I've noticed or anything." He looks back at Dev. "Particularly when they were fighting before."

Dev glances up curiously. "You were fighting?"

"He found out that I'm still in high school and didn't take it super well. That's why we left the game."

"Oh." He rubs the back of his neck. "I didn't know. You should have said something to me."

"You were excited about the win. And let's be real—we both know you aren't too invested in my relationship with *UK Ken*."

He frowns. "Sorry."

I take a deep breath. I can't believe he's been upset with me this entire week about missing the cricket game. I didn't think he cared. And honestly, does it really matter if I'm around today or not? Dev will be with his best friend and the girl he likes. I've always been the tag-along friend. I'm surprised he's not relieved to be free of me.

I lean forward on the table that separates us. "I'm not planning on making a habit of this, but . . . I couldn't refuse with things the way they are right now."

Dev nods.

"When is he picking you up?" Sage asks.

"Around noon or one."

She scans the itinerary. "Maybe we can rearrange this. I know you don't care about this." She draws a line through one of the bullets on her beautifully written itinerary. "Or this." Another swipe.

"But—" I reach out to stop her.

"And we'll move all this down here."

Dev leans over Sage's arm to examine her new scribbles. "But we're arriving into King's Cross specifically because it's close to the British Library."

"You better still leave time for Platform 9 ¾," Huan interjects.

I look at him, surprised. "I didn't know you were a fan."

He shrugs. "I'm not really, but I do love Daniel Radcliffe. And I'd rather take a cheesy picture with a trolley than spend an extra hour at museums."

"You guys don't need to change your whole plan," I say. "I'm the one messing everything up."

"It's not a big deal," she says. As if she doesn't care that she spent multiple precious study hours working on this schedule.

I sit back, my throat suddenly tight. I can't imagine Crystal ever changing her plans for me. "Thanks," I whisper.

"He better make it worth your while, though," Huan says.

"I have a feeling he will. He says he wants to make it up to me."

Huan nods approvingly.

I risk a glance at Dev. "Looks like you really know how to tutor after all."

"Maybe I should start charging for my services."

"You'd make a killing," I reply awkwardly.

I stare out the window to break the tension. When I turn back a minute later, Dev's eyes are still on me.

chapter
21

When we arrive at King's Cross station, I'm immediately overwhelmed in the best possible way. People are going in every direction. There are backpackers with bags almost as long as they are, looking haggard and happy and very cool. There are people in extremely fancy suits, parents with children, elderly couples. Different languages swirl around me, amplified by the modern domed ceiling. I adore everything about it. We all stand there, wide-eyed and grinning, and the tension from the train is immediately forgotten. There's no time to think about anything but the awesomeness of London.

We head toward Platform 9 ¾ first, but there's already a huge group of tourists waiting for their turn to take pictures with the luggage trolley.

Sage shakes her head. "We'll do it on the way out. If we're going to see Big Ben together, we need to move."

We follow Sage through the complicated procedure of buying transit tickets and finding the right Tube line. I've used the DC metro system a lot, but there's something so much more adorable about the London Underground. Everywhere I go there are signs reminding me to *Mind the Gap*. I know it's about the most touristy thing I could do, but I'm definitely buying a *Mind the Gap* T-shirt before I leave England. Maybe two.

We make it across the city quickly and as soon as we exit the Tube station, we see Big Ben.

It is breathtaking. And tall.

The entire area is so quintessentially . . . *London*. Which is dumb because *of course* London looks like London, but this feels like they took all the biggest icons of the city and crammed them together for tourists to enjoy. We allow the crowds to steer us toward Big Ben while taking in the mammoth Parliament building that borders the Thames River. Beyond that is Westminster Abbey and across the river is the London Eye, a ridiculously huge Ferris wheel. There are even fancy black cabs and red double-decker buses driving past. It's like we've been dropped in the middle of a postcard.

After a minute of gawking, Sage pulls out her itinerary and scratches something off. "Great! Okay, next on the list—"

"Wait!" I grab her arm. "Are you crazy? We can't leave yet. It's picture time!" I force everyone to smoosh together and take selfies with Big Ben in the background. Dev keeps making stupid faces and Huan tickles me so that I'm a laughing blur in the photos instead of smiling and normal. After a moment's hesitation, I post one anyway. I may look like a dork, but at least I'm a joyful dork surrounded by awesome people.

Next we wait in line for Westminster Abbey. Inside, Sage makes a beeline for Charles Darwin's grave and then Isaac Newton's. It turns out there are an outrageous number of famous people buried here. The mood of the visitors in the abbey is a strange mixture of reverence and excitement as they find their "favorites" and whisper around their tombstones, which are embedded in the walls and even the floors. Walking over graves that are set into the ground makes me wish the soles of my shoes were cleaner.

Huan elbows me and points to a large tour group making their way down the aisle we're in. I'm assuming they're Australian from the flag the tour guide is gesturing with. Huan grins and motions toward the group. I muffle my laughter and we shuffle up to the stragglers and pretend to listen and nod when the guide says something.

I peek behind me. Sage's eyes are wider than I've ever seen them and Dev is shaking his head and waving for us to come back.

The group surges ahead, following the guide out of the main abbey and into the cloisters outside. A sign on the door says *Tour Entrance Only*.

I bite my lip and follow, keeping my head down.

"What are you guys *doing*?" Dev whispers. He and Sage have run to catch up to us.

"Come on," she whispers. "Before we get in trouble."

Huan shakes his head. "Be cool. Or as close to cool as we can get."

The guide points to something behind us and the entire group turns in our direction. I almost duck. Instead, I turn and pretend like I'm looking with everyone else. We're not fooling anyone. Two women whisper to each other and give us the evil eye.

Another steps forward. "I don't remember you being a part of our rugby sevens team."

Oh, crap. The group is made up of only women. Very fit, very intimidating women.

"Um, nice to meet you?" I say.

Another girl steps up.

Huan pulls on my arm. "Come on!"

We take off through the doorway and into the chapel. We scurry through the crowds and back onto the lawn outside. I put my hands on my knees and burst out laughing.

"We almost got our asses kicked in a church."

The others are laughing now too, though Sage is shaking her head. "What were you guys thinking? What if they called the guards? What if they kicked us out?"

"Were we planning on coming back?" Huan asks.

She huffs. "Well, I'd like to have the option. They might have some database where they keep our names on file or something."

"Or maybe an Abbey prison?" I suggest.

She rolls her eyes, but her mouth crooks up in a half smile.

"Well, that was more fun than I expected." Huan gestures to Sage's itinerary. "What's next?"

I point at the London Eye. "Do we have time for that?"

"I bet the line is already crazy," Sage replies. "I mean, we could try, but . . ."

I wave away my disappointment. "Never mind. I'll follow your lead."

"Okay, well, we were going to go to Trafalgar Square next. I think it's pretty close to here."

I look at my phone. It's eleven thirty. We'll be cutting it close but I don't want to waste a minute in London. "Let's do it."

The Tube car is almost filled when it arrives at our platform. We push on, followed by even more people so that we're crammed together, body to body. Everyone shifts so that they aren't directly facing another person. My nose is inches from another woman's shoulder, and I can sense Dev right behind me. Huan and Sage are farther back. The train zooms off to the next stop, and we all sway in unison. My nose fills with the stench of perfume and sweat.

Despite claustrophobia-inducing conditions, I can't stop smiling. I study the Tube map and the fun advertisements that line the inside of the car. Everywhere I look, there's something else that I want to photograph and share online so I don't forget. When I turn to read more advertisements on my left, I find Dev watching me. His face is very close.

"You're always so happy here. I don't remember you being like that last year."

I didn't realize he'd noticed me. A tingle runs down my spine at the knowledge and I focus on his shirt rather than his gaze. "Just excited to be visiting London finally."

The car screeches and everybody lurches forward. Dev slams into me and I lose my grip on the bar. I throw my arms out, pushing into a middle-aged man.

"Oi, watch it!" the guy yells, and Dev grabs my waist, pulling me back against him before I topple anyone else over.

"Sorry!"

"That was my fault," Dev says to him. "I wasn't paying enough attention and bumped into her. I'm really sorry."

The man mutters something about tourists and straightens his coat.

"Are you okay?" Dev whispers. My back is still pressed against his chest and his arms are wound so tightly against my stomach that the heat from his fingers burns through my shirt. "I'm sorry, I—"

I look over my shoulder at him and his mouth clamps shut. We're only millimeters apart now. His eyes are fever bright and for a moment his grasp tightens against my waist. My heart does a stutter step. How did I never notice how beautiful Dev's eyes are up close?

His arms go rigid and he lets go, his gaze shifting to an advertisement to my left. I take an unsteady half step away. I look behind me, but Sage is staring at the ground. Did she see Dev grab me? Hopefully she knows better than to think anything could be going on between us. I should have stood by Huan instead to give her and Dev more time together, just in case there's still any potential there.

We stand in awkward silence as the train zooms along. Then something occurs to me and I elbow Dev. "Now we're even."

"What?"

"From when I stopped on the stairs and made you fall over." I stand up straighter. "Now I'm not the only klutz."

"No way." His expression clears and he smirks at me. "That was much worse. I could have broken my neck. You just bumped into someone."

"Someone who is probably cussing me out right now," I whisper, nodding to the man in front of me.

"Yeah, well, that guy's an asshole."

I laugh and try to ignore the fact that we're still standing close enough that I can feel his breath on my skin. I rush off the train as soon as the doors slide open. I can't make eye contact with Dev the whole way to the square and I'm grateful when he starts debating museums with Sage.

"The National Gallery has some of the most famous artwork in the world."

"So does the Portrait Gallery," Sage replies. "Don't you want to see the paintings of the royal line?"

I perk up. "Ooh, do they have any paintings of Prince Harry?"

"They do!" Sage says, nodding at me. "See?"

Dev gives me the evil eye. "You don't get a vote."

"Fine, I'm going to enjoy the ambiance next to the lions while you fight this out."

Huan comes up beside me. "That's the best idea I've heard all day."

We head to the enormous column that sits in the middle of the popular square. Four massive iron lions surround the column. There are lots of signs reminding visitors not to climb on them, so Huan and I find a seat close by.

"So, you excited to see Will?"

"I am." My stomach flutters at the idea that he'll be here to pick me up soon. I hope we can get over what happened last time and have a fun afternoon together.

Huan rubs a hand through his hair, making it stick up even straighter. "So . . . you and Dev . . ."

"Are friends," I say quickly. Did he see Dev and me on the Tube earlier? "I hope. Mostly I think I piss him off."

"You certainly know how to drive him crazy."

"What about you? I'm not the only one who knows a cute British boy living in London."

Huan grins but doesn't reply.

"Did you tell him you'd be here?"

"Yeah, he knows. He wanted to tag along but I told him I wanted it to be the four of us."

I slump, feeling crappy all over again.

"No, I didn't mean it that way. Really. It's cool, Ellie. I can tell how much you like Will. And how much this all means to you. I just don't feel the same way."

"You don't like Frank that much?"

He keeps his gaze trained on the crowd. "Frank is amazing. He's . . . well, he's not like anyone else I've met. Or am likely to meet in the future."

"So what's the problem?"

He turns, scowling. "*That's* the problem. I'm not going to be living here. And he's not going to be living in America. So, it's like, what's the point?"

I lean back, surprised. "The point is that you like him. And that you're only here for a few months."

"Exactly."

"So *enjoy these months*, Huan. Live them up. Don't overthink it."

He shakes his head. "Aren't you scared of what happens after that? When we go home? How are we going to go back to Waterford after . . . all this?"

I pause. At the beginning of the trip, my worst nightmare was going back to Waterford. The idea of seeing Andy and Crystal together was enough to keep me hopping from one European country to the next until after graduation. Now . . . I still don't want to go back, but it's not about them anymore. I'm dreading Waterford because that means I won't be *here* anymore. No more Emberton Manor, with its grand halls and rolling green fields. No more weekend trips to gorgeous cities with my friends. And, even worse, no more Will being only a train ride away.

My phone buzzes with a text from Will. He's illegally parked.

I jump down from the ledge. "Let's not think about going home yet." The only thing we should be doing is enjoying each day as much as we can. There's no time to waste.

I wave down Dev and Sage. "That's my ride." I hold up my phone. "Who won the argument?"

Dev puffs up proudly.

"Wow, impressive." I politely clap. "Well, take lots of pictures today. And have a good time looking at all the art."

"And you have fun making out a lot," Huan replies.

"Oh, I will."

Dev grimaces. "*Please*, no pictures then."

I wave and hurry away in the direction Will told me. When I get to the edge of the square, I turn around to wave again but they're already taking a group selfie. My heart stretches in two directions, pulled toward Will and my friends simultaneously. I wish I could have a few more minutes with them. And I wish I could have more days with Will. Mostly, I wish I didn't have to choose.

chapter 22

When I find Will, he's double-parked on an insanely busy road and he's leaning out the door, waving at a bus to go around him.

"I'm here, sorry!" I scramble into the car.

As soon as I'm inside, he hits the gas and swerves onto the road. "The traffic around here is shite, but it's worth it." He kisses my hand and all thoughts of Trafalgar Square fade. "I'm so glad you're in London today."

"Me too."

"We're okay?" he asks, his eyes still on the road. "You're not cross with me?"

How can I be cross when he's looking so perfect next to me and is kissing my hand and asking me if I'm *cross*? It's impossible.

"I'm okay if you are. We don't need to bring it up again."

His shoulders relax and he kisses my hand again. "You really are bloody amazing. Were your friends upset that I stole you away?"

"They'll be fine. They understand."

"I guess we could've invited them along, at least for the

afternoon. They might have liked having someone to show them around. I wasn't even thinking about them. I only wanted to spend the day with you, and Father was being mental and . . ." He pauses. "I wanted you to help distract me. You're perfect at that."

I bite the inside of my cheek. He said I was perfect—which should be the highest praise a girl can get—but I'm perfect at making him forget his life. Is that a good thing?

I shake off my concerns. "Don't worry. My friends don't need a tour guide. They already know exactly where they want to go and how to get there." I smile, thinking of Sage. "We promised to swap stories when we get back together tonight."

"Good. Because I'm not ready to share you."

I bask in that thought as I stare out the window at the shops and tourists whizzing by. The streets of the Mayfair district are lined with expensive stores, restaurants, and gorgeous hotels with multiple valets standing outside. Seeing London this way is a totally different experience. I feel like a local.

Will pulls up in front of a restaurant. "The Lady in White," he announces. "We have reservations here for lunch. Assuming you like the idea."

The restaurant looks . . . *posh*. Like, you need celebrity status or a six-figure salary to get a table. "Are you sure?"

"You deserve the best day I can give you. I thought we'd start here." Will takes a ticket from the valet. "I hope you like it. The menu is traditionally British. Not really my style, but Mum loves it."

My eyes widen as we step inside. Gilded chandeliers glint in the floor-to-ceiling mirror panels along the back wall of the restaurant. Each table is covered in linen with a bouquet of purple flowers. Thick embroidered curtains frame the enormous windows that face out toward the street. Teenagers don't eat at places like this. Politicians and lawyers and businessmen eat here. The Middletons might eat here. But not me.

"They're going to kick us out," I whisper, mortified.

"They won't. I promise."

True to his word, the hostess takes us to our table without a second glance. It's a small table, but the location is perfect. Close to the two-story windows, but situated so we can also see the rest of the restaurant. I take a deep breath and soak in the moment.

"Do you like it?" he asks at my expression.

"I—it's unbelievable."

"I'm so glad. Father got us the reservation. Mum asked him." His voice turns bitter. "They'd never turn away someone listed under his name."

"Your dad must be really successful."

He rolls his eyes. "It's easy to be successful when you never stop working. It's always something. Cocktails. Dinners. Group massages." I sit back at that and he smiles. "Who knows what he does. But, yes, he's good at his job. That's why I grew up around this."

He gestures toward the street outside. Oh, *wow*. He didn't bring me to an expensive part of London to impress me. He brought me here because this is home.

I have to stop myself from fidgeting as I read the menu. At the very top is a traditional English tea with scones, finger sandwiches, and tiny desserts. The little girl in me (which is like 90 percent of me) lights up until I see the price. It's sixty-five pounds. I almost choke. That's probably eighty dollars. I skim the menu for cheaper options. Maybe I can get a side salad?

Will tilts his menu to me and points right at the English tea. "They're known for their tea service. Does that sound good?"

"Are you sure? It's so exp—I mean, I thought you didn't like British things?"

He laughs, too loudly for the tranquil surroundings. "Are you winding me up? Obviously I like British things. *I'm* British."

I blush. "I'm sure you like yourself. I just meant . . . I don't know. Like Jane Austen and tourist attractions and stuff. You don't seem to like traditional things."

"I don't like the stereotypes. And Jane Austen can bugger off, but I'd be crazy not to like scones."

I scan the menu again, forcing myself to forget the price. "It does look good."

"Then it's settled." He pulls the menu from me with a grin.

The waitress brings out an elaborate three-tiered tray covered with tiny sandwiches, desserts, and scones all decorated with orchid blooms. I don't let Will touch it until it's been properly documented. My mom will kill me if she doesn't see *detailed* pictures of this.

Unsurprisingly, the food is as scrumptious as it is beautiful. The sandwiches—cream cheese and figs, prosciutto and Brie— melt in my mouth. And the desserts look like they were created by the Star Bakers on *The Great British Bake Off*. There are custard tartlets topped with red raspberries, tiny cups of silky orange panna cotta, perfectly cut squares of moist Earl Grey cake, and chocolate mousse swirled into milk chocolate cups. I've been transported inside my English Tea Pinterest page.

"I'm not ungrateful," Will says out of the blue. I freeze, teapot in hand. His eyes are wide, like he's trying to persuade me of something. "For this lifestyle, I mean. I hope I didn't come across that way before. I know how lucky I am. It's only . . ." His hand grips the delicate teacup too tightly. "There's always a deal to negotiate or a client to woo or some dire issue that he has to fix that minute. It's been like that for as long as I can remember. That's why Mum would plan holidays for us. She thought we could all have time together if we left the country, but he'd usually back out last-minute. She barely asks him anymore." Will speaks more quickly now. "I can't remember the last time he asked about my friends, or what I was interested in lately, or what I'm doing at the weekend. I can't remember the last time we talked about *anything* but work and school."

Will's words carry and a few people turn to look at us. I put down the teapot and lean forward, taking his hand. "I'm sorry," I whisper. "So you haven't talked about your restaurant investment either, then?"

"I tried. He listened for exactly thirty seconds before cutting me off and telling me to stop 'wanking about with witless ideas.' Every idea is stupid unless he comes up with it."

I squeeze his hand, my heart aching at the bitterness in his eyes. His relationship reminds me how lucky I am to have Mom.

"He's being horrible. How are you supposed to know what you want to do with the rest of your life if he never gives you the freedom to try?"

"*Right.*" He almost knocks over his teacup in his rush to lean closer. "It's so good to talk to you. No one else gets it." He lifts my hand to his lips and closes his eyes. When he opens them again, the storm inside him seems to have settled. I love that I somehow have the power to do that for him.

After we finish lunch, Will takes me through the ritzy Burlington Arcade—a beautiful shopping center full of clothing and jewelry too expensive to breathe on—and then we meander through the streets into Green Park. I spy some huge pine cones on the ground and almost stoop to grab them before changing my mind. It's too bad. Pine cones like that are the perfect material for fairy house roofs.

"Did you go to school around here?" I ask instead.

"No, Father insisted I go to Harrow."

"What's Harrow?"

His eyes widen in surprise. "A boys' boarding school."

"Boarding school?" I can't help chuckling as my brain fills with images of little boys in sweater vests and ties. "What was it like?"

He ducks his head. "It was . . . like another home. Frank and I met there years ago. All my friends are from there."

"Did you wear uniforms? And have houses like Hogwarts?"

"Uniforms, yes. Hogwarts houses, definitely no."

"Was it more like the boarding school in *Never Let Me Go*?"

He blinks. "Uh, I'm not sure. I don't really remember that film."

"Wait, have you not read the book? It's so good."

"I've never been much of a reader. Is it long? I can't make it through long books."

I have to press my lips together to stop from yelling out. *Please* tell me he doesn't watch movie adaptations before reading the books?

"Have you tried listening to audiobooks instead? Sometimes those can be almost better than reading the hardcovers."

"Eh, I never had any interest in them."

"Oh."

Will wraps his hand around mine and leads me down the path. "Come on, let's keep walking."

He takes me along the sidewalk that surrounds the park. I'm aggravated that he's not listening to me, but my mood softens as we walk farther.

I love seeing the families playing in the grass and the young couples strolling hand in hand. It's surreal to be one of those couples. Will points out the massive golden gate in the distance that separates tourists from Buckingham Palace, then tugs us down onto one of the benches that line the pathway and angles toward me.

"I'm so happy you came to London today. Sometimes I wonder what would have happened if Frank hadn't forced me to go to that flea market. We'd never have met." He takes a deep breath. "And you would never have rescued me."

I sit back in surprise. "I didn't rescue you."

"What do you think you're doing right now?"

He cups the back of my head and I take a shaky breath. When he leans in, I practically fall into his arms. The kiss grows deeper, his other hand wandering up my leg. There's a part of me that's aware we're out in the open for anyone to see, but I don't care. My heart beats faster with each passing second until I'm worried it'll flatline from overuse.

No one has ever kissed me like that. He clearly has a lot of experience in this area, whereas the only other person I've kissed is Jim Hartwell after our ninth-grade winter formal—and that was quick, dry, and anticlimactic. What else would Will want to do if the threat of constables wasn't hanging over us? More heat rises to my cheeks at the idea and I'm suddenly glad we're in the park. I could happily spend the rest of my day in London kissing him, but I don't think I'm ready to start buying condoms off Sage.

A vibration from my phone pulls my attention. It's been vibrating all afternoon but I haven't checked it.

Will pulls away. "You might as well," he says, gesturing to my phone while he pulls his own out. "Mum wants me to call her." He stands and walks a few paces away.

I shake my head as I scroll through my texts. Sage, Dev, and Huan have been sending me photos throughout the day. The three of them posing outside the National Gallery. Dev proudly standing next to paintings we studied in art history. All of them pouting next to a huge pile of McDonald's fries and two small ketchup packets. Clearly, it's become a game for them to send me as many photos as they can, with more and more ridiculous poses. Dev pretending to strangle Huan at the Tower of London. Huan doing a somersault near some very grumpy-looking guards in fancy black-and-red uniforms. They even roped Sage into it, getting her to pose so that it looks like she's pushing a huge bridge in the background. I laugh out loud, but I feel a twinge of sadness as well. They're clearly having an awesome day without me.

Will walks back over. "What's so funny?"

I hold up my phone and show him a few pictures.

"Looks like they're getting on well."

"They're just being dumb."

He sighs. "I've got some bad news if you were expecting another fancy meal tonight."

"What's going on?"

"I guess Father left some paperwork for me at the house and Mum wants me to come pick it up." He rolls his eyes. "I told her I was spending the day with you, but she said we should both pop over. I think she's curious about you."

My mouth goes dry. "Your mother wants to meet me?"

"You know how mothers are. They always want to know who their sons are seeing."

"But . . . but I'm not dressed to meet your mother," I say in horror, looking down at my Tube shirt, jeans, and scuffed tennis shoes. "Is your father going to be there too?"

"No, he's almost never home." He leans down and kisses me on the cheek. "And you look beautiful. She knows this is last-minute. She won't be expecting anything."

I swallow hard. So she *would* expect me to dress better had I known I was going to meet her?

He pulls me up from the bench. "Best bit is that she's ordering Indian from our favorite place. You're in for a treat. You won't get better Indian food anywhere else in the world."

I laugh, wondering if Dev would agree.

chapter
23

Will's house in London is even crazier than the country house. It's part of a long stretch of white row homes on a quiet, tree-lined street. I'm expecting the interior to match the traditional appearance of the outside, but it's ultra-modern. There are neon signs hanging on the walls next to baroque paintings. The floors are covered in huge slabs of pure white marble and the furniture is oddly shaped and looks uncomfortable. Even the quiet stillness reminds me of an empty modern art museum.

"My father again," Will whispers when he sees me checking out a Marc Chagall we studied in class. I guess my studying is paying off. "He's been collecting since he was my age."

I'm trying to imagine growing up in a place where the art costs the same as my house when his mother walks in from another room. She's beautiful. Tall and elegant and exactly how I pictured her.

"You must be Elle." She takes my hand in both of hers and squeezes it warmly. "How do you do?"

"It's so nice to meet you." My heart hammers and I wish I'd questioned Will about his mother's likes and dislikes before we got here. "I'm, um, sorry to hear you had to cut your trip short."

"Ah well, it's nice to be home. Come in and relax." She waves us from the entrance into a mammoth living room. "The food should be here soon. Beatrix!" she calls. "Come here and meet our guest."

Beatrix? I mouth to Will.

He whispers in my ear, "My sister. Mum studied British literature at university, if you hadn't guessed from our names."

A younger girl, probably twelve or thirteen, flounces into the room. She's slight and her long blond hair falls limply around her face. Her expression brightens at my presence.

"You're here! I was half wondering if Will made you up." She tilts her head to study me. "His stories didn't make you sound nearly as dumb as all his other girlfriends."

"Bea!"

"I'm glad to hear that," I say, trying not to laugh.

"He also says you're not as dramatic as the last one, which I hope is true because she was dreadful. Always crying and fussing." She shakes her head. "*And* you're American. I wish I had American friends. It would be so much fun to travel back and forth to see them." She plops down on the couch next to me, completely ignoring her brother's glare. "I've been to America, but only once. It's so *massive*. I can't keep it straight."

"Then you'd fit right in. Plenty of Americans can't keep it straight either." I tap my temple as if thinking hard. "It's those states in the middle that are always the trickiest to remember. I think Kansas should be in there somewhere . . ."

Bea squints at me for a moment and then laughs loudly.

"Ooh, you're fun!" She scoots closer to me on the couch. "You can stay."

Dinner arrives and I'm ushered to an enormous glass table covered with all kinds of food I don't recognize. I hang back, unsure of what to do, while Beatrix reaches around me.

"Have you ever had Indian food before?" Will asks.

I shake my head.

"Well, you've definitely come to the right town." He grabs a plate and starts piling food on it. "Everybody thinks that England is all fish and chips and mincemeat pies, but the real dish of England is chicken tikka masala." He hands me the plate. It has a big pile of rice and orange-brown sauce dripping over the chicken. "If you want to be British, eat that."

My first bite is tentative. Then warm spices flood my mouth and I scoop up another forkful. Why has this been missing my whole life?

"How did you like your lunch?" his mother asks.

I quickly wipe my face with a napkin before answering. "It was magical. We ordered the tea service."

"You know, I can't remember the last time I got Will to take tea with me."

"Well, truth be told, he barely drank any."

"Snitch!" Will says.

Beatrix giggles and warmth washes over me. "What else did you do?" Bea asks.

"After that we went shopping and walked through Green Park."

She sniffs. "That sounds like a boring day. My friends and I have done that loads of times." Beatrix swivels and points a finger at Will. "Why didn't you take her anyplace else?"

Will winces. "I—"

"Oh, it's all right," I jump in. "Your brother did a wonderful job. And I already saw some of the big attractions this morning with my friends. Big Ben, Westminster Abbey, Trafalgar Square. We had a great time."

Will frowns and I realize I never told him what we did this morning. Actually, now that I think about it, Will was so busy talking about his father and his trip this afternoon that he never got a chance to ask me much at all.

My gaze snags on another painting I recognize. We had to memorize it for our Italian Renaissance chapter in art history. I've already forgotten most of the paintings, but this one has stuck in my mind because it was weird staring at the naked woman in the forefront of the painting with Dev sitting right next to me.

"Isn't that, um, *Venus of Urbino*?"

Will's head whips toward me.

"Why, yes, it is. A reproduction." His mother regards the painting with fondness. "It doesn't fit with Timothy's collection, but he agreed to leave it up anyway. I bought it when we visited Italy on our honeymoon." She cocks her head at me. "Are you an art lover? I thought Will said you were studying psychology."

"Oh, well, I'm also taking European art history this semester.

We just finished a section on the Renaissance."

Will squeezes my leg under the table and I jump. Oh no, am I embarrassing him? But when I turn, his expression is surprised and pleased. His mother is also studying me with more interest than she had previously. She turns to Will.

"I spoke to your father when he dropped off the papers. He has a new client who works at UCL. He's very excited about the possibility of your being admitted. He wants you to ring him after dinner."

"UCL?" I ask Will. The happiness in his expression dries up.

"University College London," his mother explains.

"I thought he was stuck on Oxford," Will mutters.

"He's come to terms with . . ." She waves her hand vaguely through the air.

"With my rubbish marks? No, he hasn't. And it doesn't matter. They won't get me into UCL any more than they'll get me into Oxford."

She cuts her eyes to me. "We can discuss this later."

"I don't want his handouts. I don't need to go to university to do well in life."

"Willoughby, really. This isn't the time to get into this. Now—" She shifts her focus to me. "What area of America are you from? I've always been partial to the West Coast."

"I'm from Washington, DC. I've actually never been out to California." I glance at Will, who is glaring down at his food. "I'd love to go one day. I'm sure it's wonderful."

"Oh, it is!" Beatrix exclaims before telling me about her love of the Santa Monica Pier. I smile and nod encouragingly, relieved to be talking about something other than Will's college prospects (or lack thereof). I'm so thankful Mom never pressures me like Will's parents do, but all this college talk still stresses me out. At least Will and I have our indecision in common.

Dinner ends without more discomfort—thanks solely to Beatrix, because Will doesn't speak and I have almost nothing interesting to say. As soon as we stand, Will and his mother step into the kitchen with our plates and I excuse myself to the bathroom. But when I come back out, I can hear Will's voice clearly.

"He likes keeping me hostage."

His mother shushes him. "Stop speaking like that about your father. You know he wants what's best for you. He's trying to give you some work experience in Northampton."

I gingerly retreat back into the dark bathroom. Maybe I should announce my presence by stomping down the hallway or clearing my throat excessively?

"He doesn't want to give me experience," Will retorts. "He wants to keep me under his thumb out there. It's his form of jail."

"And if you'd done better on your A levels, we wouldn't be having this conversation."

"You know, all your talk of America is making me think I should move there for a while. It might be best for all of us if Father and I had some time away from each other."

"Really, Willoughby." She sighs dramatically. "What would you possibly do there other than spend more of our money?"

Ouch. Maybe I should kill a few more minutes in the—

"Elle! I was wondering where you went off to."

Beatrix stands in the open doorway with her hands on her hips and a smirk on her face.

"Oh . . . yes. I—" I swivel around for any excuse as to why I'm standing alone in the dark. "I got confused about which way to go. Your house is so large."

"It's only this way." She threads her arm through mine and pulls me with her. "They're always like this. Going on about universities and all that. Best to get used to it now."

She marches me back into the living room where Will and his mother stand side by side, stiff but smiling.

"How about some tea before you go?" she asks me.

"We can't," Will cuts in. "We already have plans."

"Fine, fine." She gives us both a double kiss on the cheeks. "Take care of our Willoughby. He certainly needs it."

"Oh—of course. I will."

I high-five Beatrix and she tells me to come back and she'll take me to all the cool spots Will doesn't know about. That makes everyone laugh.

"I assume you heard Mum and me arguing?" Will asks when we're on the street outside the house.

My ears burn with embarrassment. "I didn't mean to. I stepped out of the bathroom and—"

"It's all right. My mates are well used to our rows. You might as well be too."

"Is everything okay?"

"It is now that I'm alone with you."

I laugh shakily. "Has anyone ever told you that you're very charming?"

"On a daily basis." He pulls me tight to his side.

"So, where are you taking me now? I didn't think we had more plans tonight."

He smiles mischievously. "No spoilers."

We take the Tube since parking in central London is a nightmare, and I'm surprised when we get off and I recognize the stop.

"Isn't this—"

"Shhh! Don't ruin the surprise. Come on!"

The station is packed and it takes us a long time to make it back out. I swivel around and there it is—the London Eye—looming in the distance, as massive and alluring as it was this morning. I gape at Will with a mixture of confusion and delight.

"I was hoping to show you Big Ben for the first time, but since I apparently missed my chance, this will have to do."

"I love it," I whisper, taking in the Ferris wheel and all the hustle and bustle again.

"There's a lot of touristy stuff about London that's rubbish. But *this* I like."

My stomach sinks at the line for the London Eye. I don't know why I'm surprised since it's a Saturday night in London. Obviously it's going to be insane. I pull out my phone to check the time and see a new text and photo from Dev. He, Huan, and Sage have already made it back to King's Cross station and they're standing in front of Platform 9 ¾ without me. Huan is holding on to the luggage trolley and Dev is holding on to Huan like a strong wind is about to blow him away. Sage poses normally next to them. My throat tightens. I can't believe I missed this. I read his text.

We decided to get a photo while there was a lull. We'll get one with all of us when you get here. On your way?

"All right?"

I jump. For a moment, I'd forgotten where I was. "Yeah. Sorry." I shove my phone into my pocket before he can see the picture. I don't want to know what he must think of that touristy "rubbish."

I nod at the line. "This is such a sweet idea, but I don't think we'll have time."

He grins triumphantly and holds out his phone, showing me two tickets. "Timed, fast-track tickets. I don't wait in lines." He grabs my hand and we scurry to the entrance. His laughter helps me forget about King's Cross. In no time, a worker scans our tickets and ushers us into an oval, glass-encased capsule. A handful of other people get on with us but I barely register them. The view is all I see.

The Thames is below me and the Parliament building stretches out across from us. Big Ben, which looked so impossibly tall this morning, shrinks inch by inch as our capsule rises. All of London surrounds me and I feel small and towering at the same time. I take a deep breath and revel in this moment.

Hands wrap around me from behind. Will kisses me gently on the cheek.

"Welcome to London, Elle."

chapter

24

I've got less than ten minutes before my train leaves by the time we get to King's Cross. Will kisses me goodbye and I race through the underground Tube station, up the stairs, and into the train station, my bag banging against my leg. I find my train on the display screen—Platform Two—and push through the turnstile. I hurl myself through the first open door I can find. A few people jump at my sudden appearance. After taking a deep breath, I check my ticket again for my seat number.

Carriage E, seat forty-one. And I'm in carriage A. Awesome.

People glance up at me as I walk through each of the carriages. I'm only to the second one when the train jerks to a start and pulls slowly out of the station. I fall backward at the unexpected movement, but manage to grab on to a seat before I land on my butt. I'm reminded of how Dev caught me on the Tube earlier and a tinge of heat rolls down my spine. What a weird few seconds between us. I just hope Sage didn't see anything and misread the moment. I know how observant she can be. And even if she's not interested in dating someone right now, I'd hate to ruin the opportunity between her and Dev because she thought something was going on between us.

When I make it to carriage E, I'm surprised to find all my friends on their feet. Sage is typing something into her phone, Huan is craning his neck to look out the window, and Dev is faced away from me in the back of the car.

I hurry forward. "I'm here! I made it. Barely."

"Way to make a dramatic entrance." Huan heaves in a breath. "We thought you were stranded back there."

"Didn't you get my texts?" Sage asks.

I scoot into my seat and I pull out my phone. Sure enough, Sage has texted me six times since I left the London Eye, even going so far as to look up alternate train tickets for me. My heart fills with love at the sight.

"I'm so sorry. There wasn't service on the Tube and then I was running and I didn't—"

"Christ, Ellie," Dev interrupts. He stands in the aisle, looming over me.

I clench in preparation for whatever judgmental comment he has. Instead, he sags into the seat across from me and pushes the palms of his hands into his forehead.

"We thought something happened. You weren't responding and we didn't know where you were . . ."

"Oh." I bow my head. "I didn't think about it like that. Will and I got caught up and I was rushing to get here in time. I didn't mean to make you worry."

"What were you and Will caught up doing?" Huan asks with an eyebrow waggle. He's clearly already over my late arrival. "Making out at some fancy club?"

"The London Eye." I can't keep the joy from my words.

"You got to go?" Sage says. "And I was sure we'd see more today than you would. How long was the wait?"

"He got us timed tickets."

Huan nods appreciatively. "He's smooth, I'll give him that. But you still missed an awesome day."

Sage yawns. "I'm going to be so tired tomorrow. And we've got that anatomy test to study for. We should have taken the earlier train."

"*Anyway*, did you get our pictures?" Huan asks.

I laugh and scroll through more photos. I guess they spent the evening walking through a market.

"Covent Garden," Dev says before I can ask. "Really cool. They had great street performers."

"I can tell." I pull up a picture of him with his arm slung around the shoulder of a man covered in gold paint.

He lifts his arm like he wants me to smell his armpit. His shirt is smeared with gold. "Totally worth it."

"Don't wash that!" I laugh. "That's the best souvenir I've seen yet."

"Speaking of souvenirs . . ." Huan reaches into a bag and pulls out a tiny stuffed toy. "Something for you since you missed out."

It's a tiny white unicorn with a rainbow mane.

I squish it to me. "Oh, I love it! You bought this for me?"

"We all pitched in."

"No," Dev says. "He's being modest. You're sitting next to our very own street performer."

I spin to face Huan. "What? Did you—"

"Oh, he beatboxed. He had a crowd around him too."

"It wasn't a crowd," Huan argues. "It was maybe a few people at the most."

"A half dozen," Sage murmurs with her eyes closed.

"But still!" I say. "That's awesome!"

"He earned enough to get that." Dev points to the stuffed animal.

"But . . . ," I falter. "You didn't have to spend your money on something for me. I didn't know we were doing this. I didn't think to get you all something."

"Don't worry about it. I wasn't going to get you something with *my* money. But since it was other people's money, I didn't mind so much. Plus, you were the one pushing me to perform in public so . . . I figured it made sense."

I hold out the unicorn. She's perfect. I didn't realize they all knew me well enough to pick this out. I throw my arms around Huan. "Thank you. You're amazing."

Huan hugs me back quickly and fidgets away. "Since you didn't bring us presents, you better have some good stories. What happened with Will? You've clearly made up."

I begin with his insane house and soon we're all sharing details from the day. We talk the entire train ride back to Northampton. It's only when we get on the Emberton van to go home that we lapse into silence. Sage curls into a ball in her seat and Huan stares out the window. Out of boredom I open Instagram, but it's not nearly as interesting as it once was. I don't care about any of the people I'm following. Mostly my feed is just Andy's and Crystal's incessant posts and a bunch of photos from clubs and football games. I close it and pull up my own photos instead. I pause at one from the London Eye. Will's back is to the camera and he's looking out at the river with Big Ben framed in the distance. It's a gorgeous photo, both of him and the city. Like something out of a movie.

Someone touches me and I jump. Dev leans across the aisle and hands me a small plastic bag. "Here." His eyes don't quite meet mine as he says it.

I frown and open the bag. Something is wrapped in tissue paper at the bottom. I unwrap it and inhale. It's a tiny figurine of a fairy. I recognize it immediately because it's one of my favorites—the Rose Fairy by Cecily Mary Barker. I turn it over in my hands, admiring the details. I can't believe Dev knew to buy this for me.

"I saw it in a shop at Covent Garden. I thought you might like it for your fairy garden."

"You know about that?"

He gives me a look. "It's kinda hard to miss since it's sitting on your window seat. And it reminded me of that booth at the flea market. So . . . you like it, then?"

I open and shut my mouth, looking down at the fairy. "Of course. You shouldn't have."

"Ellie, I'm sorry I snapped at you this morning."

I meet his gaze. "I'm sorry I blew off your game."

We stare at each other for a moment before both looking down at the ground. I want to say more. To thank him or ask him what else he knows about me. But he shifts toward the window and it's clear he's done talking. I hold my fairy—she's going to be *so* pretty nestled in the leaves back home—when he twists around again.

"We missed you. It wasn't the same without you today."

I squeeze the fairy in my fist. "I missed you guys too."

chapter

25

I was living in a dream during our London trip, but Monday brings me back to reality like a slap to the face.

"Can't we take a break?" I ask, and slump onto the Formica table in the cafeteria.

Next to me, Dev, Sage, Huan, Sam, and Kelly hunch over an open chemistry textbook. Laptops cover the table, along with cold cups of coffee, forgotten sandwiches, scribbled notes, and artfully rendered flash cards (my contribution to the study fest). Everyone is freaking out so much over our upcoming chemistry test and group presentations that they won't stop studying to eat. I don't know why, though. As far as I can tell they already know everything.

"Ellie, you're the one who needs to be listening here," Sage says without looking up from the textbook. "I know you didn't understand chapter eight."

"My brain can't take any more. Didn't your parents ever tell you it's rude to read at the table?"

Sam snorts. "And didn't your parents ever tell you to get your grades up?"

I glare at his back. My grades have actually improved a bit since the first weeks here. Bs in psychology and art history, a C in British lit, and a C- in chemistry. I know a lot of the honors kids freak out if their grade drops to even an A-, but I'm damn proud of these scores. I've worked harder here than I ever have before. Grades were never something I cared much about in the past, and I did decently in my non-honors classes with minimal effort, but that's not going to fly here. And I can't face my mom if I come back with Ds and Fs.

Kelly asks something about ionic chemical bonds and everyone starts talking at once, trying to explain. I check my phone again, but there's nothing new from Will today. His father decided last-minute to bring him on a two-week work trip to Manchester, so now he won't be back in Northampton until early November. Will thinks it's payback for going on holiday to Belgium rather than staying to work. All I know is that it sucks. I'd really been hoping to spend *more* time with him after London, not less. I sigh and shove my phone into my pocket.

"Hey, Ellie?" Huan points to the textbook. "Are you feeling okay about this chapter? We're nearly done with this but we could spend some extra time going over terms if you'd like."

I shrink back into my chair. I know he's trying to be nice, but his offer only makes it worse. I *hate* that I'm the only one still struggling with the material.

"No, I'm good. Thanks." I hold up a half-eaten grilled chicken sandwich. "Um, better throw this away."

I hurry over to the trash cans before he can argue. Maybe if I kill a little time, the conversation will move on to something less discouraging. When I turn back, everyone is leaning toward Sam. I hurry over, wanting to hear whatever rumor or secret is being shared.

"I just wish Dr. Allen wouldn't have put her in my group. She can't keep up," Sam whispers.

"Jesus, don't be a prick. She's our friend," Huan says.

I stop behind him before anyone notices I've returned. I wrap my arms around myself. There's only one possibility of who Sam's talking about.

"I know she is. And she's nice enough if you're sitting around talking about nothing, but not when you're in a presentation group with her. How the hell is she supposed to help write the Power-Point on the decay of radioisotopes if she can't even understand the damn definition? She shouldn't be here. But she is, so now I'm left carrying the whole project myself and she'll get an A because of my work. Not that she doesn't need it."

I suck in a breath and Huan turns, followed by Dev, Sage, and Kelly. Their eyes bulge and they shift their glances to Sam. He's the last to turn around and when he does, his expression is unnaturally calm.

"Hey there. I—uh—didn't realize . . ."

I bob my head, too humiliated to speak. Every fear I've had about taking classes here explodes in my mind. Sage reaches toward me, but I can't stay. I don't want to hear Sam's excuses or fake apologies. I don't want to smile and nod while Sage and Huan tell me that I'm trying hard and that's what counts, like I'm a god-damn kindergartner or something. I just have to get away.

When I reach the conservatory, I'm surprised to see a few people chatting and sipping drinks around the fountain. I debate leaving, but something about the humid air and the tangle of leaves and flowers is too calming. I walk to the other side, letting my fingers trail along the palm leaves as adrenaline and anger course through me.

"Do you like the changes?"

I jump. It's the gardener I met last time. She's wearing dark green pants and shirt with a name tag. Miriam.

I force myself to push Sam from my mind and inspect the space. My mouth drops open. There are cushioned chairs . . . tables . . . I can't believe she took my advice. The weight on my chest lifts slightly. I may be horrible at school, but that doesn't mean I'm horrible at everything.

I turn to Miriam and she smiles.

"No point avoiding good advice just because I didn't think of it." She waves a hand toward a group clustered around the pond and whispers, "I can't get the students to leave nowadays. They make a terrible mess, but it's nice that the place is being used. Did you bring any of those fairy gardens you mentioned before?"

It takes me a second to remember what she's talking about. "Oh. No, I didn't. I kind of . . . I didn't get a chance to run by my room."

"Hmm." She gives me an appraising look. "What's your name?"

"Ellie Nichols."

"It's nice to meet you. I'm Miriam Powers. I have something you might like. Follow me."

She steps behind one of the larger palm trees to reveal a door, painted green to blend into the surroundings. A long narrow greenhouse lies beyond. The cement floor is smeared with dirt, the windows are streaked, and masses of potted plants sit along shelves. A spot of joy breaks through my previous mortification.

"Few people get to see behind the curtain," she says with a smile, surveying her surroundings. "Not much to write home about, but I thought you might find a few things you could use in your gardens."

She gestures to the other end of the greenhouse, where trays of tiny ferns, baby tears, Irish moss, and other plants I don't recognize wait. I hurry over, pulling the pots from the trays. I've never had so many plants to choose from before. I started gardening in sixth grade, when we moved from a house into an apartment and I realized houseplants made my small dark bedroom come alive. I've spent a lot of time in garden nurseries since then, but they always have the same things. Not here.

"You don't mind?"

"It seems you need a place to escape to," she replies. "You're welcome to come down here to make your fairy gardens . . . as long as you put in a little work."

I drag my eyes from the plants, my mind already racing with everything I could do. "What kind of work?"

She sets a maidenhair fern down in front of me—it's seen better days.

"Nip off some of the brown bits at the bottom." She hands me gardening shears like I'm her new apprentice or something. I hesitate, but honestly, gardening sounds like a great break from everything happening on the other side of the conservatory doors.

We work together in silence. When I finish with the maidenhair fern, she points to another one behind it, then has me repot a half dozen fishtail palms. The work isn't difficult but it is consuming, and thoughts of Sam fade. Finally, I stop to stretch my back and hand her the shears and trowel. A bit of time spent in the conservatory again and I already feel better.

"It's nice having an assistant." She nods at the plants in front of me. "Especially one who knows what they're doing."

"Eh, I don't know about that."

She puts down her trowel and looks at me. "Have you ever considered doing something more serious with this hobby of yours?"

"Fairy gardening?"

"Gardening in general. I don't know what ambitions you have for the future, but you clearly like it here. It's worth looking into gardening programs or internships when you get back home. Just to see what opportunities you might have."

"Oh . . ." I shrug. "I don't know. I've never thought that much about it."

"Well, you should."

I nod and add it to the endless to-do list in my mind. Explore career paths. I'll get right on that.

When I shuffle into my dorm room, I'm surprised to find Dev and Sage alone together. I avert my eyes, all the humiliation from before whooshing back.

"Oh . . . hey." I step back into the hall. "I'm just—"

"What are you doing? Come in." Sage waves me forward. "We

were just talking about you."

"There seems to be a lot of that going around today."

"Sam is a self-involved jerk," Dev says. "Now get in here and shut the door so we can start talking about him."

I sit on the edge of Sage's bed since Dev and Sage have taken both chairs and fiddle with my phone. "I don't want to talk about it. There's nothing to say and I don't want to sit here while you guys patronize me with compliments."

"I wasn't going to do that," Dev says.

"You weren't?"

"No. I know you're struggling with the classes. There's no point pretending otherwise."

My shoulders relax. I appreciate that he's not going to act condescending.

"*But*—" He points at me. "You struggling and Sam being a jerk are not mutually exclusive. He's one of the biggest complainers I've ever met. He loves to blame his problems on other people. If I know him, he was only saying that stuff so he has a ready-made excuse if you guys get a bad grade on the presentation."

"Totally." Sage nods. "Before every test he tells us how he didn't get much sleep, or he had to help his mom with something, or he's sick, as if that can excuse him for any bad grades he gets. It's incredibly tedious."

Tingling warmth creeps through me as they speak. I want to pull them into an enormous bear hug. "That does sound a little desperate." I give a weak smile.

"Very."

I sigh. "I know I'm the odd one out here. And the rest of you know it too. I've just been so scared that everyone was judging me and then to hear him say that . . ."

"Screw everyone else," Dev says.

I purse my lips. "You know what I'd like to do? I want to finish that entire goddamn presentation by myself and shove it down his throat."

Dev and Sage exchange excited looks.

"Hell yes!" Dev pumps his arm in the air.

"And that's going to take *a lot* of studying." I stand and walk to my desk. "I'll grab my stuff and go to the library. I don't want to interrupt you two anymore."

Sage shuts her laptop and pushes back her chair. "Actually, I think I need a break. I'm going to get a shower."

"I—" I glance between them nervously.

She grabs her bathroom stuff and heads for the door. "I'll be back in a while." She closes the door and leaves us in the silent room.

"Sorry for the interruption." I twiddle my thumbs. "At least you two had a little time alone?"

Dev shrugs one shoulder.

"I don't think you should give up hope. I know she likes spending time with you—I bet everything else will fall into place with time."

"Mmm, yes, it's all coming together. In fact, she could barely control her lust as we talked about protons and electrons. Couldn't you tell?"

I laugh. "Well, if the only thing you were talking about was protons, that might be the problem. You need to step up your flirting game."

"Because you know so much more than me about flirting?"

"I might."

He smirks and shakes his head.

"No, really, I want to hear this." I sit down and cross my arms. "You think *you're* a better flirt than me?"

"I could probably learn a couple of things. But I don't think you're the one to help me in that department. Well, unless you want to help me pick out a different name, *Elle*? Should I go by Devid? Or Deviel? Or maybe you could help me pick out some interests?" I throw my chemistry notebook at his head and he ducks, chuckling. "Hey! I'm only joking."

I wave at the door. "Go on, get out of here. I'm going to need every ounce of free time I can get to finish this by Friday and you're wasting precious minutes making fun of me."

I pull out my textbook from a messy pile on my desk. To my surprise, Dev pulls up a chair next to me.

"What are you doing?" I ask.

"What does it look like?"

"Sage won't be back for forever, you know." I flip open my book. "She takes weirdly long showers, considering how short her hair is."

"Actually, I didn't come to your room because of Sage. I was waiting for you."

I look up. "Why?"

"To make sure you were okay. And to study. With *you*."

My heart does a small flip in my chest. I'm not sure why since we've studied together plenty of times over the last few months. Maybe it's the realization that I was hoping he was going to stay to study, but didn't want to admit it until now. Plus, for once he's not even making a snarky comment.

He retrieves my notebook and lays it on the desk. "Studying next to you keeps me focused."

"Really? I didn't realize my study habits were so helpful."

"They're the opposite, actually. I know if I say something you'll start talking and we'll never finish our work. I've learned to keep my mouth shut when I'm around you."

And there it is.

I shake my head. "I guess I've done the whole world a favor, then."

chapter
26

"Ellie?"

I stop and turn to find Dr. Allen in the hallway outside the cafeteria. Dev and I exchange a quick glance. Earlier this afternoon in chemistry she handed back presentation grades to all the groups and I'm still on a high from our grade. I worked my ass off all last week to nail that presentation and am ecstatic to get an A-, especially since the only reason for the deduction is that Sam confused the nuclear equations for the alpha and beta decay reactions when he was presenting his portion to the class. Seeing her now makes my stomach flutter, though. Dr. Allen doesn't speak to students outside of class. *Please* tell me she's not rescinding our grade.

I give her a weak smile. "Hi, Dr. Allen."

"Good afternoon. I was hoping to talk to you for a moment. I've been thinking a lot about your presentation."

"Oh?" My palms begin to sweat. What if she thinks I cheated? Or did Sam say something nasty about me?

"I was really impressed, Ellie. Really impressed. I know you struggled at the beginning of the semester, but you turned it around. I'm sorry that I underestimated you before."

My eyes widen and Dev's do the same. "That's . . . no problem at all, Dr. Allen. Thank you."

"Well, your principal at Waterford Valley asked us to look out for exemplary students that we could recommend as tutors at your high school. I already have a few names in mind, but I'd like to add you to the list. I think your struggles and successes in the class could be inspiring to other students who are intimidated by chemistry."

My eyes bulge out. *Me?* Be a *chemistry* tutor? I almost turn around to make sure this isn't another Andy situation and Dr. Allen isn't talking to a different Ellie standing right behind me.

"Um . . ."

There's no way I'm doing that. I can't possibly be a tutor. I'm barely holding my own in this class. I only worked so hard on that presentation out of spite. I look to Dev and he gives me a subtle thumbs-up.

"Well, I mean, thank you. That's really amazing to hear. But, um, I don't think it's a good idea right now."

Dr. Allen cocks her head. "You know the tutors are paid, don't you? And it's always a good addition to your college résumé."

"Oh, right . . . but no thanks. I think it's just too much to take on senior year."

"Hmm, okay." She frowns. "Let me know if you change your mind."

She walks away and I give a *can-you-believe-that* look to Dev as we walk into the cafeteria. "Has she lost her mind?"

"Have *you*?" he asks. "Why didn't you say yes?"

"Because it's chemistry, Dev! I hate chemistry. I can't imagine how much work it would be to tutor other people in it when I'm drowning already."

Dev mumbles something, but I don't respond. I have no interest in getting into a debate about this. I mean, it's a huge compliment that she'd think of me as a possible tutor. I can't believe all my work has actually paid off. Maybe, if I really dedicated myself, I could keep it up next semester at Waterford. Or even in college eventually. But that doesn't mean I want to dedicate myself to *chemistry*. Life's too short for that.

Once I've grabbed a slice of pizza, I sit down at our usual cafeteria table for dinner. Sam and Kelly sit farther down the same table. They aren't officially unwelcome—Kelly's pretty nice actually—but Sam has kept his distance since the incident last Monday.

Huan is looking at photos on his phone and I lean over his shoulder to see. "Wow, that's gorgeous!" He hands it to me and I find more postcard-perfect pictures of Oxford University. "Did you get to take a tour?"

"Frank offered since he knows some people there, but I didn't want to spend the whole day thinking about college." He shakes his head wistfully. "Though Oxford is really amazing."

"Is it too late to apply for next year?" I ask.

"Um, I don't know. I hadn't really—"

"Yeah. The deadline was October fifteenth," Sage says as if it's not weird to have university application dates memorized.

Huan's shoulders sag a bit.

"Well, there's always the following year." I nudge him. "In the meantime you can just enjoy hanging out with your *boyfriend*."

"Oh, you made it official?" Sage asks.

He perks up. "Just this weekend. But Frank's been trying to convince me since he came for the cricket match."

"I'm glad you finally listened to reason," I reply. "But if you guys didn't spend the day in Oxford *at* Oxford, where did you go?"

"Keep swiping," he replies with a chuckle.

Dev leans closer to the screen. When I move to the next photo, we both pull back and laugh at the same moment.

"Seriously, man?" Dev says.

"What?" Kelly asks loudly from the end of the table.

I hold up the phone.

"You went bowling?" she cries. "In Oxford?"

"Why not?" He tips a bag of Walkers crisps into his mouth. "Have any of *you* been bowling in England?"

"No, because we're in England," Dev replies.

"Yeah, you're all really living it up here—sitting in the school cafeteria eating nasty pizza."

I almost argue, but I'm too happy for Huan to care if he lords it over the rest of us.

"Ladies and gentlemen, if I may have your attention."

We all turn in unison toward the voice. The headmaster of Emberton, Mr. Odell, stands at the front of the cafeteria, still looking every inch a British gentleman despite the salad bar and trash cans next to him. This is the first time I've seen him since he welcomed us when we arrived.

When there's perfect silence in the room, he begins again. "As you all must know, we're over halfway through the semester and now Thanksgiving break is only a month away. In accordance with the American holiday, we will be preparing a traditional dinner for those of you who aren't flying home."

At this, Huan rubs his stomach and mouths, *Yum*.

"It has also come to my attention that many of our high school students would like to travel over the long break. While we usually have a strict policy against minors traveling overnight, we are loosening that policy for the holiday." The cafeteria goes from silent to boisterous in under a second. Everyone turns to their friends, whispering and high-fiving. Mr. Odell clears his throat and the room goes silent again.

"*However*, there will be strict rules that everyone must follow if they wish to travel. You will need to submit a proposal to me by the first week in November. If your trip is approved, you will need to purchase all flights, train tickets, and hotel rooms ahead of time and provide us with a complete itinerary, including travel times, confirmation emails, and phone numbers where you can be reached. I will also need written parental permission. Finally, during the trip, you must check in with the school at the beginning and end of each day you are gone."

Abstractly, I'm aware that this is a lot of work to do in a short amount of time. (Nothing associated with Emberton comes without homework.) But I couldn't care less. Soon I might be standing in the shadow of the Eiffel Tower . . . or the Colosseum . . . or maybe on the quiet canals of Amsterdam. If only Will could come too . . . My heart thumps at the thought. That would make the trip perfect.

If Mr. Odell says anything else, I can't hear him. The noise of the cafeteria explodes like a sonic boom as everyone tries to talk over one another. Someone yells *red light district* and *smoke shop* at the next table.

"Is anyone flying home?" Huan practically shouts at us.

I shake my head. Mom's already made plans to spend Thanksgiving weekend with Aunt Aubrey, baking and shopping way too much.

"Okay." Huan rubs his hands together. "Let's get planning!"

After thirty minutes of debate, there still isn't a clear decision. We've narrowed it down to France or Italy, but we decide to meet later to hash out the rest. All I want to do is get back to my computer and start Googling, but Huan catches up with me in the hall.

"So, do you think you'll ask Will to come?" he asks in a low voice. "Frank will definitely want to when I tell him about this, but it might be awkward since he doesn't know you guys well. But if Will comes too . . ."

"Look at you! First Oxford and now this trip."

"You were right. How many times are we going to experience something like this?"

"Exactly!" I grab his arm and do a little shimmy. "You really think it'll be okay? Omigod, this changes everything! Will and I actually *traveling* together!" My grin matches Huan's. "But wait, do you think Dev and Sage will agree?"

Huan thinks for a moment. "I'm sure we can get them to, but they may not love the idea at first. Maybe we should get everyone together and bring it up then? They'll be a lot less likely to argue against it if Frank and Will are sitting right in front of them."

"That's devious and I love it. So we get Frank and Will on board first, then Dev and Sage?"

"That's the plan."

We high-five and continue chatting the rest of the way back to his room, debating the relative merits of Paris vs. Rome. Dev is already there when we arrive, sitting in front of his computer. Three young faces are smashed together on his monitor. Oh god, I'm interrupting a Skype session with his family. I stop in the doorway, flustered, and take a step back. From the kids' grins, though, it's clear I've already been caught.

"Are you allowed to have girls in your room?" his brother asks. His face gets even bigger in the monitor as he leans forward to see me better.

Dev turns. "Oh, this is Ellie."

"Ellie? I want to meet her!" says his youngest sister, Riya. "Tell her to come here."

Dev motions me over with an apologetic expression on his face.

"How do they know who I am?" I whisper to him.

"You're his new friend, right? The one who really likes fairies and unicorns and stuff?" she says in reply. "He talks about you all the time."

I cut my eyes to him and he shakes his head. "No, I don't. Just a normal amount."

"I love unicorns!" she says. She's so cute that it's hard to stay embarrassed. "Anaya and I play with them every day."

Anaya, whose a few years older, glares at her little sister. "I only play because you make me. Unicorns are for *little* girls."

"Anaya!" Dev exclaims.

My face goes red but I force myself to smile. She's not totally wrong. "Well, Dev likes fantasy stuff too. In fact, I have it on great authority that he really, *really* likes Quidditch." Dev kicks my foot.

"You're so lucky," Sahil says. "I hope I get to go to England when I'm a senior so I can hang out with my girlfriend all the time and slack off."

"Oh, so he's told you about Sage?" I say in a teasing voice.

The sisters exchange confused looks. "Who's Sage?"

They don't know about Sage? Then who are they talking about? They couldn't possibly think that Dev and I . . .

"Oh, um, she's my roommate. I thought you were talking about . . ."

"The only girl he ever talks about is you," Anaya says.

Me? I clear my throat and I look over for Dev's reaction, but his gaze is fixed to the screen.

"That's because Ellie is new. I've been in the same classes with everyone else for years. Now, can we move past the part of the conversation where you all try to embarrass me?"

"No, that's the only reason we call."

"Sahil, be kind in front of Dev's new friend," a woman says.

All the children turn and an older Indian man and woman come into view. They are sitting together on a couch in the back of the room. They wave at me and I wave back, though my stomach is a bundle of nerves now. Couldn't Dev have given me the heads-up that his parents were listening in? What if I had said something stupid or inappropriate and given them a bad impression of me?

"Hello, Ellie," his father says. It's a little hard to hear because he's so far away from the screen. "We've heard you've been such a help to Dev this semester. Did you come over to study again? We can let you go."

"Oh—no—I mean, I don't want to interrupt."

"Anyone who helps our son in school is not an interruption," his mother replies.

I nod, even more confused. How have I helped Dev? "Well, still, I should let you guys get back to talking." I take a step back. "It was nice to meet you."

Riya pouts but no one argues. I'm halfway down the hall when I hear my name.

"Hey. Sorry about that," Dev says as I turn.

"Oh, um, it's no problem." My hands are weirdly shaky. "They're really sweet."

"Thanks." He rubs his foot on the carpet. "Listen, don't pay attention to what they were saying. About . . . you know. I just don't talk about Sage around them because there'd be even more teasing. It's not like I said—"

"No, I know. Just kids being kids." I fumble for my cell phone and drop it on the ground. "Well, I'm going to go dig up every detail I can find on Paris now."

"I can't wait for the trip."

"Me either."

"It'll be nice to get away from everyone for a while."

I nod. The hallway is practically silent. I chew on the inside of my cheek, suddenly aware of the intent way Dev is watching me. He opens his mouth as if to say something and then clamps it tight and shoves his hands in his pockets.

"What is it?" I ask. Was he going to say something more about our trip? Or what happened with his family?

He shakes his head. "Nothing."

"Okay. Well, um, see you in the morning."

"Yep. Good night."

chapter

27

Friday afternoon I'm back in the conservatory, trying to decide whether the second walkway from the acorn house should lead to the pond or the tiny swing. Ever since Miriam gave me access to her greenhouse, I've been coming as much as my schedule will allow. Miriam insists on displaying whatever I put together, and it's so relaxing to be here after hours of classes. Maybe she's right about looking into a future with this. I would kill for a job like hers. Or even something on the side if I couldn't get a full-time job. I haven't forgotten how fun it was helping out at the fairy garden class in the park. Something like that wouldn't feel like work at all.

My phone rings. I assume it's Mom since we've been playing phone tag, but it's Will. My stomach rolls and I squeeze the pebbles in my palm. I was so excited to have Will come on the trip when Huan and I talked about it at the beginning of the week, but now a few days have passed and I still haven't said anything to him. It's a big step—what if he says no? I'm not sure I can deal with the disappointment.

"Hello!" I exclaim too loudly into the phone.

"Hello yourself," Will says. *Oh*, his voice.

"How was your trip with your father? Are you back home yet?"

"If you mean Northampton, then yes. He dropped me off before catching the first train back to London. I hoped to go with him, but he wants me out here for the next few weeks to help with some of his clients."

It hurts that he'd rather be in London than close to me, but I swallow it back.

"So I had something I wanted to ask you," I say.

"Actually, I do too. Can I go first?"

"Um . . . sure."

"I saw a video online last night and . . . I could have sworn it was you."

"You did?" I sway and sit down hard on a bench. "What was it about?"

"From the looks of it, there was a party and this girl . . . she looked exactly like you. She has to be you. And you ran up and threw yourself at some guy."

My forehead falls toward my lap as I curl into a ball. *Nooooo!* He's seen the video! That horrible mortifying immortal video. Will I never live that down? I think about denying it, but who am I kidding? It's clearly me and if I refuse to talk it'll make it seem like a bigger deal than it is.

I take a deep breath and push down my fear.

"Oh, yeah, that video." I try for a laugh, but it sounds like a parrot squawking. "That is me. It's just a stupid video taken by stupid people at a stupid party. They posted it online and . . . you know, it made the rounds on the internet. I wish it didn't exist, but there's nothing I can do to control that so I just don't talk about it."

We're both silent and I imagine he's processing the fact that the video is of me. Finally he says, "You really threw yourself at him." His voice is softer than usual.

I squeeze my eyes shut in embarrassment. "I—it's a long story. Obviously, I thought he was talking about me. But he was leading me on." I clutch the phone tighter. "Please don't worry about that video. That was so long ago now. It feels like a million years ago."

"When did it happen?"

I grimace. "Before I came here."

"So not that long at all."

"It feels like it to me. Are you mad?"

"That some wanker posted a video of you without your permission? No. But . . . I don't know. You never mentioned the video before. It's not because—you don't have a thing for—"

"No!" I practically yell into the phone. The idea turns my stomach. The most ironic thing about all this is that Andy is single again. He and Crystal both posted about it a few days ago. They had seemed so happy online, but I guess they were overcompensating with their constant mushy pictures. It's crazy to think that if I'd waited around in America I'd have another shot with him now, but the idea couldn't be more repellant to me. I don't even feel the vindictive joy I thought I would about their breakup. If their relationship had turned out to be something real, then at least I could try to be happy for them, regardless of how it began. But I lost a friend and Crystal lost the chance to study here, all for a relationship that didn't last three months. What a waste.

"Believe me, I *really* don't have a thing for him. I just don't like talking about it. Would you want to go around telling everyone you met about the most embarrassing moment of your life? I'd blot it from reality if I could."

"True. Those comments . . ."

I cringe. The first rule of going viral: *never* read the comments. "So we're cool?"

"Yeah, we're cool. But . . . there's nothing else you should warn me about, right? No more videos floating around online?"

I bite my lip, thoughts warring with each other. There's plenty he still doesn't know about me, but nothing like this. Nothing important.

"No more videos."

"Good." He exhales into the phone. "So what did you want to ask me about?"

I'm still so caught up thinking about the video that it takes me a second to remember. "Right, um, do you want to have dinner tonight? A bunch of us are going to the pub on Derngate around six."

"As much as I like your friends, I'd rather spend the evening alone with you."

"I want to spend time alone with you too, but there's actually a special reason I thought you might want to come." I pace in front of a palm tree, nervous. Maybe this isn't the best time to bring it up. I wish I'd waited until we were together to mention it, but it's too late now. "So, um, we're thinking of traveling over our break and . . . well, we wanted your opinion. Since you've traveled so much." I scrunch up my face. Ugh, spit it out! "And, I mean, if you're interested, you could maybe come with us. And I think

Huan is asking Frank, so maybe he'll be there too. It'll be a bigger group, but it could be fun. Unless you're sick of traveling, which would totally make sense. So no pressure if you don't want to, but—you know—I just wanted to mention it."

I'm about to hyperventilate, but luckily Will chuckles and says, "One phone call to you and my whole week turns around. The idea of going somewhere with you sounds brilliant, even if we're in a crowd of hundreds."

I collapse back onto the bench. Thank god he didn't want to FaceTime.

That night I slide into a seat next to Will at the pub with the rest of the group. We're crammed around a few small tables we had to push together to make room.

Will squeezes my hand. "I've missed you," he whispers.

"I missed you too."

Will waves cheerfully to the others and we scan the menu. When I came to England I was expecting fish and chips and not much else, but the options are amazing. Who knew you could order fried squid at a pub? The conversation turns from Emberton classes to the differences between British and American TV and I take a breath in relief. Will doesn't seem different after learning about the video. No weirdness at all.

"So, Will?" Dev says when there's a lull in the conversation. "I heard you're thinking of investing in a brewery. Have you made any progress with that?"

"Oh, I've been off that for a while. Actually, I had a new thought while I was in Manchester—sustainable energy sources."

He turns to me, his eyes wide with excitement. "It's clear that's where the world is headed."

"There's some cool stuff being done out there," Huan replies. "Have you heard how they can produce energy from ocean waves? It's amazing."

Will shrugs into his beer.

Frank snorts. "I can assure you he has not. Believe me, it's best not to spend much time investing in Will's *investments*—he's always on to the next thing." Despite the harsh words, Frank grins over at Will good-naturedly. "He's been like that since we were lads together."

Will chuckles. "He's not entirely wrong, but I'm serious this time."

"So you're a big environmentalist, then?" Dev asks. I can easily hear the sarcasm in his tone, but Will seems oblivious.

"Not particularly. But if it can make me money and get my father to leave me alone, then I'm all for the environment." He laughs and Frank joins in, but Dev stares at his drink, his eyes narrowed.

Sage raises her eyebrows at me and I squirm in my seat. Sitting here, it's hitting me how little time my friends have spent around Will. Almost zero time, really. And this topic isn't bringing out his best side. If everyone knew more about his rocky relationship with his dad, they'd understand why he's desperate to be independent of him. Still, a tendril of doubt creeps into my mind. Maybe inviting Will on the trip wasn't my best idea.

"Anyway, enough chitchat." Huan eyes me meaningfully and leans into the table. "We have more important matters to talk about—like our trip."

"For Thanksgiving," I add.

"Yes, I've heard of it." Will winks at me. "There's usually turkey, right? And stampedes for cheap tellies?"

"Not just TVs. Cell phones too," Huan adds.

"Sounds brilliant. Thanks for including me."

Dev frowns and Sage cocks her head. I elbow Huan.

"Right," Huan says. "So, um, we were thinking it might be fun if Will and Frank came along too. If everyone's cool with it."

"I think the question is whether Mr. Odell is cool with it," Sage replies. "If he doesn't approve our proposal then none of us are going anywhere."

"I don't see why *Mr. Odell* needs to know anything," Frank says. "You lot go on your trip and Will and I will go on our own. If we happen to wind up in the same city, at the same hotel, then so be it. Merely coincidental."

Sage slowly nods. "True."

Huan leans closer to Frank so their bodies are touching from shoulder to hip, and I can't help but smile.

There's only one person left to convince.

"Dev? Are you fine with it too?" Huan says.

But Dev doesn't look at him. His gaze fixes on me and my pulse skitters at the intensity. For a moment I swear I see a glint of longing in his eyes. The second stretches thin. Then—*snap*—it recoils and Dev turns to Will.

"If you've been invited then I certainly won't stand in the way."

I play with my drink, my whole body flush with heat. Surely I misread him. He couldn't be *longing* for me. Though maybe he's longing for a trip *without* Will . . .

"So, what are the options?" Will asks, and rubs his hands together.

"A lot of people are going to Amsterdam," Huan says.

Will and Frank share a look. "Anywhere else?"

"What about Paris?" I blurt, pushing thoughts of Dev from my mind.

"Mmm," Will says, and takes another swig of his beer.

"Not a fan of the French?" Dev asks.

"No, no. Paris is wonderful. It's a beautiful city. Great food."

Frank leans forward. "Excuse him. Willoughby's pretentious levels have grown so extreme we might need to wear protective suits around him now. I should have mine somewhere around here." He pretends to rummage around in his coat. "I carry it everywhere. . . ."

"And I left my eye gear back at the manor," Huan says. "Even after you reminded me and everything."

Will shakes his head. "I'm not being pretentious. I'm only saying that Paris is . . . the conventional choice."

Frank smiles and puts out his hands like he's showing us proof. "In other words, it's *common*."

"And how many times have you been to Paris, Frank?"

"Oh, bugger off."

"That's what I thought," Will replies with a smirk.

The waiter comes then and we all put in our orders. When he leaves, Dev says, "While it's great that you both spend so much time in Paris, none of us have been there. It definitely won't be common for us."

"I didn't mean to imply it was," Will replies.

"So you really don't think Paris will be fun?" I ask.

Will takes my hand. "It's not that it won't be fun, but I think there might be other places that could be better. Were you thinking of any place else?"

"Well . . ." I hesitate, not wanting to be shot down again. "Maybe Italy?"

Both Will and Frank nod at that. "What about Venice?" Will asks.

Venice.

Venice.

I know Paris is supposed to be the most romantic city in the world, but suddenly I'm imagining Will and me with the sinking buildings and the lapping water and the gondolas. I squeeze his hand.

His face lights up. "Yeah? I understand if you'd like Paris more." He leans his head toward me and whispers, "But I've only been to Venice once—when I was a little boy. I'd love to explore it with you." He kisses me lightly on the lips and my face warms. It's one thing to kiss Will in the privacy of a public park or a crowded London Eye capsule, but it's another to kiss in front of my friends. When I pull back, Huan waggles his eyebrows suggestively.

"Won't there be a lot more travel time with Venice?" Sage asks, always the voice of reason.

"And it'll be more expensive too," Dev says.

"But the gondolas!" Huan argues.

"A gondola ride does sound rather magical." Will leans close to me and I kiss his cheek.

"Think of the culture!" I say to Dev and Sage. "World-class

museums and architecture, delicious food . . ."

"It shouldn't take long to get there if we fly," Will says.

"And we could get cheap rooms at a hostel to save money," I say.

Frank pales at that suggestion but doesn't argue.

Dev shrugs. "If everyone else is on board, then I am too. Some authentic pizza does sound good."

The others take the van home after dinner, but Will drives me. I love having the extra minutes alone with him, but I can't shake the guilt that comes with it, like I'm subtly telling my friends that I don't want to spend time with them. Hopefully this trip will help me balance everything better. I want it to feel natural when Will and I are with the others. Right now it still feels like an either-or decision between them.

"Are we sure about this trip?" Sage asks when the four of us are back at Emberton later that evening. She and I sit on her bed, while the boys have taken the chairs. "We have so much studying to do and we'll be gone for so many days."

"But there are so many educational opportunities," Huan says, and winks at me.

"That's true. We need to be well-rounded," I add.

"I guess so. Mom has been hounding me to take advantage of these opportunities. I think she's worried I'm going to burn out if I keep working so hard." She shakes her head.

"Yes! We'll all take a break. We'll get away and do something fun and make great memories!"

Dev leans back in the chair and props his feet on my desk. "I'm not going to argue that it'll be a great trip. There's some art there that I'd love to see in person. But I didn't like how UK Ken strong-armed you into going to Venice." He shakes his head.

"He didn't do that. I can't wait to go to Venice with him."

"Eh, you'll be sick of him after one day."

"And I'll be sick of you in one hour."

Dev chuckles but I scowl at him.

"Why aren't you hounding Huan about this? He's only known Frank for a few months too!"

"Hey!" Huan replies.

Dev waves away my question. "He and Frank will be fine. They're clearly made for each other."

"And Will and I aren't?"

"Ellie, I've been tutoring you on how to talk to him. I think we both know the answer to that."

I round on him, but Sage comes between us. "Stop messing with her. And it's none of our business how Ellie acts around her boyfriend. If they want to take their relationship to the next level, then we should respect that. How else are they ever going to have a night alone?"

"Exactly! Thank you, Sage! I—" Sage's true meaning comes to me and I freeze. "Wait, what?"

Huan snorts with laughter.

She tilts her head like it's obvious. "We'll be in Venice during the day *and* night. With no real supervision. So I assumed it'd at least occurred to you that you could . . ."

Oh god. How had this *not* occurred to me? More importantly, why is she bringing this up in front of Huan and Dev?

I hold my hands up. "He doesn't want to take me to Venice just to have sex with me!"

"Holy shit, I do not want to have this conversation." Dev bolts up from the chair.

"There is no conversation! He only wants to spend time with me."

My entire body is so hot I feel like I'm about to melt into the floor. I'd be lying if I said I'd never imagined anything more with Will. Thoughts of that kiss in the park float through my mind often. But there's *more* and then there's *MORE* and I'm not sure how I feel about that yet. And I sure as hell don't want to talk through my feelings with Huan and Dev.

"Look . . ." I take a deep breath to calm myself. "The trip is not about sex. It's about having fun." I force myself to make eye contact with everyone even though I'm having a hard time keeping my voice steady. "And even if . . . *that* was happening, Sage is right. It would be none of your business."

Dev fiddles with his shirtsleeves. "My greatest wish is to never hear another word about it. I need to review for anatomy." He heads for the door. "Huan, are you coming with me?"

Huan gives my shoulder a quick squeeze. "We'll see you guys tomorrow."

"But—we're decided on Venice, right?" My voice is too high. "Because we have to start figuring out flights and hostels?"

Dev is already out the door when he calls, "Yeah, it's decided." Huan waves half-heartedly and follows him.

chapter

28

A week and a half later, I wake to find a DM from Crystal.

Your trip looks like a dream. And OMG that guy you're
with at the pub—I can't believe I gave up all that for such
a dumbass. Hope we can still be cool. xo

I stare at the message, shocked to hear from Crystal after all
this time. Seeing her name doesn't make me angry or sad or . . .
anything now. Except sorry for her that she missed all this. I'm
not sure what picture she's referring to until I look back through
my posts. It's one of the whole group last Friday when we met
to discuss the trip, and I guess it does look like the kind of perfect travel photo you'd see on a tourism website. We're cute and
smiling, but it doesn't show how uncomfortable it was having
Dev and Will at the same table or the awkwardness of the conversations.

I hesitate, wondering what to say to her, and then write back:

> It's been life-changing. Thanks for
> reaching out. We're cool.

And we are cool. We're not friends anymore, and we won't be again in the future, but I don't hate her. I'm really thankful to her, actually. I wouldn't be here otherwise.

When I look up from my phone, I find Sage watching me. "What's up?"

"Nothing. Just . . ." She shrugs.

"What? You're never one to hold back your opinion."

"I was just curious if you'd thought any more about Will and the trip? You know, since you were teasing me so much about my condom earrings before." She flicks one of her dangling earrings and I can't help but laugh again.

"I'm . . . still thinking it through."

To be honest, ever since Sage mentioned Will's possible reasons for coming to Venice, I haven't been able to get the idea out of my head. The whole situation is unbelievable to me. Coming here, my biggest relationship hopes were taking some cute selfies, going on fun dates, and maybe a kiss someplace utterly European and romantic. I never thought I'd be debating losing my virginity. Every time I think about the possibility, my heart races and blood rushes to my face. It could be amazing. But it also feels fast. *Really* fast.

I say as much to Sage, my face burning, but she only nods sympathetically.

"I mean, I've only known Will for a few months, and even then it's not like we've been able to hang out every day. Or even every week. There's still so much I don't know about him and even more he doesn't know about me."

"So what are you going to do?"

I slowly put my notebooks for psychology and British lit into my book bag. I think there's only one thing I can do. "I've got to be myself around him. My real self, dork and all. We're going to have all this uninterrupted time together on the trip—it'll be the perfect place to come clean. And if that goes well . . ." I shrug. "Then I'll think more about everything else. Plus, we'll be on an island so even if he goes running for the hills after he sees this other side of me, he won't get far."

Sage laughs, but despite my bravado I'm so scared that's exactly what's going to happen. I already know how he feels about my Jane Austen and Cicely Mary Barker obsessions. I have no idea how he'll react when I tell him about my fairy gardens and unicorn wardrobe, but given his previous comments, I'm not feeling optimistic. It's possible I'm about to ruin everything by doing this, but I don't have much choice. It's now or never.

In British lit later that morning, I hunch over the open pages of *Alice's Adventures in Wonderland* and try to focus on Dr. Florence as she describes the metaphoric elements of Alice's changes in size. I'm feeling a bit like Alice nowadays. The closer I get to coming clean with Will, the more it's like I'm shrinking after a sip from the cordial bottle. I can't figure out *how* I'm going to tell him all these details about myself. Should I just stride up to him in my unicorn hoodie, rainbow mane streaming down my back, and announce that I'm in love with Captain Wentworth from Jane Austen's (very underrated) *Persuasion*?

I try to catch Dev's eye, but he doesn't look my way. Things have been a bit awkward since that insane conversation in my room a week and a half ago. Not *bad*. We're not fighting. Just weird.

I force myself to take notes on plot structure for the rest of class, since the next round of exams will be starting in a few days and I need to nail them. I bolt to his side as soon as we're released. "You want to walk outside?" We have fifteen minutes between our classes.

He agrees and we walk down the ornate hallway, through the double doors, and out into the east garden. Without speaking, we head to a bench a few feet away. It has a nice view of the lion fountain. We sit for a minute and then I turn to Dev.

"Are we okay?"

He frowns. "Yeah."

"Okay. Good. Because you seemed a little distracted lately and . . ."

"It's nothing. My parents are just getting on me about grades. Plus, I told them about Sage's research position and now they think I need to find a position too."

"Do you have time for that?" I'm surprised how my mood plummets at the idea of Dev spending less time with us.

He stares at the fountain. "Maybe. I'd need to drop cricket. And Quidditch." He gives me a small smile. That's still our secret.

"You can't quit Quidditch!" I lower my voice when his eyes widen in alarm. "Or cricket. You love that stuff!"

"They're only extracurriculars, Ellie."

"But colleges want extracurriculars. You can write your application essay about how playing Quidditch makes you a better person."

Dev chuckles as he shakes his head.

"Do you even want to do medical research? You don't sound excited about it."

His smile fades. "I'm sure I'll like it in time."

"That means you don't like it." When he doesn't argue, I throw my hands up. "Why are you doing something you don't like?"

"Because my parents have been dreaming of me being a doctor since the moment I was born. It would make them so happy. And not just my parents—my grandparents, my aunts and uncles—" He reluctantly pulls his gaze from the countryside and turns to me. "Sahil, Riya, Anaya. You should see their faces when I talk about going to med school."

"I *have* seen their faces. They look at you that way all the time. Imagine how they'd look if you told them you were going to be a professional Quidditch player."

That makes him laugh again.

"I mean it. That sport has got to turn pro soon." I nudge him. "Have you even told Sahil about the fact that you're playing? Or the rest of your family?"

"Only you."

I bite my lip to keep from smiling too big. I know it would be better if he shared this with his family, but it's fun sharing this secret with him.

"I don't know, Ellie. I don't think everyone else will get it. I know it's a dumb hobby to have."

His words make me think about what Miriam told me when I said something similar about fairy gardens. "It's not dumb if you love it."

He stares at me for a second, his expression turning serious. "I'm really glad you found me at Quidditch practice that afternoon."

"You are? You seemed kinda pissed."

"I was embarrassed. But I'm glad you know. It's nice to have someone I can talk to without having to watch my words."

I feel this completely. It's such a rare thing to have someone you can talk to without censoring yourself in some way . . . and thinking about this makes it even more apparent that I don't feel like this around Will. There's so much I have to edit with him. I have to come clean in Venice.

I don't want to bring up Will right now, though. "You know, if you want to have people to talk to about Quidditch, there is a simple solution. You could just invite all of us to a game."

"Nice try, but no thanks." He stands up. Our time is almost gone already.

"I'm serious, though," I say as we walk back to the manor. "About inviting us to Quidditch stuff, but also about everything else. You need to find something that makes you happy, even if that's not medicine."

"And what about you? What are you going to do that makes you happy?"

I pause, taken aback by the sudden reversal. "I don't know. Can I make a living writing Jane Austen fan fiction?"

"I bet a lot of people already have." He shoves me lightly. "But what about your fairy gardens?"

"Um, aren't we finished talking about embarrassing hobbies? There's no more future in that than professional Quidditch, despite what everyone else seems to think."

"What do you mean?"

"Oh, Miriam—the woman who takes care of the conservatory— is pushing me to look into gardening internships and jobs in America."

"Have you?"

I shrug.

"You should do it. She made it a career, so why can't you? And just look at what you've done to the conservatory."

I hesitate outside the door into Emberton. "How do you know that?"

"I spent a few hours studying there and she told me about the bright student who suggested the changes. She's very impressed by you." He ushers me inside. "I am too. It's so much nicer in there now."

"Oh. Yeah." I fidget with my ponytail, unsure what to think about this unexpected compliment. "So, um, are you still excited about Venice?"

To my surprise, Dev brightens. "Absolutely."

"Has Sage said anything to you about getting tickets yet?"

"No. You'd know more about what she's doing than me."

"I'll get on her about it. I know how disappointed you'll be if she doesn't come."

Dev messes with his shirtsleeves, a nervous habit I hadn't

noticed before. "Actually, let's drop the whole Sage thing, okay? You don't need to worry about that anymore."

My shoulders slump. It was my job to help Dev and Sage get together. That was the deal. He held up his end—*more* than held up his end—and I'm letting him down. Despite what he said, I'm not ready to forget about it yet. There has to be more I can do.

I spend most of chemistry thinking about Sage and Dev. Maybe if I can get her to spend some time alone with Dev—quality time, not *how many thoracic vertebrae are in the human body* time—then she'll finally feel that spark she's been missing. And there's no place better for spark-inducing interactions than Venice.

I hurry over to her in the hall after our class. "Hey, did you book your flights yet?"

"Actually I bought them during the lunch break."

"Great!" I do a little skip next to her. Knowing that Sage will be by my side makes the whole trip more exciting. "I was worried you weren't going to come. Were you able to get on the same flight?"

"No, I'm on a different one."

"Ugh, seriously? It was already sold out? I hope Mr. Odell's going to be okay with that since we were supposed to have everything turned in last week. I think he wanted us all flying together so the school can keep better track of us."

"I got it approved. Hey, so I've already made my niece two crocheted blankets and I think three is a little much. Can I make you a scarf? We could go through patterns tonight. And I bought so much yarn when we went shopping last that you'll have tons of colors to choose from."

"Um . . ." I pause. "Yeah, that would be cool, if you don't mind. Do you have Christmas patterns?"

"I could get them online."

"Awesome!" Sage unlocks our dorm door and I drop my bag onto my desk. "So what time is your flight?"

Sage doesn't answer. Instead she pulls a huge bag from under her bed. "Why don't you look through the yarn first? Then we can choose a pattern once I know the yarn weight."

My eyes narrow. "What's going on?"

"Trying to stay busy. Dr. Reese gave me five more articles to read before our lab meeting next Friday so I want a new project while I read."

"I mean about the trip. When are you flying out?" I say the last sentence slowly.

"Eight a.m."

"Oh." Relief floods through me. "Your flight's actually before ours. Maybe you can wait at the Marco Polo Airport for—"

"Friday."

I blink. "Friday?"

Everyone else is flying out Wednesday morning. The flight and travel into Venice will take the majority of the day, which leaves us Thursday, Friday, and Saturday in Venice before we have to fly back Sunday. But if Sage isn't even leaving until Friday morning . . .

"You'll miss everything! And you'll be alone on Thanksgiving!"

"I won't be alone. I talked to Dr. Reese and we decided that I should really be at the university during break. Another professor from Stanford is giving a talk Thursday and—"

"But . . . but you'll miss everything." My heart sinks. Nothing will be the same without her. Plus, I've been secretly working on a whole itinerary so we don't miss any of the sights—Doge's Palace, the Galleria dell'Accademia, Ca' d'Oro. I'd scheduled Thursday chock-full of historic sites and museums for Dev and Sage.

"Is it really so important for you to be at this talk? I know you want to get into med school eventually, but I can't see how missing one speaker is going to matter."

"This isn't about padding my résumé for college or med school applications—I'm staying because I *want* to be there. I love being a part of something larger than myself, something that could affect the future of medicine . . . even if my part is minuscule right now." Sage shoves the yarn back under the bed with a sigh. "It won't even be a big deal for me to come late. Venice isn't that large and I read it's easy to get around. This way I can still have a fun weekend, but I don't miss anything academically."

I open my mouth to argue, but there's no point. The way her arms are folded across her chest tells me that. "Have you told Dev?" I blurt.

Sage bristles. "So I can get his permission?"

"No. No, that's not what I'm saying. I just think he'll be disappointed."

She snorts and turns on her laptop. "And I think you don't know Dev half as well as you think you do."

"What's that supposed to mean?"

"Ellie . . ." She cocks her head in pity. "You're being purposely naive. If you spent a little less time looking at Will, then you'd notice how much someone else has been looking at you."

My only response is a sarcastic grunt. Inside, though, tension crawls up my spine as I think back to our dinner at the pub. But that was different. Dev was upset we'd included Will in our plans. He wasn't *looking* at me. His only looks are exaggerated eye rolls and grimaces when we're studying. Plus, he likes Sage. Maybe she's being purposely naive.

chapter

29

"Let's go!" Dev stands in the doorway of my room, tapping his foot impatiently. "Ellie, if we miss the van to Northampton then we're going to miss our train, which means we're going to miss our flight."

"I know, I know!"

I grab my passport and water bottle, throw my carry-on over my shoulder, and snatch the handle of my suitcase.

Dev steps back to let me pass, but I can feel the judgment pouring off him. He's managed to pack for a five-day trip with nothing but his book bag. Boys.

I duck back into the room. "See you soon," I call to Sage.

"Have a safe trip!"

"You do know that you aren't moving to Venice, right?" Huan asks as I lug my suitcase into the hall.

"I couldn't decide what to bring. Will's taking me to a nice restaurant one night so I had to pack some fancier stuff, plus I wanted layers. I read that Venice will be colder because it's on the water."

"Pretty excited, then?" he asks.

I take a deep breath, trying to put my mood into words. My feelings are a jumble inside me. I *am* excited. A break from schoolwork, traveling in Europe, spending time with one of the most gorgeous guys in the world. This could end up being one of the best times of my life. But what if Will's upset when I tell him our interests aren't as similar as he believes? What if he doesn't like the "new" me? Between the viral video and my age, I've already kept way too much from him.

"I can't wait for the food," Dev says. "Followed closely by the art."

"Forget all that," Huan replies. "I'm grabbing the first slice of pizza I see and waiting in St. Mark's Square until pigeons sit on my head."

"That's disgusting," I reply.

"It's not a real visit without the pigeons. I don't make the rules."

Heathrow is alive with controlled chaos. From a distance I can make out Frank and Will waiting for us near the check-in kiosks. I draw in a quick breath. All around us are passengers in every shape, size, and type, but Will and Frank stand apart, like two movie stars in a sea of extras.

Frank sees us first, and he whoops and waves us over. Will strides to my side and kisses me before shouldering my carry-on. "Now I can relax," he whispers.

My smile is tight. If only I could relax too.

It takes a while for all of us to get checked in and through security. At one point Frank thinks he lost his passport and we all go into panic overload, searching his bags and trying to find phone numbers for lost and found, before he realizes it was in the outside pocket of his bag the whole time. It's a miracle when all five of us finally make it to our gate.

"I need coffee," Frank says, looking around. "Anyone else?"

"*Yes*," Will says.

"Should we all go?" I ask.

Dev shakes his head and drops his bag at the end of a row of seats. "You guys go. I'll watch the bags." His voice is different— dejected. Looking at our group, it's clear why. Dev's the odd man out, at least until Sage meets us in a few days.

"I'll bring you back a coffee," I tell him. "Extra sugar, no milk, right?"

He holds my gaze a moment. "Thanks, Elle."

I bite my lip at the name. Will's already heading to the nearest coffee shop so I give Dev a brief smile and run to catch up. Will's phone rings then. He pulls it out, curses, then shoves it back in his pocket.

"Everything okay?" I ask.

"It's my father. I'm ignoring him until after the trip."

His phone rings again while we're waiting to pay for the coffees and a third time when Huan makes us stop to buy a Milka chocolate bar. The fourth time it rings, Will jerks it out and takes the call. A moment later he ducks his head and says, "*No*. Absolutely not."

I scurry over to Frank and Huan. "Will's father keeps calling him," I whisper, gesturing over to him. Will is pacing in the terminal with a mutinous expression on his face.

Frank frowns and slowly puts down the Queen Elizabeth

bobblehead he was inspecting. "Something's wrong."

We inch closer and the second Will finishes the call, I move to his side.

"Are you okay? We were getting worried."

"Elle . . ."

My heart clenches. "What's happened?"

"Elle, I'm so sorry."

Immediately my throat goes tight. I sense Huan step behind me protectively.

"I can't even tell you how sorry. My father is being an absolute arse. I tried to change his mind, but . . ."

"He doesn't want you to go?" I whisper.

"I swear to god, I said everything I could. I tried every promise, used every tactic. I threw a fit like I was a toddler. But he won't budge. He has a client who wants to sell his son's flat in London. The man's also on the admissions committee at UCL and now Father's insistent that I come to the lunch. He says I need to charm him into liking me so he'll overlook my 'subpar academic performance.'"

"When's the lunch? You know Sage is flying out late. You can come late too. It'll be fine."

I know I sound desperate. Will's already trudging back toward the gate where we left his bag, but I refuse to give up hope. There has to be another solution. He can't just *leave*.

"I already tried," Will says. Everything about him is so controlled right now. His voice, his expression, even the way he walks. "The lunch isn't until Friday, but Father thinks it's too risky. And I'd have to fly back tomorrow anyway so there's not much point."

"There's nothing we can do? No way for him to reschedule?"

"This is another punishment." His control cracks and his voice gets louder, sharper. "He doesn't trust me. He thinks I'm wanking about every minute I'm not with him."

"What if . . ." I hurry to keep up with his pace. "What if you, you know, came anyway? I mean, I know he's your father, but you're also eighteen. You don't have to do everything he says."

"Then I'd get to Italy and have no place to stay. And no money to eat. I might be an adult, but I still . . . well, I still rely on him financially. I know he'll cut off my credit cards if he has to. He's done it before."

"But . . ."

Dev sees us and comes over. "What's going on?"

"I have to stay in London," Will says, his voice harsh. "My father is insisting. He's sending a car."

"I'll walk back to the entrance with you," I say.

He wipes the tears off my cheeks with the back of his hand. "You'll miss your boarding. Ring me when you get there. And I got my father to agree not to cancel the hotel reservation, so you lot should feel welcome to use it instead of staying at your hostel. It's already paid for."

"What if I came with you instead? Maybe we could spend the time in London? I'm sure there's so much more to visit."

His expression is so pained that more tears come and I have to turn away.

"I don't think that's a good idea right now."

"The school will go ballistic if you change plans," Huan adds.

He's right, but I don't care.

A flight attendant announces that our flight will be boarding soon. Will wraps his arms around me and kisses me on the top of the head.

"I'll never forgive him for this. But I'll also never forgive myself if I've ruined your holiday. Try to enjoy it. Don't let him mess it up for both of us."

I nod and try to speak, to argue, but Will is kissing me again. Then he walks away. There's a small corner of my mind that's relieved I won't have to reveal everything to him this weekend, but I push that aside. This was supposed to be our time together. There's another announcement, and passengers stand and move toward the gate. I search for Will but he's already been swallowed by the crowd.

Huan and Frank step into line, but I don't follow. Will's not coming. He's already gone. Dev puts a hand on the small of my back and guides me forward. In front of me, Huan's and Frank's backs are blurry through my tears.

"Your ticket?" Dev whispers, and I pull it from my coat pocket. I hand it to the attendant in a fog, only moving down the ramp and onto the plane when Dev steers me forward.

"Here." He points to a seat on my left. I sit and he hesitates, looking back and forth between the empty seat where Will should be and a seat beyond mine. "Do you . . . maybe you want to be alone?"

"I forgot your coffee."

"You can buy me two when we get there." He points to the seat. "Should I . . . ?"

"Please."

He sits down and people push past like a dam just broke. The seats are tight and even though Dev is lanky, our arms keep brushing as he tries to get his luggage situated and his seat belt on.

"I'm sorry." His voice is so quiet that I can barely hear it over the roar of the engine.

A horrible thought pops into my head and I can't stop myself from saying it aloud. "What if he got cold feet about the trip?"

Frank's head pops up over the seat in front of me. His long golden curls flop over his eyes, but his expression is serious. "He didn't, I promise. I haven't seen Will that gutted in a long time."

Some of the pressure on my chest lifts.

"He's definitely not missing the trip on purpose," Dev says. "If he had even the slightest chance of sleeping with you, he wouldn't have left here unless his life literally depended on it."

I burst out in embarrassed laughter, and Frank and Dev follow.

"Thanks for the encouraging thought." I wipe the tears out of my eyes and lean back in the seat. "God, this sucks."

"It doesn't have to." I glare at Dev and he shakes his head. "I'm not saying you shouldn't be upset. But remember, we've got five days off from school. No classes, no homework, no obligations." He knows he has me now and leans closer. "Authentic food. Canals. Shopping—"

"Pigeons," Huan calls out. "And lots of them."

I laugh quietly. "Well, I guess I can't let the pigeons down."

chapter 30

I send Will a stream of photos once we touch down at the Venice Marco Polo Airport. Will replies back almost entirely in emojis—usually some combination of sad faces and hearts. I like the hearts the most. The only time he writes, it's to reiterate that he wants me to enjoy the trip and keep sending as many photos as possible. *Bonus points for smiling selfies.* Which sounds pretty doable since I can't stop myself from smiling when I see the water bus that will take us from the airport into Venice.

Huan comes up next to me. "This is really something, huh?"

I nod, wide-eyed. The inside of the water bus looks a bit like a regular bus, with rows of seats and an aisle that cuts down the middle. Except outside there's rippling blue water lapping up against the boat instead of pavement. Soon Venice comes into view. The buildings rise from the water like we've been transported into some magical world.

As we get closer, Dev leans toward me and points out the window. "Gondolas," he whispers.

At least a dozen are tethered to the canal docks, covered in blue cloth, bobbing with the undulations in the water. I press my forehead against the glass.

"Look!" Huan calls.

We're passing St. Mark's Square now. Even from the water I can see masses of people milling around. I've looked at dozens and dozens of photos of it online since it's one of the most popular attractions in Venice, but they didn't do it justice.

Finally, the water bus stops close to the Rialto Bridge and we get off. The white stone bridge spans the Grand Canal and is another one of the most popular spots for photos. We huddle together on the sidewalk, overwhelmed. I snap photo after photo, partially for Will and partially because it's impossible to stand someplace so breathtaking and not take pictures of it.

Huan rubs his hands together. "All right, this is gorgeous and all, but I'm dying to see this hotel Frank's been telling me about. Lead the way, sir."

Frank bows. "My pleasure."

We get lost a few times—well, more than a few times—because Venice is beautiful but also meandering and confusing. When Frank announces that we've made it, I think he's joking. We crane our heads to look up at an impressive salmon-colored building that sits directly on the Grand Canal. I take a deep breath, missing Will more than ever.

The interior is as spectacular as the exterior. Massive marble columns adorn the room, and domed fresco paintings of saints peer down at us. No one speaks in loud voices or moves too quickly. The trickle of water from two carved fountains provides most of the sound, while the click of expensive heels on the tiled floors adds the rest.

"I can't believe this is where you and Will were planning to stay," I whisper to Frank. "It's about a billion times nicer than our hostel."

"Which is exactly why you have to stay here instead."

Another issue occurs to me then. How would we even check in without Will to give his name, and more importantly, his credit card? But Frank waves off my concerns. "I'm very persuasive." He strides off to explain our situation to the front desk.

"No problem," he whispers when he's done. "Will already called and got your names added to the reservation."

Of course he would have thought ahead about this. I text him a thank-you with more hearts and pictures of the lobby.

The bellboy takes us up to the rooms on the third floor. I'm confused when he opens the doors to three rooms instead of two and asks which luggage should go into each. I hesitate and point to rooms randomly.

"What's all this?" I ask Frank after the bellboy leaves. "Was the reservation messed up?"

"No. I reserved this room and it looks like Will reserved those two," Frank replies with a raised eyebrow.

I frown. Will had reserved an extra room here? I knew there was a pretty good chance he'd ask me to stay with him at the hotel instead of my hostel, but I hadn't decided if I was ready for that or not. The fact that he'd thought to get me a private room rather than pressure me to sleep in his makes me ache for him even more.

"Looks like we all got upgraded for this trip," Huan replies, rubbing his hands together.

"What? No." Dev takes a step back. "I've already got a reservation and I don't want to get in trouble with Emberton for changing plans."

"Then check in at the hostel but sleep here."

"I'll be fine at the hostel."

"Have you *been* to a hostel before?" Frank shivers dramatically, his curls falling in his eyes. "The chainsaws, the maiming, the murder . . ."

"You're thinking of the old horror film about a hostel," Huan reminds him.

Frank grins. "Oh, am I? You're probably right. Well then, I'm sure you'll be totally fine there all by yourself, mate."

"Completely safe," Huan agrees. "No need to worry at all."

Frank ushers Dev down the hallway. "Right then, no need to linger. Off you pop."

Dev looks back at me, eyes wide. "Um, maybe I'll just have a look around here first."

"Will you? Suit yourself." Frank winks at me. "We'll just start getting unpacked."

I follow Dev into one of the rooms. It's like nothing I've seen in real life. The space is so grand—larger than Mom's and my living room, kitchen, and dining room combined. An enormous bed with a gilded headboard and canopy takes up most of one wall of the bedroom. Upholstered chairs and a table with inlaid marble fill the adjacent sitting room. But it's the windows that make Dev and me gasp. They reach from the floor to the ceiling and overlook the Grand Canal.

Dev comes up beside me and we stare as boats of all sizes bob past. "You've got to be kidding me," he whispers.

"You can't fault his style."

He grunts. "Are you sure I should stay here? I can't imagine Will would like it."

"Of course you should stay here. He told us to use the rooms, he's already paying for them—how could you *not*?" I gesture at the opulence. "And bonus, no chainsaw-wielding murderers."

"That is true." Dev steps toward the window and leans his head against the glass. "But this view is to die for." He pauses for effect and then gives me a wicked grin.

I groan loudly. "You're lucky these windows are locked or I'd throw you out of one."

We all check in with Emberton, then Dev heads to his room to send an email to his family, and Frank and Huan go back to their room to do whatever it is that they're going to do. I send Mom a long series of texts (brushing over Will's absence) and a bunch of photos. I think about posting everything on Instagram too, but then decide I don't care. Who am I trying to impress on there anymore? I don't really know any of those people.

Finally, I call Will. He picks up on the first ring. "How's the hotel?"

"Will, it's . . ."

"Is it too much? When I suggested this hotel to Frank he told me you'd think I was trying to buy your happiness."

I climb onto the bed and literally sink into the layers of blankets. "If you were, it worked."

"Good. I just wish I could see that very costly happiness."

I snap a selfie of me beaming on the bed and send it to him. A few seconds later, he laughs. "I've never liked technology more."

"I'll document the whole trip for you. You'll get so many pictures you'll think you're here."

"I'm holding you to that promise."

"Thank you," I say softly. "This really is too much, but I love it anyway."

"You're worth it."

chapter
31

We start that evening at the Rialto Bridge, then walk down through the city to St. Mark's Square. The sadness of being here without Will still lingers, but he made me promise to enjoy the trip and there's lots to enjoy. The storefronts are filled with goods both gaudy and fabulous. Lots of them sell Murano glass chandeliers and vases that come from the nearby island. Those are beautiful, but it's the display of colorful glass fish nestled into coral reefs that really catches my attention. I can't imagine how anyone could create something so delicate. I make a mental note to search for a present for Mom tomorrow. I don't have much money to spend, but hopefully I can find her something small for Christmas.

Eventually we arrive at St. Mark's Square. Huan, true to his word, immediately heads off to buy food so he can feed the pigeons, with Frank trailing behind. Dev and I skirt around the edges, checking out the cafés that ring the enormous square and admiring the extravagant domed basilica.

Dev points to four bronze horses above the entrance. "You

know they stole those. Well, they'd probably say they won them, but really they took them from Constantinople during the Crusades. Though those are replicas."

I bump his shoulder with my own. "Is this part of our art history material? Because I thought I was finally caught up on my reading."

"Don't worry, no studying while on vacation." He puts his hands in his pockets and moves closer to the basilica. "I just read about it before coming here."

"Light reading in your spare time?"

"Something like that." His eyes rove over the intricate architecture. "There are supposed to be the most amazing mosaics inside."

I study his profile and take a deep breath. "I know you don't like talking about this, but you're really good at art history."

"I love talking about how good I am at stuff," he says without taking his eyes off the building.

"Then you won't mind me saying that you should major in art history next year instead of going premed. Have you looked into that at all? The program at Columbia is supposed to be particularly great."

"How do you know that?" he asks with a frown.

"I was thinking about our last conversation. I know your parents have always pictured you being a doctor, but I was curious about art history, so I looked some stuff up."

He stops and turns to me. "Really? Thanks." He shakes his head. "But I already know what they'll say and they're completely right. What am I going to *do* with a degree in art history? It doesn't matter how interesting something is if I can't use the degree.

College is too expensive for me to major in something that won't get me a job."

"You need to get your PhD and teach, of course." I can't believe how much I sound like Sage right now, already talking about graduate school when we haven't even finished high school. She's clearly rubbed off on me. "You'll still get to be a doctor."

He chuckles and begins to meander again. "Nice try, but not exactly what they were envisioning."

"Then help them envision it. Dev"—I take his arm and force him to stop—"I really think this could be what you're meant to do. Just imagine it for a second. You could spend *your life* studying art. Wouldn't that be amazing? I can already see you as a professor at some elite private college—harshly marking up papers in red ink, lecturing your bored students about the brilliance of Picasso. You love to lecture people!"

His eyes shine when he laughs. "You know me too well."

"Exactly. And I know this could be perfect for you. Have you told your parents how much you like it?"

"Let's go back to talking about how talented I am."

"That'll be a short conversation." He rolls his eyes. "Promise me you'll talk to them. You owe yourself at least that."

"Maybe. I'll think about it." He catches my hand and squeezes. "Thank you."

I blink in surprise, then pull away as Huan and Frank appear before us. Frank is wrinkling his nose, but Huan is pure exhilaration.

"Done and done." He points to his shoulder at a pile of white bird poop.

"Eww!" I back away.

"I may end up regretting this trip," Frank says.

"Party poopers." Huan bursts out laughing. "See what I did there? Okay, that fancy marble shower is calling my name. But first, take my picture."

After eating way too much at the hotel breakfast the next morning, we set out with our itineraries in hand. We head back to St. Mark's Square first so we can get in the front of the line for the basilica and Doge's Palace. I send photos to Will as we walk. Then we head west for the Guggenheim. Dev recognizes half the art and takes the rest of us around like we're on a guided tour. In fact, a few clueless tourists trail us for a bit. By the time we're done, my head is spinning.

"Okay, next up is the Accademia Gallery," he announces.

Huan and Frank exchange glances.

"That sounds great and all, but maybe we could do something a little less . . . cultured?" Huan asks. "Like shop for cheap souvenirs?"

Dev groans.

"Yeah, we've seen enough art to last us a year. I'm knackered," Frank replies.

"I could do with a slice of pizza," Huan adds.

"Plus, I promised Sage we'd save some of this for when she gets here," I reply. "You know she's not going to want to shop for Venetian masks."

"Damn, I hate it when you're right."

"Your heart must be full of hate, then."

Dev snorts but doesn't argue, so we head over to a small open-air market. I snap a selfie in a sequined masquerade mask for Will, but he only replies with a quick laughing emoji. His father must be keeping him busy because I haven't heard much from him all day.

Frank and Huan leave to get lunch alone and I find a glass rose that'll be perfect for Mom. Dev is nowhere to be seen. It reminds me of when we were all at the flea market together and Dev left only to return with a pamphlet for Quidditch shoved in his pocket. What's he snuck off to find now? Maybe there's an Italian team?

Someone touches my elbow and I spin. Dev is in front of me, practically vibrating with excitement. "Come with me!"

We push through the crowds, but there are so many people that I can't keep up with him. He reaches back and takes my hand. It isn't lost on me that this is the second time we've held hands in as many days, but I brush it off. We're not *holding hands*. We're just ensuring that we don't get swallowed alive by the horde.

Dev pulls me down a narrow alley and stops, triumphant, in front of a small shop. One look and my hands are over my heart. It's a miniature fantasy world in glass. Tiny trees and flowering bushes. Herds of unicorns in white, pink, and blue. Tiny fairies with wings so thin you can see through them. Each figure is so small, I can't imagine how anyone could make such a thing.

I look up at him. "It's . . . everything."

"Yeah, pretty much. As soon as I saw it, I knew I had to rush back to get you. It basically screams Ellie." He waves me closer to the window. "Let me get a photo of you."

He takes a few and then we go back to studying each piece. I expect him to get restless, but he seems as interested as I am. I guess this is artwork, like anything else we saw this morning.

"Let's go inside. Maybe you can find something for your fairy gardens?"

I nod, eager to see more, but I can't imagine I can afford anything here. Some of the glasswork out in the stalls was reasonably priced, but this is a specialty store directly from Murano and it's clearly pricey. Sure enough, the unicorns and fairies are forty euros or more. Way more than I can afford.

"What about this?" Dev holds up a red toadstool. It's tiny—shorter than my pinkie finger—but it's beautiful. And it's only ten euros.

"Perfect."

After I buy it, Dev and I wander down more streets, pointing out window displays and reveling in the fact that we're here. Eventually he gets caught up looking at small pieces of art for sale. I try calling Will but it goes straight to voice mail. Next I call Mom to wish her a happy Thanksgiving. It's hard to believe that millions of people back in America are sitting down to turkey and football right now. A lump forms in my throat as she describes her favorite cheesy floats from this year's Macy's Day Parade. This is the first holiday I've ever spent away from her.

"When you get home, we'll pick a Saturday and make an entire Thanksgiving feast. It'll be like you never missed it," she says, sensing my melancholy.

"That sounds wonderful."

"I miss you. But you'll be back home before you know it. For now, soak in every second of Italy."

I wish we could celebrate Thanksgiving at one of the gorgeous waterside cafés, but I'd need Will-level money for that. So instead we meet back up with Frank and Huan, grab huge slices of pizza from a sidewalk vendor, and head back toward the Grand Canal.

Dev's chomping on pizza and talking with them about an older James Bond movie that was filmed here.

"A little better than Pizza Hut, huh?" he says to me with a small wink before turning his attention back to the conversation. Absently, he pulls a few pepperonis off his slice and puts them on the edge of my paper plate. He only likes pepperoni if it's thin and crispy—if they double layer it, then I get the extras. I pop one in my mouth and study his profile. When exactly did I discover that about him? When did we become the kind of friends who share food without asking? I never even noticed us slipping into these patterns . . . probably because it's all so simple with Dev. Teasing and bickering and laughing like we've known each other all our lives. Somehow, over the course of a few months, he's become one of the closest friends I've ever had.

"Any word from Will?" Frank asks me.

"What? Oh . . ." I pull out my phone, feeling guilty that my thoughts were on Dev. The last text was a picture of his lunch with some smiling emojis. Indian takeout at his parents' like we had together in October. "Not for a few hours."

"He's probably too gutted to write much," Frank says sympathetically, and my stomach twists. I hope that isn't true. I hate to think of him being so unhappy . . . particularly when my thoughts aren't exactly where they should be.

"Ride?" a voice calls out.

We turn toward a gondolier who waves at us from a distance. He looks a little desperate for more business before he wraps up for the night. Next to him stands another gondolier, plus a row of gondolas already covered in blue tarps.

"Want to?" Huan asks. "We can't leave Venice without a gondola ride."

"That could be fun," Frank says. "Do you guys mind if we split up?"

"Of course not."

It's very clear from the way Huan and Frank are looking at each other that they have no interest in sharing a gondola with us, and I can't blame them. They walk to the next boat and we head to the gondolier who called to us.

"Ahhh." He grins and motions between Dev and me. "Love is in the air tonight, is it not?"

Dev's eyes go wide. "Oh, no. Not for us. No, you can send the air over that way." He mimes waving the air toward Huan and Frank.

The gondolier raises an eyebrow at me. "Hmm, you're sure? Well, no matter. Men always come around when the sun goes down." He winks.

My cheeks flame and I take a step back. What is he talking about? Is that why he called us over here—because he thought we were together? I mean, that would make sense—most of his business probably comes from couples. There's just the small issue that we're definitely *not* together and have no business looking like we are. I stare into the boat. There's one seat at the back, covered in

255

embroidered red velvet with matching pillows, where we're clearly supposed to sit. It's a very small seat.

I take another step back.

This is wrong. I shouldn't be riding in gondolas with people when I'm dating Will. I shouldn't even be thinking about it.

Dev glances between me and the gondolier, confusion written on his face. "I don't—"

"Actually, I changed my mind."

"What? But I thought you loved this kind of stuff."

He's right, but the fact that he knows this is only making it worse. I shake my head. "No, not tonight. I—I have a headache. And I promised Will I'd call him. I'll see you back at the hotel."

I push past him and dive down the Venetian sidewalks. Dev calls after me, but I don't stop. I just need to be alone.

chapter

32

I rush down a tight sidewalk between buildings and cross over a tiny bridge that connects the small islands Venice is built on. I need space and time to think. I don't like that people could assume Dev and I are a couple. It feels too close to cheating on Will, even though I know that's irrational.

"Ellie, stop!"

Dev's voice makes me pick up my pace. I don't want to see him like this, not when my emotions are a jumble inside me. He knows me too well. He'll know something is going on.

"I'll meet you at the hotel!" I yell. My shoes echo loudly in the quiet, announcing my impending arrival to anyone who happens to be around. I've left the Grand Canal behind. It's freezing and my feet are throbbing.

"Slow down! You're going the wrong way for the hotel." Dev's footsteps quicken. "You can't wander around alone in a strange city at night."

"Yes I can!"

I slip between two buildings and dash over a small arched

bridge into an open courtyard. There's a church and a little grocery store that's already closed for the night. Two old men sit on a bench to my left, speaking in Italian. There are a few passageways leading from the square but I have no idea where they'll take me. My desperation gives way to fear. I've gone so far now that I have no clue where I am.

I turn back and find Dev has stopped a few yards behind me. "What the hell is going on? Are you running away from me?"

"No. It's just—I wanted time alone." He's breathing fast and so am I.

"Why? Was it that creepy gondolier guy? I don't blame you for not wanting to ride with him, but you could have just said that—you didn't have to run halfway across the city." He closes the distance between us and looks around. "Where are we?"

"Venice."

He rolls his eyes. "Nice. What we are is lost."

"It's an island. You can't get lost."

"Great, then why don't you lead us back to the hotel?"

"Because, like I've been trying to tell you, I need some space."

Hurt flashes on his face. "Is the idea of sitting in a gondola with me that repulsive to you? I didn't realize you hated my company so much."

"I don't hate your company." I rub my hands over my eyes and walk slower down a sidewalk. "It's just—I miss Will. Everything would be better if he were here. Easier."

Dev's expression darkens. "Right. If only Willoughby were here to brighten your day with his wit and culture."

"What's your problem with Will? You've had it out for him since day one."

"That's not true." He shoves his hands into his pockets. "All right, fine, it's absolutely true. But come on, he drives a *Jaguar*? That's excessive."

"I didn't know you cared so much about cars."

"I don't."

"Then what is it? Really?" I stop on the sidewalk and turn toward him. Suddenly, I want to know what he actually thinks of Will. My hands shake and I don't know if it's because I'm cold or because I'm nervous about what he's going to say.

"Ellie, let's drop it. This isn't a good conversation for us to have."

"No, tell me. I want to know."

"You really don't . . . but fine. I don't like him because he has everything that the rest of us want and he wastes it all. Money, connections, opportunities. It's like he doesn't even care." He heaves a big sigh and meets my eyes. "But mostly I don't like him because he's not good enough for you. He's not even close to what you deserve. And I think he knows it. That's why he does all this."

My throat tightens and the shaking spreads down my legs. "You've got it turned around. He's too good for me."

His shoulders hunch. "I hope someday you see yourself the way the rest of us see you."

I can't hold his gaze. I walk away, but Dev keeps pace with me. Rather than think about what he just said, I focus on our surroundings. Our walkway dead-ends into a narrow canal. It's only wide enough to get a small boat or gondola down. It is pitch-black here, the dark half-masking our faces from each other.

"We are so lost." Dev sighs and sits on the steps leading down into the canal.

I sit as well. My body feels weak and my feet are screaming at me after walking the whole day. We sit for a few minutes in silence, listening to the lapping water and distant hum of a motor.

"Should we try to head back?" I ask finally. "I bet we can find our way eventually. Or maybe we could ask someone. *Ci dare indicazioni?*"

"You mean, *Ci puoi dare indicazioni?*"

"You're intolerable."

He bumps my shoulder with his. "Aw, I feel the same about you."

I stand and he tugs at my arm. "Let's stay a little longer. I mean, unless you really do need to call Will."

I should call him, but I don't have to do it this instant. And despite the fact that it's bitterly cold and the water smells like mildew, there's also a charm to this forgotten canal. I hesitate and then sit back down. I should be freaking out that I'm lost in the middle of a foreign city, but . . . I'm not. I don't feel lost with Dev here.

"Are you still glad we came to Venice despite no . . ."

"Absolutely," I say. "Venice is magical."

"It is. Thanks for forcing me to come."

"And it's about to get even better. Sage should be in tomorrow afternoon."

He stiffens. "Why are you so invested in me and Sage?"

"Because you asked me to get you guys together. That was our deal."

"I never asked you. You offered and I wasn't going to turn you down, though I never thought anything would happen. I've been in school with Sage since we were ten. I always knew it was hopeless."

"But . . . that was how I was going to pay you back."

"The time we spent hanging out wasn't billable hours."

I eye him. "Well, you certainly seemed annoyed about helping me."

"That's because it was annoying helping you be someone you're not. But we're friends, Ellie. I like hanging out with every version of you."

My throat gets tight and I can't reply.

Dev fidgets next to me. "Can I ask you something without you getting pissed at me?"

"Probably not." But I nudge him so he knows I'm (mostly) kidding.

"Why do you like Will, really?"

"Because I feel special around him," I whisper.

"And . . . you think he's the only one who could make you feel that way? No one else will do?"

His voice is soft and gravelly. All of a sudden I'm aware of how close we are on this narrow step. His lips are only inches from mine.

A window slides open on the second floor of the building to our left and a woman leans out. She shakes a blanket and gives us a curt nod.

I pull back, startled by her presence.

"I bet she heard us fighting before," I whisper. "She probably thinks we're lunatic American tourists."

"Eh, she's Italian. She probably just thinks we're in love."

My breath catches even though I know he's being sarcastic. But all my senses are heightened now. I can feel his body heat radiating on my skin and smell the mint from his gum. He shifts slightly and our knees touch. He doesn't pull away and neither do I.

When I look up, his eyes are already on me. Warm brown in the cold black night. I lean away.

"We should go," I whisper.

He nods. "Happy Thanksgiving, Ellie."

"Happy Thanksgiving, Dev."

We retrace our path—with a few wrong turns along the way—until we get back to the Grand Canal and use that to guide us to the hotel.

"This was fun," he says when we arrive an hour later. "Well, not the part where you ran away for no reason. But I liked getting lost with you."

Getting lost wasn't the part of tonight that I liked the most, though. It was the feeling of being found.

I toss and turn all night, despite the cloudlike bed. I find a text from Will when I wake in the morning.

Father continues to be impossible. I hope I haven't missed anything too fun. Can't wait to see you.

I run a hand through my hair, guilt coursing through me. I know it's stupid because nothing happened between me and Dev last night . . . but at the same time it kind of feels like something did. It's like I saw him in a way I'd never allowed myself to before. Could he be feeling the same way? I shake my head in annoyance.

My brain is being dumb. I'm really happy with Will. It doesn't matter what Dev is feeling.

I text Will back to say that I miss him and wish he were here, then roll my shoulders back. Today is going to be a good day. A *great* day. Thank god Sage is arriving. I've missed her so much.

Dev comes up to me as soon as I walk into the breakfast room. "Are you coming to Ca' d'Oro with me?"

"*Don'tdoit*," Huan coughs into his hand.

"Ignore them. They wouldn't recognize art if it slapped them in the face."

At that, Frank spins toward Huan and slaps him. I suck in a breath, but Huan grins and grabs Frank in a tight hug. "*Art!* How are you? It's been so long!" He holds Frank out to get a good look at him. "You aren't nearly as pretentious as I remembered you being."

They dissolve into laughter and Dev rolls his eyes. "Yeah, yeah, get back to buying your overpriced souvenirs from China."

"Hey, I'll have you know I've been invited to beatbox in St. Mark's Square."

"Whoa, really?" I ask. "Who invited you?"

"A group of hip-hop dancers from France," Frank says proudly. "They're hoping the tourists will take some videos and it'll go viral. We watched them yesterday. They're quite good."

"They said they'd split their earnings with me."

Dev cocks his head. "And what are you going to spend your money on?"

"Overpriced souvenirs, obviously."

"Obviously." Dev turns to me. "You won't abandon me, though, right? You're the only one who'll appreciate the museum anyway."

"Um . . ."

I shift from foot to foot. I want to spend the morning with Dev, but another wave of guilt hits me. Is spending all this time alone with him wrong? Should I force Huan and Frank to stay with us? But as soon as I think that, I know it's ridiculous. We're only touring a museum, not going for candlelit dinners or . . . gondola rides.

So we split up, agreeing to meet at the Rialto Bridge at one, when Sage should arrive.

The museum is housed in an unreal palace on the Grand Canal. The interior courtyard is a masterpiece of intricately carved columns and mosaic tiles in shades of terra-cotta, green, and cream. I'd be happy to spend the rest of the day right here, but Dev assures me there's much more to see.

He takes me through the galleries like this is his museum and these are the paintings and sculptures he's carefully curated over time. I'm in awe of the details he remembers about the artists. Dates, places of birth, tidbits about their lives that even I have to admit are pretty interesting. He seems to remember it all so easily, as if he was born with the knowledge instead of having to learn it.

I keep my eyes on the art, or on the plaques next to the art, or on the arched walls and tiled floors. I don't stare at Dev. I don't notice how his eyes sparkle with excitement when he points out gory details in the Renaissance paintings. I don't notice the way his jeans fall low on his hips or how his hair is curling into waves along the nape of his neck. I don't notice because I *can't* notice. I have a boyfriend waiting for me back in England. *It's only Venice*, I tell myself. It must do funny things to people's brains.

chapter
33

Will calls me when we're waiting for Sage by the Rialto.
"Elle! I'm glad you picked up. You never called me."

I wince. "Oh god, I'm sorry—I've been so caught up in everything . . ."

"Well, things have been horrid over here. Father has kept me running from meeting to meeting since I arrived in London, then pestering me with advice for the lunch whenever we're alone. It's a nightmare."

I make a sympathetic noise, relieved that he isn't going to grill me about how I've been spending my time here.

"When is your big lunch?"

"Soon. I'm at my parents' right now. I have to do a fashion show so Father can approve my clothes like I'm a child. He wants to make sure I look professional."

Tourists bustle around me and I duck against a wall to get out of the way. "I'm sure you'll be as debonair as James Bond. Are you nervous?"

"A bit. I don't care about the school, but I don't want to deal with his wrath if it doesn't go well."

Dev's comments about Will from last night come back to me. Is it possible that Will really doesn't care? But no. Just because Will doesn't have the same goals as Dev doesn't mean he has no goals at all. His parents expect a lot out of him, and it's probably even scarier to fail when you have so many opportunities. He has so far to fall.

I wrap my coat tighter against the cold wind that slips between the buildings and into my bones. "You're going to wow this admissions guy. I can't imagine any other outcome."

"I wish you were coming with me. It would make this whole thing so much more tolerable. Plus, if they met you, they'd find me more tolerable I'm sure."

"Oh?" I imagine Will standing in front of me, his mouth quirked in a smile. "You think I bring out your charm?"

"Most certainly," he says. "I have to be at my most charming to keep you around."

Dev waves crazily in my direction and I know that means Sage is getting off the *vaporetto*.

"Will, I'm sorry, Sage just arrived so I've got to go. But good luck with your lunch!"

We say goodbye and I run over and throw my arms around her. She squeezes me back. This is the first time we've ever truly hugged and I've never needed it more.

"You're here! Finally! Were the flight and boat ride all right?"

"No issues." She turns in a little circle, dazed. "It's so gorgeous here."

"You just wait," I say. "You haven't seen anything yet."

She claps her hands together. I've never seen her so elated. "I have the *most* wonderful news. Yesterday, Dr. Reese and her grad students went out to a fancy dinner with Dr. Patel—the speaker from Stanford—and they asked me to come along. We started talking about the work I've been doing with Dr. Reese on the effects of RAS mutations on melanoma and Dr. Patel said he was really impressed! *So* impressed that he offered me a position as an undergrad assistant in his lab if I get into Stanford! Can you believe it? Having a letter of rec from him could be the thing that gets me into grad school. Thank god I already got my application in. And to think I wasn't sure about applying!"

"That's amazing!"

She and Dev start talking about assistantships and research opportunities and all their plans for the future. Hearing them reminds me how far behind I still am. I started researching gardening internships and jobs like Miriam suggested—including some pretty amazing opportunities with the United States Botanic Garden in DC—but then I got intimidated and stopped. I have *zero* real experience—how would I be competitive for something like this? I'm nothing like Sage, who's been raking up volunteer experience since she was first learning the alphabet.

Sage laughs at something and I can't help but peek at Dev's expression. Is he upset that she's already making plans years into her future—particularly plans that include Stanford—a college on the opposite side of the country? If he is, I can't tell.

Sage turns around again, taking in the view with an excited

smile. She points to a gondola floating down the Grand Canal. "Should we take a gondola ride sometime or is that too tacky?" I glance at Dev before I can catch myself and Sage notices. "Or did you guys already do that?"

"No, we didn't. Ellie and I stayed behind."

She looks between us and I know her brain is churning. Sage really is too smart for her own good. I turn away before she reads anything else from my expression. Close by, people are practically hanging off the side of the Rialto Bridge to get the perfect photo of the canal. It's weird to think that they're all going to go home and show off their photos as if they're unique when really fifty other people have the exact same shot of this moment. How many people in the world must have identical pictures that they think are one of a kind? Or even identical experiences? Maybe everyone here gets lost in the back alleys of Venice. Maybe they all sit under the stars. But maybe that doesn't matter because it's no less special when it happens to you.

We update Sage on the trip while walking over to the hotel so she can drop off her bag. It turns out she wants to see Doge's Palace first, and Huan is meeting up with that dance group again, so everyone agrees to go back to St. Mark's Square. Since I've already toured the palace, I decide to walk around on my own for an hour.

I head to the back alleyways again. I find a little neighborhood grocery store and buy way too much stuff—Italian chips and chocolate and weird drinks I've never heard of before. Will texts me to say that the lunch went well and his father is very happy for once. I'm glad for him. At least he didn't miss this trip for nothing. But my mind keeps returning to Dev and Sage. Is he happier now that Sage is here? Is he having more fun with her than with me? Stupid, pointless thoughts.

I meet up with the group and we spend the rest of the day together before splurging on a real dinner in a restaurant. The five of us squeeze around a small round table, slurp pasta, and stare out at the chilly canal. A dusting of snow falls over everything and I've never seen a place so beautiful. We take a thousand pictures together and I post a few, but I'm not so worried about what everyone else is going to think. Other people don't need to like my photos in order for me to know how amazing this trip has been. Just looking around will tell me that.

Afterward, we meander along the canal. Huan and Frank lean into each other, chatting and laughing quietly. Dev, Sage, and I walk behind in an awkward row.

"So, uh, did you actually want to try the gondola?" Dev asks Sage, and gestures to some gondoliers in front of us.

She shrugs. "When in Venice . . ."

"Yeah? Okay . . . well, great." He pauses for a moment before jumping to action. He calls to Huan and Frank, keeping his back to me.

Huan whispers to Frank before slipping his arm over my shoulder. "I'd like to go one more time. How about just you and me, Ellie?"

I snuggle into him. "Perfect."

Dev and Sage get into the first gondola and Huan and I follow behind in the next one. The boats are so low in the water that it's like I'm stepping inside the canal. The gondoliers push off and I'm surprised by how close they stay to each other. There's clearly a path that all the gondolas take and soon we've caught up to three other boats. We all float along, one right after another, like a gondola caravan, and it's less romantic than I was expecting. Not that I need romance with Huan.

"So are you enjoying the trip even without Handsome McBritain here?"

I elbow him. "You're one to talk about Handsome McBritains. And yes—it's magical. I don't want to leave."

"Good. I was worried at first." There's a pause. "And how's everything with you and Dev?"

"We're fine. It's been fun."

"Mmm."

I can tell he wants to say something else, but I don't want to talk about Dev. I want to soak in every second of this experience. We've left the Grand Canal and are slipping down smaller canals and under the arched bridges I walked across last night. The city is quiet, but a few people stop on the bridges to watch us. Old stone buildings tower on either side. There are places where I could reach out and scrape my fingers against the walls or climb out of the boat and through one of the doorways into someone's house. Everything is dazzling but it's teetering on the edge between decadence and death . . . between being one of the most beautiful things I've ever seen and crumbling away into the sea. I have a sudden thought that falling in love feels similar.

"You're quiet tonight," Huan says. "Do I need to start beatboxing to cheer you up?"

"Instead of having the gondoliers sing? You could start a new fad. It would pull in a whole younger generation."

Huan laughs and does a little riff, which makes the gondolier turn in surprise.

"Frank will kill me if he finds out I did it without him. He was goading me the whole ride yesterday."

"You guys seem to be having a good time." I nudge him playfully.

"You could say that. It's hard for me to imagine being happier than I am here."

"We're pretty young to have already hit our peak."

"Frank is . . ." He shakes his head. "He's one of a kind. I'm not going to find someone else back home like him."

"So don't look for anyone else."

He chuckles. "I don't want to be single forever."

"Then don't be single either. Maybe long distance can work if both people really care about each other. And clearly that's true for both of you." I lean against him. "If you really like Frank, you should give it a chance."

"The same goes for you."

"Oh, believe me, I've been giving it my best try with Will."

Huan's expression grows serious. "Maybe I wasn't talking about Will."

He looks to Dev's gondola and I follow. Dev and Sage have

their backs to us. They aren't touching, or at least I can't see them touching, but they're sitting close and every once in a while one will lean over and whisper something to the other. It feels inappropriate to watch them, like I'm intruding on something intimate. My stomach twists.

"We're just friends," I whisper.

chapter 34

Saturday goes by in a blur and before we know it, we've packed our bags, loaded onto the water bus, and are heading back to the airport. We arrive extremely early so I peruse the duty-free shop with Sage.

"Why are we walking through here again?" she asks. "Are you planning to take a huge bottle of vodka back on the plane with you?"

"No. But we should walk through anyway—it's like a requirement when you fly internationally." I hold up a fifty-euro bottle of perfume. "And we could buy this instead."

She wrinkles her nose. "No thank you. Perfume gives me headaches."

A scent catches my attention. It's an expensive men's cologne in a small blue bottle. "I think this is what Will wears." Just a whiff of it brings back memories of standing with him in the London Eye and snuggling close to him at the pub in Northampton. But those memories feel far away now.

Sage comes over and takes a tiny sniff. "Eh, could be worse. Have you decided what you're going to do about Will?"

"What do you mean?" I ask even though I know what she's hinting at. It's been on my mind all morning.

"The pledge you made to try out the 'real Ellie' around him—are you still going through with that now that Venice is behind you?"

I mess with the cap on the bottle rather than answer her. Everything made more sense before this trip. I was going to tell Will about myself and we were going to bond and kiss and eat from the same plate of spaghetti like in that Disney movie. But spending all this time with Dev has confused everything. I can't forget his words from the night we got lost or the way it felt to be so near him. Like I was exactly where I was supposed to be. But Will is waiting for me back in England and I'm not ready to let go of him either.

"Ellie?"

I shake my head. "I'm . . . conflicted."

"Obviously. The guy running the cash register can see that."

I turn to her. "Tell me what to do about Will." My words are loud—a command.

"What? No."

"Yes, please. Just give me your opinion. You always have a better handle on things than me."

She heaves a big sigh, as if she wishes she could be anywhere but here, having this conversation with me. "I'm not going to tell you what to do with your life. But . . . I do have an observation, if it helps anything." I nod eagerly. "I know you think Will makes you happy. But sometimes . . . well, you seem happier when you're not with him."

"What am I like with him?"

"You're . . . on edge. Sanitized." Her tone is matter-of-fact. "You're *Elle* instead of Ellie."

My stomach drops. I am? Sage says it like it's so obvious. My mind spins, trying to compare my time with Will to my time at Emberton.

She touches my arm. "Have you two even talked about what happens when we go back to America? Has Will said he wants to date long-distance?"

"No. He . . . I don't think he likes to plan much into the future."

She raises her eyebrows. "Well, if that's the case, then I'm not sure the rest of this matters."

My conversation with Sage plays in my mind the entire flight back. She's right. If Will and I are destined to break up in a few weeks, it doesn't really matter what I decide to tell him. And I can't see any other outcome but that. I know some people can make long distance work with texts and calls and lots of FaceTime, but we can't always find time to see each other when we're thirty minutes apart. There's no way we can make this work when we live in different *countries*, and I have zero money for another trip abroad. Which means that the only real question is whether I want to spend my last weeks here in a relationship with an expiration date. Maybe that would take the pressure off. We could just have fun—no expectations. Or maybe it makes it sad. I can't decide.

Sage takes a seat alone on the train back to Northampton, saying she wants to use the time to study (of course she brought her notes on vacation) so Dev and I sit together. I'm a little nervous to be close to him again, but as soon as we start comparing photos, I relax. It turns out he took photos of artwork, but almost none of Venice itself, so I send him all of mine.

"Do you have any big plans tonight when we get back?" he asks.

"Other than staring at these photos and wishing I could teleport back in time? Nope, my calendar is wide open."

"Do you want to study together? I think Sage has the right idea."

More time alone. I'm not sure that's a good idea . . . but then again, he only wants to study. And he's never explicitly said he wants to be more than friends. For all I know, he's oblivious to what's going on in my head.

"I guess we can study. But I reserve the right to stare at Venice photos every thirty minutes."

"I wasn't sure about this trip," he says. The creak of brakes is shrill as the train pulls into the Northampton station. "But I have to admit you were right."

I stand straight up and almost drop my bag on my foot. "Wait. You're admitting—without coercion—that I was right about something? You did hear that, didn't you?" I ask Huan.

Frank stayed in London and Huan's been quiet the whole train ride, but he perks up at this. He pulls out his phone, opens up a dictation app, and sticks it under Dev's nose. "Could you repeat that once more, sir, slowly and carefully? We need it for our records."

"Shut up." He pushes Huan's hand away good-naturedly. "I've learned my lesson. Never bet against Venice."

We're still joking and laughing when the van drops us off at Emberton. Probably we're giddy with exhaustion. Out of the corner of my eye, I see *blue*. Shiny, recently washed blue metal. My chest tightens with shock and I spin.

Will sits on the hood of his car. A ridiculously large flower arrangement rests on the ground beside him. As in, I'm not sure how he got it into his car and I have *no* idea how it'll fit on my tiny desk upstairs.

My hand goes to my mouth. "Omigod!" On instinct, I look at Dev, then Sage and Huan. Sage has a small frown, but Dev and Huan have no expressions at all. "What are you doing here?" I ask him.

Will jumps off the car and spreads his arms wide. "Can't a guy miss his girlfriend? Come here!"

I hurry to him and he wraps me in a big hug. He smells just like the duty-free cologne.

"Did you miss me?" he whispers in my ear.

I nod and he kisses me. It does feel good to be in his arms again, despite everything, but I'm also aware that the others are staring at us.

"How long were you planning to stay? Do you need to get back or—"

"I cleared my schedule." Will's smile is blinding. "I thought we could spend the evening together. It feels like I haven't seen you in an age." He drops his voice. "You didn't exactly keep your promise to send me constant photos at the end there."

I flush. Different emotions fight for control. It's so sweet of him to surprise me and bring me flowers . . . but I wish he would have texted me first. I need more time to think about our relationship and these last few weeks.

Dev, Huan, and Sage linger, clearly unsure whether they should wait for me or not. Sage is holding one of my bags and Dev has another. I hate feeling so torn.

"So, um, I think Will and I are going to get some dinner. Do you all want to join us?" I raise my eyebrows to Dev, hoping he can read the apology in my expression.

"No, I'm going to drop onto my bed and not wake up until tomorrow," Huan says. "Good to see you, Will."

Sage declines, but Dev pauses and for a second I think he might actually agree. I try to imagine the three of us sitting together at a small table, Dev and me regaling Will with stories from Venice and talking about life at Emberton. It sounds unbearable.

"I'll pass." Dev jerks his head in Will's direction. "Looks like you've got your hands full."

I blink, thinking that was a snarky comment about Will and me, but then I realize he's talking about the flower arrangement.

"Too right, mate. It was rather rough getting it into the front seat."

I inspect the arrangement for the first time. It's the type of thing you'd see in the lobby of a fancy hotel or at a wedding. There must be at least fifty red roses, plus hydrangeas and green berries. It's wider than I am and probably half my height. I don't even want to think about how much it cost. Dev's words about why Will spends so much money on me return.

I turn back to him, but he's gone.

"You really didn't have to buy me flowers," I tell Will.

He waves away the words. "I left you stranded at an airport. It still wouldn't be enough if I delivered one to you every day for a year."

"But the mone—"

"Don't bother about it. I put it on my father's business account. He should be the one sending you flowers anyway."

I smile, but his words make me twitchy. Does his father even know he spent all this money? Or is it so little money to them that they don't notice the expense? Either way, I'm not sure I like it.

Will carries the arrangement into the front hall, managing to wobble only a few times from the weight and size, and then we head toward Northampton. Will flies past the fields and hedgerows even faster than usual.

"I got us reservations at the best steakhouse in Northampton—the one I was telling you about."

I raise my eyebrows. If I'm thinking of the same one, then it's crazy expensive. "Do I need to change clothes?"

"No, it's fine." Of course Will looks impeccable while I'm once again in my travel clothes. I'm getting used to looking slovenly in comparison to him. "I have amazing news and I thought it deserved the right atmosphere."

"You do?" I swivel toward him. "What is it? Did you hear something about UCL already?"

He waves my words away. "No spoilers! We'll be there soon and

279

then I'll tell you the whole thing."

I sit back in my seat, excited for him but tense at the same time. This must be related to him getting away from his dad—there's not much that would make him happier. What am I going to say if he tells me he's going to college at UCL? Or that he's found some other job, possibly one in London? I mean, I'll be absolutely thrilled for him, of course, but it makes it even more obvious that his life is just beginning in England when I'm a few weeks out from leaving. Maybe it's not worth bringing up the possibility of long distance at all. Maybe he always assumed we were temporary and I just didn't get the memo.

The restaurant is rustic, with lots of stone and barn-wood paneling. It's also packed for a Sunday night. We practically have to yell to hear each other.

"Do you like it?" His eyes are wide and he's practically bouncing in his seat.

"Yes, absolutely. But I want to hear your news!"

"I chose this place for a reason." He looks around, as if for a waiter, and then throws his hands in the air. "They haven't taken our drink order yet and I'm probably going to get interrupted in two seconds, but I can't wait." He reaches out to take my hand across the table. "You know how unhappy I've been with Father. I've been casting about for a way to separate myself and then over the weekend the greatest idea occurred to me. I'll move to America for school." He puts out his hands as if to say *ta-da*. "The more I think about it, the more I realize it's perfect. I'll be in uni like Father is lusting after, but I won't have my every move choreographed anymore." He squeezes my hand. "What do you think, Elle?"

I suck in a breath. Of all the things I expected Will to say, this one wasn't even on the list. I open and close my mouth. Then do it again.

"I . . . wow . . . you really think you'd be able to do that?"

"Yes. I don't think my parents will be terribly happy, but I mentioned it to Mum and she didn't shoot me down. If I'm at a reputable university overseas, then I don't think they can be too cross." He speaks quickly, like there's so much bursting to come out of him. "I already looked and I haven't missed all the due dates for next autumn, although it may be too hard to get everything together in time. But even if I can't start in the autumn, I'm thinking I can move early to find a flat and a job to make some money. I'm determined to wean myself off Father's money. Frank was right—it's the only way."

I nod, only half comprehending. "Yes, true. That makes a lot of sense." My brain is chugging as hard as it can, trying to process all this and what it means for him. And for us. The boat, plane, and train rides must have wiped me out because I can't wrap my mind around it. Will? In *America*?

"You think so? Are you excited? I want to live where you'll be, Elle. I know we never talked about it—and if I'm being honest, I wasn't sure we could stay together after you left England—but now we don't have to worry about that. We'll be together again soon."

I keep nodding. Will and me in America. Together . . . indefinitely? As soon as I think that, Dev pops into my head. What will he think when I tell him? And why does it matter what he thinks?

But Will is watching me expectantly, so I push Dev from my mind and smile brightly. "Yes, I'm totally excited! I think this could be amazing for you. I bet you'll love living in America."

Maybe this *will* be amazing. We could apply to the same schools, live in the same city. He could meet my mom and we'd have the time for him to get to know me—the real me this time. A tiny voice in the back of my mind reminds me of my concerns from before. What if Will doesn't like the real me? But the joy on his face sucks me in. Will is the dream and it looks like now I get to keep him.

"I knew you'd think so! I'm so glad." He gestures around the restaurant. "Do you get it now? Why I brought you here?"

I squint in confusion.

"It's an American steakhouse! The beginning of many more American dinners together."

It's close to curfew when I finally make it back to my room. Will and I ended up staying at the restaurant forever talking about America. He had a thousand questions about American colleges—most of which I couldn't answer—so we got on our phones, looking up admission deadlines and procedures. It was easy to get caught up in Will's excitement, but now that I'm alone, I realize we talked about nothing else tonight. He didn't ask to hear more about the trip or my last few weeks of classes. But then, he was ecstatic over his new plan for his future. It's not fair to judge.

When I get to my room, the first thing I see is the flower arrangement, which someone has set on the ground next to my desk. It's so large that I have to turn sideways to get around it.

Sage smirks at me. "Welcome to our floral shop."

I can't help but laugh. It *is* pretty ridiculous. The door opens and I'm surprised to see Dev walk in with two mugs.

"Oh, hey. I was wondering if you were going to miss curfew."

He hands one mug to Sage and then sits down at my desk. I hadn't realized until now that it's covered with his laptop and notebooks.

"Why are you studying here?" I ask.

"Huan's a little down about being away from Frank. I came over here to give him some space." He raises an eyebrow. "You know, since *someone* bailed on me."

I cringe and sink onto Sage's bed. "I'm sorry about that."

"How's Willoughby?"

I bite my lip. "He's good. Actually, he's great. He's, um . . ."

Sage turns to give me her full attention. Nerves tighten my throat and dry my mouth. "He's . . . decided to move to America. For college."

They both lean back, eyes wide, like they choreographed it. I try to read their emotions, but their expressions are blank except for shock.

"Where's he applying?" Sage asks. Her voice is quiet.

"He's not sure yet. That's why we were out so late. I was helping him look into options. He says he wants to go wherever I'm going."

"But you don't know where you're going, right?" Dev asks. "Or has that changed in the last three hours too?"

I shake my head. I'm still not sure where I want to go, but I know I want to try for college. This semester has shown me that I can survive it if I put the work in.

Sage breaks the silence. "Well . . . that's exciting for him. Maybe this is exactly what he needs. And you're feeling good about it?"

"I am, yeah. It was a shock for sure. But it would be really fun to have Will in America. I can hardly believe it."

My mood falters when I look at the flower arrangement. I'm reminded again of Dev's words.

But mostly I don't like him because he's not good enough for you. He's not even close to what you deserve. And I think he knows it. That's why he does all this.

I glance at Dev, hoping for a small smile or positive word, but he doesn't look at me. He's too busy packing up his stuff.

chapter
35

Sage was right—taking a five-day vacation so close to the end of the semester was *not* a smart choice. We've returned just in time for the ramp up into finals week. The halls are quieter, the classes are tense, and the dining hall is never more than half-full since students are too busy studying to bother with food.

And, as usual, I'm in over my head.

I have a British lit paper due next Monday, my psych and chem finals that Tuesday, and a huge art history paper due next Thursday. My brain is bursting with to-dos when I'm not texting with Will about America or worrying about how this move is going to go. All around me are tiny noises that scratch at my mind. Shoes shuffling, pages turning, small sighs and whispers. It's hard to concentrate with everything else going on. I rub my hands over my face and push back from the crowded library table.

I heave a deep breath in the hallway. I don't want to go back to my room yet. Sage is there writing her British lit analysis and she's going to want total silence. What I'd like is to study with Dev. I don't know where his head is at, though. He hasn't said anything about Will moving to America. Honestly, he hasn't said much at all this last week.

When I don't find him in his room, I go looking in the only other place I can think of: his secret study room. I have to backtrack twice, but eventually I find it. The fire is roaring and Dev is there by himself, head down, earphones in, surrounded by books. He doesn't see me. I stand in the doorway, watching him. He's tapping his foot like he always does when he's studying. The room is hot and he's wearing only a thin T-shirt—it's one of his favorites, the blue one with the logo of the Indian national cricket team on it. He's hunched over his desk, the curve of his spine and shoulder blades visible through the fabric. Dev isn't muscular—he's skinny and tall and a bit gangly—but he is fit. It must be all that cricket and Quidditch.

He looks up and jumps. Heat rushes to my face. Oh god, does he know I was staring at him? He pulls out his earphones.

"Hey. What's wrong?"

"Nothing." I hurry into the room and sit down across from him. "Just trying to find someplace to study. I think you've found the only quiet place in the manor."

"Probably because no one knows it exists."

"Luckily for us," I say, and then flinch. That sounded like flirting. "Do you mind if I join you?"

"Uh, no." He pushes some of his books out of my way but I notice his hesitation. I'm hoping he'll ask me what I'm studying right now, or even suggest that we work together, but instead he puts his earphones back in. It feels like a rebuke.

I pull out my chemistry notes. I've been helping Dev organize his chicken-scratch notes lately and it's taught me how to take better notes myself. I used to not write much, but now I write down everything the teacher says, plus my own thoughts and examples. That means I basically never stop writing in my classes. I've already warned Dev that I'm suing if I develop carpal tunnel syndrome.

I've also started outlining every chapter of the textbook and then using both sets of notes to study. Dev convinced me to start studying way sooner than I used to (the night before the test) so I can memorize the notes rather than only read over them. It's a *hell* of a lot of work. And I hate it. But I got a B on my last chemistry quiz so I haven't complained. Well, that's not true. I've *definitely* complained, but not as vehemently as I could have.

I start reviewing chapter eighteen (chemical thermodynamics) but my brain immediately shuts down. These last chapters are the hardest in the entire book, plus the final is cumulative so I have to restudy everything. Professors are the spawn of Satan. I inspect Dev, but he doesn't notice. I tap his book.

He stops chewing his gum but doesn't take out his earphones. Okay.

"Hey, do you want to study together?" I ask, my voice loud to compensate for his music.

"Um, maybe later, okay?" He goes back to highlighting his notes without waiting for my response.

I sit back. Dev never acts like this.

"Is everything okay?"

He huffs in annoyance. "Not really. I'm trying to study and this crazy girl keeps interrupting me."

"Maybe we should talk."

"I'm busy right now, Ellie. And stressed. I need to ace all my finals to make sure I keep my 4.0."

"Then let's study together. Come on!" I reach over and shake his notebook. "You can lecture me on chem just the way you like! I'm going to flunk this final exam if you don't help me."

He drops his highlighter on the table. "You don't need me. You're just scared to do the work on your own."

"What? No, I'm not."

"Yes, you are. It's your pattern." He waves at my notes. "You never see things through to the end. As soon as something gets hard, you get scared and run away."

"I don't do that."

"No? What happened after that crap with Andy? You ran off to England rather than deal with it. And when Dr. Allen wanted to nominate you for tutoring? You immediately said no even though it could've been a great opportunity. And I bet you haven't looked further into your gardening either. Who knows where that could take you if you'd push yourself to really explore it? But you're always running away to something new and easy and superficial."

I sit back in shock.

"You're so afraid to let yourself *try* for anything, Ellie." He leans across the desk toward me, his dark eyes flashing. "To really put yourself out there and see where the chips fall, even if that means you fail and have no excuses."

"Do you not remember my infamous video, Dev?" I whisper. "*That's* what I get when I risk it all and put myself out there. I get squashed like a big fat bug."

"Screw that video! Who gives a shit what that jerk did? Are you going to let that define the rest of your life? Are you never going to go after anything you really want?"

"And who are you to judge? You're sitting here studying anatomy when you know damn well that you don't even like medicine!"

"It doesn't matter what I like. I'm *good* at anatomy. I'll be a good doctor. Not everything can just be about me, me, me all the time. Maybe you have that luxury, but I have to take my whole family into consideration. What they want matters too."

"So you've talked to your parents and they've said absolutely no to art history?"

He clamps his mouth shut.

"They've told you they'll never forgive you if you pursue something other than medicine?"

His eyes narrow into a glare.

"Exactly! I knew you hadn't brought it up."

"Oh please, you're one to talk."

I splay my hands on the table and half stand. "What the hell do you think I've been doing here, Dev? Taking the leap to come here when I knew nobody? Joining classes that are harder than anything I've ever done before? Believe me, I'm trying. And if you've got me all figured out, then how do you explain Will? Are you saying it's not a risk to be with him?"

His expression darkens at my last words. "Oh, don't get me started on Willoughby."

"Stop calling him that."

"Stop calling him by his *name*? Should I stop calling you Ellie too?" He rubs a hand down his face. "Do you even realize how absurd that is? That this guy doesn't know which name you go by? And now you're going to keep this up in *college*? If you really think you're taking a risk with him, you're more screwed up than I thought."

I stand and Dev stands with me, both of us arched toward the other. Our faces are close enough that I can smell his peppermint gum.

"He. Doesn't. Know. You. Your entire relationship is a charade because you're so scared that if he knows the slightest thing about you, he might not like you anymore. And you'd rather be in a fake relationship than try for something that might be messy and difficult and *great*."

I jerk back. We stare at each other in silence. My heart is racing and my hands are shaking and I'm too angry to think straight.

I grab my things. "I'm not going to stay here and listen to this anymore. I'm leaving."

"Of course you are." He throws his hands in the air. "Why stay and talk about something real when we can fill our conversations with meaningless chatter and bullshit?"

"Nothing I ever said to you was bullshit." I shoot him one last glare and rush out the door.

chapter
36

I slam my dorm door behind me. So *that's* what he's thought of me this entire time? That I'm some spineless girl who's too scared of her own shadow to take any risks?

"What's with you?"

I spin toward Sage. "Dev is an asshole."

She sits back in surprise. "That's not what I thought you were going to say. What happened?"

"All I wanted was to study with him and instead he thought he'd take the opportunity to list all my faults and tell me what an idiot I am."

"That doesn't sound like him."

"Yeah, well . . ." I glare at her. "This is all your fault."

Sage glances longingly back at her notes before returning my gaze. "What's my fault? Why am I even a part of this?"

"Because he liked you!" My voice is too loud. "Why couldn't you have liked him back? Then everything would be perfect."

"Perfect for whom? Me and Dev, or just you?"

I groan. "I don't know. For everyone. You two could be happy,

Will and I could be happy . . ."

"Why do I have to date Dev in order for you to be happy with Will?"

I grit my teeth. "I . . . ugh, never mind."

I drop into my chair and whip out my glue gun. The idea of gluing a bunch of crap onto a birdhouse right now sounds blissfully mind-numbing.

Sage sighs and turns back to her notes. "It's not that difficult, Ellie. If Dev makes you this mad, then stop hanging out with him. You'll be happy, he'll be happy, and I can study in peace. Problem solved."

The suggestion stops me cold. As much as I want to wring his neck right now, the idea of not being friends with Dev is unbearable. I try to imagine it—passing him in the halls without acknowledging him, sitting next to him in class and not peeking over at his notes or complaining about the teacher after. My stomach twists at the idea.

"That's what I thought," she says.

"What did you think?"

"That he means a lot to you." She lowers her voice. "And I don't need to be a mind reader to realize how much he cares about you either."

Flutters tickle my rib cage at her words. I can't deny that *something* is going on between Dev and me. *Something that might be messy and difficult and great.* The flutters rev into trembles. Was he talking about us back there? Was he saying that we could be something great together? I drop my head into my hands. It doesn't matter either way. I shouldn't be having these thoughts at all. I'm with *Will*—my charming, handsome, dreamy boyfriend. The one who is moving to America. That's all I should be focusing on.

"You want my advice?"

"Probably not."

"Great. Maybe you should spend more time thinking about classes and less time thinking about Will and Dev. You're proving my point that boys are only distractions."

"You're not wrong about that. But you make it sound so easy."

"Easy? It's the opposite of that. But I want every contact, every tenth to my GPA, every piece of advice I can get and I'm not going to let anyone stand in my way. I *have* to make this trip worth it for my dad."

"Is he on your case about grades?"

She stares at me for a second and then slumps back into her chair. "I figured someone had told you by now."

"Told me what?" I reply, suddenly anxious.

"That my dad passed away a few years ago."

I slap a hand over my mouth.

"It was before you came to Waterford. There's no reason for you to know. I just assumed Dev or Huan had mentioned it by now." She picks at her nails as she speaks, her shoulders hunched. "Lung cancer. Weird thing is he never smoked a day in his life."

Thick silence fills the space between us. My mind races back through all the previous conversations we've had, searching for other times I might have inadvertently mentioned her father. "I'm so sorry," I whisper.

"Everyone has problems."

"I wish I'd known sooner. Why didn't you say anything?"

"I never talk about it."

I walk over and hug her before she can shrug away, which she totally does.

"I got obsessed with medicine when Dad was in the hospital. I was constantly asking the doctors questions and trying to follow them during rounds. They didn't like that very much." She gives me a tiny smirk. "But what I really wanted was to be the person who discovered the new treatment. The one that would have saved Dad if we'd had it in time. I told Dad I was going to make sure other families never had to go through what we did. And that's still my goal."

"Sage, my god." I sit back. "You're amazing."

She shrugs. "More like determined. Afterward, I concentrated on school more than ever. It became my number one priority, above boys and even friends. I was planning on keeping my head down here too, but then I got you as a roommate." She smiles at me. "I couldn't stay locked up in my room all the time with you around."

"I guess I can be a distraction sometimes too."

"Not a distraction—a respite. But Mom's trusting me to make this trip worth it. She would have rather I saved the money and used it for college tuition next year, but I convinced her that with this research I'd get into a better college, maybe even get more scholarships. She finally relented. So now . . ." She looks up at me.

"Now you need to deliver."

She smiles slightly. "Something like that."

"You must think I'm the most idiotic, superficial person you've ever met."

"No, I don't think that. You and I are just . . . different."

I swallow hard. We *are* different, in most every way, and it's pretty clear which one of us is better.

"That's not what I meant." She squeezes my hand, somehow knowing my feelings without asking. "I'm not trying to make you feel bad. I just don't want you to get sucked into what everyone else wants from you. I know you all think I'm boring sometimes"—I shake my head in protest and she arches an eyebrow—"but I'm doing what's best for me. You need to do that too. Stop thinking about what everyone else wants from you and concentrate on what makes *you* happy. You are awesome as you are, with or without a boy in your life. You're funny and smart and the most joyful person I've ever met. Don't let anything pull you down. Don't lose yourself."

I wrap my arms around her. This time, she doesn't let go.

chapter 37

Somehow I almost manage to keep up with my work during the next week. I finish my big British lit paper and make flash cards for social psych. I reread my chemistry chapters. The only time I come up for air is when Will calls me, which is becoming more frequent. Now that he has a plan to get out from under his father, he can't stop thinking about it.

"What about George Mason University?" he asks as soon as I pick up. "Have you heard of that one?"

"Um . . ." I close my psychology notes. "Yeah, but I don't know anything about it."

He sighs. "Father wants me to have a plan before he fully agrees and this is all turning into so much work. How about I come pick you up and we can run away from our obligations for a bit?"

Getting away from my literal pile of work is so tempting, but both Sage's and Dev's words echo in my mind. I shake my head. "I'm sorry, I can't. I've got so much to do still."

"Come on, Elle." His voice turns soft and pleading. "Can't I persuade you? What happened to the girl I met at the flea market?

The one who said she was here to have fun?"

"That girl realized she needs better grades if she wants to make it into college. You have no idea how many chem chapters I still need to study. I don't know how I'm going to get it all done in time."

"Oh, I'm sure it'll be fine. You'll work it all out. But we have something much more important to discuss—when we can see each other again. We only have this week left."

I frown. I wish Will would slow down so I could tell him more about what's going on. I need someone to vent to without that person worrying (like Mom) or telling me to start working (like Sage). Hopefully it isn't like this next year.

"I can't until my finals are done. But I'm free on Friday."

"Then Friday will have to do." I can almost see his pout from the manor.

I go back to studying, but by late afternoon my brain is too exhausted for homework. Usually I'd go find Dev, but that isn't an option anymore. We still aren't speaking. We don't walk together in the halls or tease each other. We don't share class notes or steal food from each other's plates at lunch. And I'm nauseous over it. Every time I see him, my stomach lurches and my heart seizes and I want to grab his shoulders and yell, *Talk to me!*

But I don't.

I'm not sure what we would say. I don't want him mad at me, but I also don't want to apologize. I wish we could rewind to before all this weirdness happened between us. But that would mean erasing Venice and I can't do that.

I don't know what I want.

So instead, I head down to the conservatory. I've been meaning to visit more since returning from Venice, but school has been so hectic. And, if I'm being completely honest with myself, Dev was right about me running away. I haven't wanted to face Miriam since I abandoned my search for internships.

A bunch of students are here, including Nicole and Heather, who wave and then go back to studying. I don't think we're ever going to be friends, but I don't care anymore that they were obsessed with that viral video at the beginning of the semester. No one has mentioned the video in weeks. I guess my internet fame is coming to an end.

"Ellie," Miriam calls from the other side of the conservatory. "Come look at this."

She's surrounded by orchids. They're beautiful—colorful, delicate, and tantalizingly exotic, especially when set against the backdrop of a chilly British winter.

"I was thinking of hanging these above the ferns in the corner there. And maybe including a little touch of the fairy magic you've sprinkled through the rest of this place."

I laugh self-consciously. "You don't have to keep all this stuff here. I know it's silly."

"Take a look around," she says. "What do you see?"

I hesitate. "Um, lots of plants."

Her eyes narrow. "What else?"

I scan the room. There are plants everywhere, even more than when I arrived, and my fairy houses and decorations peek out from in between leaves and nestle below foliage. But, more than all that,

I see people. Nicole and Heather sit in a shady corner. There are students from my psychology and chemistry classes and another group of college students I don't know.

"There's, um, a lot of people here."

"Exactly. Students. Everywhere I look there are students. They're already here when I come in to water in the morning and they stay until who knows what time at night. They drop food on the ground and I know they're feeding my koi even though I explicitly told them not to. And they're always in the way when I'm trying to prune." She shakes her head in disgust.

"I—"

"It's the best thing to happen here since I was hired."

My eyes widen in surprise.

"Did you know Mr. Odell was thinking of closing the conservatory? He said it was a waste of resources. But now . . ." She sweeps her arm in front of her. "He actually mentioned raising my budget for next year. Only by a few hundred pounds, but still." She puts a hand on my shoulder. "So I won't be taking out the fairy gardens. And I won't be removing the study tables."

My cheeks warm with happiness and I survey the room again with fresh eyes. Nicole elbows Heather and points to one of the fairy houses I made. I brace myself for her to snicker or roll her eyes, but she doesn't. Instead, her eyes light up and she takes a picture with her phone. My chest tightens.

"They're adorable, aren't they?" Miriam calls out to them, and then side-eyes me.

"So cute!" Heather replies. "Are there more of them here?"

"All over." Miriam gestures around the conservatory. "It's like a treasure hunt trying to find them all."

"Cool!"

Miriam leans in. "I told you, you shouldn't underestimate yourself."

I take a deep breath. "Actually, I was thinking about starting a fairy gardening class for kids when I get home. Parents are always looking for fun stuff to do with little kids and I thought some of the local greenhouses and craft stores would be interested if I shared the profits with them. What do you think?"

"Oh!" She nods enthusiastically. "I think that sounds like a wonderful idea."

"Yeah?" Her enthusiasm pushes me to keep going. "And I also found a possible position at the Botanic Garden in DC, but I haven't applied yet. College internships too. I was worried I didn't have the experience, but . . . maybe I should try anyway."

"Of course you should. I interned while I was in college. I think that's a great idea for you. Maybe you could even come back to England sometime. We do have some of the loveliest gardens in the world, according to me at least."

I nod eagerly, the weight in my chest lifting. "That would be amazing. Thank you for everything. You don't know what it means to me."

"It was a pleasure. This place is going to miss you."

"I'm going to miss it too."

"Keep at it. You have a real knack for this." She pats me on the back and heads for the greenhouse.

I stand there, my mind filling with dreams of working at a conservatory for a living. Maybe they could be more than dreams someday. Absently, I break a dead piece from one of the ferns, then pull out my camera. I've spent hours and hours working in this conservatory and I've never taken a single photo of my handiwork. I think it's time that changes.

I go through the conservatory meticulously, getting photos of every detail of the fairy gardens, down to the tiny pebble paths and the rope ladder extending up a large palm tree. I hesitate, then post them online for the world to see. It's scary, but it also feels really good to put that side of me out there.

Nicole and Heather walk past me on their way out.

"Don't you love this stuff?" Heather says, and points to the fairy village I just photographed. "So adorable!"

"Yeah . . . actually, I made it."

She exchanges a glance with Nicole and they both smile. "Really? That's cool."

Yeah. I guess it is.

chapter
38

I'm late for my last art history class of the semester. Dr. Lotfi closes the door just as I come around the corner, which is her not-so-subtle signal that class has begun. Crap, it's *so* awkward walking in after the door closes. She stops talking and everyone turns and stares, just to rub in what a disruption you're making.

I'm sorely tempted to go back to my room and start working on the final paper that's due tonight, but I know Dr. Lotfi or someone else will just come looking for me if I don't show up soon. No one skips class here. I've really been trying to keep up with all my work, but with two finals and my British lit paper due earlier this week, there hasn't been time. I'm in for a seriously long night.

I open the classroom door as quietly as I can and, sure enough, every soul in the room turns to stare like I'm in some D-list horror film. My eyes find Dev's on instinct. I expect him to look away—or at least frown in disapproval—but his forehead furrows in concern.

"Sorry," I whisper, and hunch over like that'll make me less obvious.

"I was just giving a last reminder about the paper, Ms. Nichols." Dr. Lotfi waits until I'm seated before continuing. "But I'm sure you started it early like everyone else, yes?" She raises a skeptical eyebrow.

At least one person giggles. God, I'm so screwed.

When class ends, I expect Dev to walk past me like he has for the last week and a half. Instead he stops in front of my desk, his tall frame looming over me. "Hey. Can we talk?"

I shove my books into my bag and try for a neutral expression. His voice is like a balm for my frayed nerves. "Uh, sure. Here?"

"I was kind of thinking someplace more private. If that's okay?"

"Maybe we could walk around the manor? I've been meaning to do that one more time before we leave. I want to commit every inch of this school to memory."

We walk side by side, silently taking in all the details that make this place so special. I don't know what I'm going to miss the most. The daily flower arrangements on side tables or the cherubs carved into everything or the secret passageways from one classroom into the next. Mostly, I think I'll miss the strange sensation of being at home in a place that couldn't be farther from my own home. But that doesn't matter when you're surrounded by the right people.

"Ellie . . ." Dev fiddles with his shirtsleeves. "I'm really sorry about what happened before in the study room. I never should have said those things."

"They were your opinions. Even if they pissed me off."

"Have you ever agreed with one of my opinions?"

I smirk despite myself. "I believe we're both in agreement about pizza toppings. And Quidditch."

"I actually have my last game Saturday, if you're around. I'd hate for you to lose out on a chance to make fun of me."

"That is one of my favorite activities." I rub my hands down my pants. "I'll try to make it. I might be seeing Will since that's our last full day in England . . ."

"Right, sorry. I should have guessed that." Dev squeezes his backpack strap tighter. "About Will—"

"Let's not talk about it." We've stopped in one of the empty gilded classrooms. I take a step back toward the door.

"No, listen." He puts out a hand to stop me. "I've been thinking about this and I need to get it out. First, I'm really sorry for blowing up on you like that. That wasn't fair to you. I just . . ." He shakes his head. "Anyway, I'm sorry, and I want you to know I'm done fighting with you. I hate it."

"I hate it too."

"This last week has been absolute misery. I didn't realize how much I'd miss you. How much I don't want to lose you." He closes the space between us. "Without you, I . . . I don't even know what to say. You're . . ." He trails off, his voice hoarse.

Wait. My breathing goes shallow. Is he . . . is he about to say he loves me? Could that be possible? His whole body is radiating energy and heat and suddenly I know that's what he's thinking. *He loves me.* I can see the next seconds playing out—how he's going to pull me toward him and the way my heart's going to leap at the proximity. The fear on his face when he says it for the first time. And what I'll say in return. Everything sharpens with sudden clarity. I *want* him to tell me. I want him to kiss me.

I want him.

"I'm what?" I whisper, barely able to get the words out.

"You're my best friend, Ellie."

I freeze. I'm floating and sinking at the same time. Yes, that's true. We're best friends. No one gets me the way Dev does. But . . .

"Your best friend?"

"I mean, don't get me wrong," Dev continues, clearly oblivious to my inner turmoil. "I still love Huan like a brother. He's been there for me through so much. And I know you have Sage—and Will, obviously—so you probably aren't looking for a best friend. But when we weren't talking . . . it made me realize how much I love hanging out with you." He shoves his hands in his pockets.

"I . . . yeah, me too."

"And I want you to know that I'm going to be cool about Will from now on. No more *Willoughby* or any of that. I know I had my opinions before, but if Will is willing to move to America to be with you, then clearly he really likes you. I'm sure you'll figure everything else out with him."

He gives me a small, hopeful smile and my heart disintegrates into ooze and starts to drip onto my liver. He's not going to say he loves me—because he doesn't love me. He wants to make sure we're still friends. Omigod, I did it again. It's like I'm back at Andy's party, waiting for him to say something that he's never going to say. How could I be so *stupid*? How could I let myself do this all over again? I want to slap myself. I've learned nothing. I'm no better now than I was all those months ago.

"You'll forgive me?" he asks. He's frowning now. I'm apparently not reacting the way he thought I would.

"Yes," I say quickly. "Yes, of course. Completely forgiven."

The worry slides off his face and he smiles. "Thank god. You had me worried for a second." He wanders out of the classroom and I follow him back toward the main corridor. He rubs his hands together. "Okay, so I had another thought. Do you remember how you asked me to tutor you in cricket so you could impress Will?"

How could I forget? The irony of that now. I force myself to nod.

"Well, I was thinking it was time for you to return the favor. Things didn't work out with Sage, which is fine. I'm happy to be better friends with her now, but I still need a girlfriend." He raises an eyebrow. "I'm determined to have a date for prom this year. A real date, not a pity date like last year."

I can see where this is going and my whole body revolts at the idea. I want to slap my hand over his mouth before the words come out. *Please* don't ask me.

"So, what do you say? Can I enlist you to help me when we get back to Waterford? I'm useless on my own, as you love to point out."

Find a date for Dev? *No!* I can't do that. But the alternative is to blurt out what I'm feeling and I can't do that either. He's just made it abundantly clear that we're friends and he wants to date other girls. I'm not strong enough to throw myself at him and watch his expression change from shock into pity. It was painful enough with Andy. Having that happen with Dev would crack my heart in half. I wouldn't survive it.

I plaster a smile on my face. "Yeah, okay. Sure. I'll start looking when we get back." An idea pops into my head that makes me genuinely laugh. "Maybe I can set you up with Crystal."

Dev's laughter fills the empty room. "Oh god, can you imagine? We could go on double dates together."

It feels so good to laugh with him, but also like my whole body is fraying into a million strands. Someday that's going to happen. He'll start dating someone and I'll have to go on a double date with them. Me, Dev, some girl, and . . . Will? *Will.* My stomach sinks. Oh god. I can't keep dating Will when I'm feeling this way about someone else. I push my hands into my forehead and then through my hair. What am I going to say to him? He's going to hate me.

"So I'll see you at dinner soon?" Dev's tone is still mercifully light. "You can't avoid me anymore."

"No dinner for me. I haven't started our art history paper yet so I'm barricading myself in the conservatory until I have something decent to turn in."

"Do you want some company?" he asks.

"Isn't your anatomy final tomorrow? I figured you'd be studying with Huan and the rest of your study group all night."

"Oh, I—" He frowns and shakes his head. "I don't have anything going on. That is, if you don't mind me hanging around."

My heart squeezes painfully. Of course I don't mind. But how the hell am I supposed to act normally around him now? Why does everything have to be so hard?

An hour later we're together again in the conservatory. It's busy here, but we manage to snag a small table in the back.

"You're doing your project on John William Waterhouse?" Dev grabs one of the books I found in the library, props his feet up on the armrest of my chair, and starts flipping through it. "I should have known."

My mind isn't remotely interested in art history right now, but I force myself to be normal. Dev is my friend and I need to be able to have conversations with him without morphing into an embarrassed ball of goo.

I point at a photo of *The Lady of Shalott*, one of my favorite pieces from Waterhouse. "He's the perfect choice. His art is gorgeous—each painting feels like I'm stepping inside a fantastical world—plus he's British. You know I'll get brownie points for that."

"You do have something there. Maybe I shouldn't have chosen Giorgione."

"Which one was he again? That name sounds familiar."

"Ellie!" Dev's absolutely aghast and it makes me smile. "We talked about him in class. *And* we saw his *La Tempesta* in Venice. Don't you remember? I told you all about the academic debate that surrounds it because experts can't agree about which biblical story it's depicting."

I avert my gaze. I was too distracted by *other* thoughts in Venice to remember the details of that painting.

"You're lucky I recognize his name."

"And you're lucky I don't pull out the flash cards and start quizzing you right now." He shakes his head in disgust. "She can remember every flower fairy drawn by Cicely Mary Barker, but she doesn't remember Giorgione. Art historians are rolling over in their graves right now."

"You're just grumpy that our class is over."

"I can't believe they don't offer a single art history class at Waterford," he mutters.

"Only *you* would complain about the lack of classes. Well, you and Sage." A thought occurs to me then. "Do you think we'll have lunch at the same time next semester?"

"We better." He looks up from the book. "It might not be too late for you to get into an AP class next semester. Then we'd all be together again. I'm sure they could move you around if your mom asked."

The idea scares me a bit, but not nearly as much as it would have at the beginning of the semester. It would be so great to have a class with Sage, Huan, and Dev again. I might even enjoy AP classes a bit . . . assuming it isn't more chemistry.

"I'll look into it," I tell him. "Mom will think I've lost my mind, though."

I focus on my biography of Waterhouse and Dev gets caught up reading through my reference books. I know I need to buckle down if I expect to finish a ten-page paper in one night, but I keep sneaking glances at him while he reads. Will it be like this when we get back to Waterford? Or will our study sessions fall by the wayside once he starts dating someone new? Maybe our friendship will fade altogether. It's hard to be best friends with one person while you're dating another . . . as I well know.

Dev looks up and catches me staring. His lips twist in a small smile. "Having a hard time concentrating?"

I turn to the pond, flustered. "Just wondering what it's going to be like to leave all this."

"*Hard.* Particularly leaving these views." He glances around the conservatory. "You really did an amazing job here."

My chest puffs with pride. "Actually, that reminds me. Do you remember that afternoon I caught you playing Quidditch and it was the best day ever?"

He chuckles. "How could I forget?"

"Well, I never told you I was at the park that day for a fairy gardening class. It turned out to be for little kids, but it got me thinking about teaching my own classes when we get back home. I've sent out a few emails to local businesses that might want to host me."

"That sounds *perfect* for you, Ellie."

I beam. "Yeah? I don't know, it seemed kinda crazy at first—me basically starting my own little business—and childish too. But I don't care about that now. Why not teach classes if that's what I like to do?"

"Can I bring my sisters to it?"

I squeal and clap my hands together. "Yesssssss! And bring Sahil too! You never know who's going to love fairy gardens." I dance in my seat, thinking about the different projects I could teach. Maybe I could even expand it into a monthlong class and the kids could build a whole fairy garden in time for the summer? I can't wait to get started planning. The fact that Dev and his family might come too makes it even better.

I grab one of the reference books to look up more facts about Waterhouse's life, but only one fact stays in my head. I'm seeing Will tomorrow and when I do, I have to break up with him. I can't pretend I feel the same way about Will that I do for Dev. I was so oblivious for all these months and now it's so clear. Dev's snarky humor and his teasing smiles and the way he always knows exactly what to say to get under my skin and make me laugh at the same time. I don't know how I was so blind before . . . or why Dev is still so blind now.

chapter
39

The next morning, I'm too jittery to sleep. Will and I aren't meeting in Northampton until noon for his lunch break, but I decide to leave early. The city is even more charming in December. Twinkling Christmas lights and wreaths decorate the storefronts and there's a festive, cheery energy in the air. Will gave me an address, and I'm expecting it to be a restaurant, but instead it's an open-air market like the one where we met, except this is a Christmas market. Pine and cinnamon waft through the air and wooden stalls decorated with garlands line the walkways. I'm surrounded by a sea of lights and Christmas trees and enough ornaments and knickknacks to fill a cathedral. I might as well be standing in the North Pole. It's delightful but I'm too nervous to truly enjoy it.

He didn't specify a particular meeting spot in the market, and I'm close to an hour early, so I distract myself with shopping. I find a knitting needle ornament for Sage and a bowling ball for Huan. He'll get it, even if no one else remembers. I continue meandering up and down the aisles before eventually stopping in my tracks at a blown glass ornament of a snitch. Memories of Dev and me laughing hysterically in the rain flood through me. He'll love it. I can already imagine his expression when he first opens it. The shine in his eyes, followed by a mischievousness at the secret he's kept from everyone but me.

My heart squeezes at the image and it strengthens my resolve. After I've talked to Will today, I have to suck up all the courage I have left and tell Dev how I feel. He might have other plans for the end of his senior year, but I don't want to spend these next months pretending around him the way I did with Will. I'm willing to risk the heartbreak again. Because he was right about me all along—I've been running and hiding and changing myself to fit molds I don't even recognize. I'm done running now. And if that means getting hurt, then so be it. It's better than trying to be someone I'm not.

"Elle?"

Will strolls down the aisle toward me, still so handsome in his peacoat, but my heart doesn't leap at the sight like it once did. Instead, cold dread rolls through me.

"What do you think?" He gestures around us at the stands. His eyes are bright with excitement, his cheeks pink from the cold. "Isn't it great?"

"It's beautiful here." I quickly hand the snitch to the person running the booth.

"What's that?" Will asks. "You're buying a flying ball?"

I stare up at him. He's still gorgeous and charming and breath-takingly British. But he's also very, *very* different from me.

I sign my receipt with shaky hands and walk down the path a few steps.

"Can we find a place to sit? I thought we could talk a bit."

"Yes, definitely," he replies. Either he doesn't notice my tone or he's ignoring it. "There's a place up ahead that's supposed to have the best mince pies."

I let him lead me to the stand but pull him to an outdoor table before we can order. I take a steadying breath and force myself to meet his eye. I can't believe I'm about to do this—or that I'm in this position to begin with—but I know I don't have a choice.

"Will, you are such an amazing person, but . . . but I don't think we should keep dating."

His eyes bulge. "Wait . . . *what*? Are you . . . you can't possibly be breaking up with me?"

"It's just . . ." My mind flails for something to say that's truthful but not hurtful. I don't think those words exist. "I'm just not sure we're compatible. We . . . we have different interests and things."

"What are you going on about? We have the same interests."

"Those are your interests," I whisper. My face is hot and my throat burns. "I make fairy gardens. And I like unicorns, and Jane Austen, and *Mind the Gap* shirts." I take a deep breath. "And I don't like beer . . . or cricket. I just learned about it to make you happy."

"You did?" The pain and confusion in his voice make me nauseous.

"I am so, so sorry," I whisper. "I never meant to hurt you. I . . . I didn't think you'd like me if you knew much about me."

"Because I'm that much of an arse?"

"No, the opposite. You were too perfect."

"This is about someone else, isn't it? That wanker, Dev."

I can't deny that. But it's not only about Dev. Without knowing it, Will forced me to figure out who I really want to be. And I don't want to be Elle any longer.

"Did you even care about me?" Will whispers furiously. "Or was I just a way to make him jealous?"

"No, of course not! I would never do that."

"How should I know? It sounds like you're a pretty skilled liar." He glares into the distance. "And I've seen how he looks at you."

"I'm so sorry, Will. Truly. You are an amazing person. I never meant for it to be this way."

He sits back. "And I was going to move to America. . . ."

"You still should," I say urgently. "Maybe major in business so you know how to invest in all those awesome ideas you have."

He snorts.

"Seriously, don't give up on it. You'll be *insanely* popular there."

We sit in silence for a moment, and then Will pushes away from the table. I stand up with him. Then he swivels to me.

"It was Venice, wasn't it?"

I freeze. "What?"

"I should never have left you at the airport. If I had gone . . ." His hands drop limply at his sides. "Things would be different if we'd been together in Venice."

Maybe he's right. It's hard to not be affected by the romance of the lapping water and hidden canals and cold, starry nights spent with another person. But then I think about Dev and me laughing over Quidditch and studying in his secret room. How he caught me on the subway and took care of me on the flight. How he immediately drove me crazy. How I did the same to him. And it makes me think Venice was only fuel added to a fire.

chapter
40

Acid pools in my stomach as I get off the van and walk into the cool corridor of Emberton. The reality of what I'm about to do sinks in. Oh god. Oh *god*. I have to talk to Dev. I debate taking a brisk walk around the manor first, or maybe grabbing a snack from the cafeteria, or locking myself in a bathroom stall and not coming out until everyone is back in America. But I know if I wait, it'll only get harder to be around him. I take a breath and force my legs to move.

As I walk up the stairs to his floor, my mind fills with the memory of meeting him here on my first day. I think my heart will explode by the time I finally knock on his door.

Huan opens it, looking tired. "Hey."

"Hey. Is, um, I mean, can I talk to Dev?"

He squints in confusion. "Dev's still finishing his exam."

Some of the pressure lifts from my chest and I suck in another breath. "What exam?"

"His anatomy exam. He didn't talk about it last night?"

"I mentioned your study group but he said you weren't doing it."

Huan snorts. "Oh, did he? Well, that's a big fat lie. And I'm officially blaming you for my lack of sleep."

"What'd I do?"

"*You're* the reason Dev skipped out on our study group. Instead he stayed up until four a.m., studying and waking me up to ask asinine questions about our material." Huan nods down the hall. "Speak of the devil."

I turn and my stomach lodges itself firmly in my throat. Dev strides toward me and it's all I can do not to launch myself into his arms. When I turn back to Huan, he's already shutting the door.

"Ellie, what are you doing here? I thought you were spending the day with Will?"

I try to speak, but my throat is too tight. My entire body is trembling. I force myself to take a deep breath. This is Dev. No matter what happens, he's not going to hurt me.

"I broke up with Will."

His eyes go wide. "What? Are you okay?"

"I'm not sure yet."

"Did he do something to you?" He steps protectively toward me. "Is that why you're—"

"No," I say quickly. "It wasn't anything like that. I broke up with him because . . . because of Venice. And art history and Quidditch and secret study rooms. And fairy gifts. And late-night study sessions when someone *should* have been with his study group."

His mouth, which had been clamped shut, drops open slightly in shock. He doesn't look upset or disgusted, though. I take that as a good sign and keep going.

"I'm so glad you consider me your best friend. And I know

I'm probably about to mess everything up, but I can't pretend that I only want to be friends. It took me way too long, but I finally realized I want to be with someone who *gets* me. Someone who likes my quirks and obsessions and makes me laugh until I can't breathe. Will could never do that." I swallow hard. "Not like you do."

He transforms in front of me then. His furrowed brow and stiff posture melt away. His eyes turn soft and warm, a beautiful deep brown just the way they were when we first met on the stairs. He takes a step forward and all my fears evaporate. We're close enough now that I need to look up in order to see his face, and I realize that my mom was right all those months ago. Nothing compares with the look on someone's face when they realize you love them as much as they love you.

"You broke up with him for me?"

I nod.

"You can't imagine how many times I've hoped you'd say that. It's been killing me pretending I don't care."

"Pretending? But what about prom and double dates and all that stuff?"

He laughs roughly. "You believed that? I must be the best actor in the world."

Tears spring to my eyes and I blow out a shaky breath. I'm about to collapse with relief and happiness. "I'm sorry it took me this long," I whisper. "I should have known how you felt. How *I* felt."

He combs my hair away from my face, making me shiver. "And how do you feel?"

"Like you're still standing too far away from me."

His lips spread into a roguish grin I've never seen before. Then he pulls me to him, pressing his mouth to mine like he's suffocating and I'm his only source of oxygen. Heat and light explode behind my eyes. I wind my arms around his neck and he falls back against the wall. His hands slide up my sides to the back of my neck and twist into my hair. I kiss the corner of his mouth and skim my lips along his jawline. He groans, low and hoarse, which only makes me kiss him harder.

Eventually, we loosen our holds on each other, our chests heaving and bodies shaking. We stare at each other in dazed wonder. How have we gone so many months without doing this? We should have been kissing from the moment we met. It's as if we *have* been kissing since that moment. As if our mouths were created for this purpose alone.

"I didn't think it was possible for this to be better than I imagined it," he says between uneven breaths.

"Oh, so you've imagined kissing me before?" I run my lips down his jawline again and his fingers dig into my back.

"I haven't done much else in weeks."

Obviously that makes me kiss him again. This time he spins me so I'm pressed up against the wall. I'd be happy to never leave this spot.

The door cracks open. "Ughhh. You guys do know I can hear everything you say out there."

We both jump. I'd forgotten about everything but Dev.

"I'm happy you've stopped torturing yourselves," Huan

whisper-calls, "but some of us are trying to nap after a brutal exam."

"Get some earplugs, then," Dev calls back, and dips his head to kiss my neck.

"Get a room. One that doesn't already have someone sleeping in it."

Dev is about to retort, but I tug his hand. I have an idea. "Do you think your secret study room is empty?"

That perfect new grin of his returns. "There's only one way to find out."

chapter

41

The next morning, I'm back in the Long Gallery of Ember-ton. This is where Mr. Odell made his welcoming speech on our first day and I couldn't concentrate from nerves and elation. I still can't concentrate, but that's because I'm waiting for someone.

People stream past toward the breakfast room. Among the students is a knot of professors. One of them breaks off and walks over to me. Dr. Lotfi.

"Ellie, have you seen Dev this morning?"

"Um, actually I was waiting for him. Is something wrong?"

"Just tell him to find me later today. I have the information his parents wanted about undergraduate programs."

"Oh, um—you do?"

She shrugs. "A lot of parents are scared of the humanities at first. But he shouldn't worry. They usually come round."

"Right. Good to know." My thoughts swirl as she walks away. He actually talked to his parents about art history? Just when I thought I knew everything about Dev, he surprises me again.

It's surreal to walk onto the sidelines of the Quidditch field holding Dev's hand. Mostly because I never thought I'd date anyone
who ran around a field with a broomstick between his legs. But
then, I don't have room for superiority, since I've got my unicorn
hoodie on, rainbow mane flowing down my back. Dev and I make
quite the pair.

I lean in and kiss him again. I can't seem to stop doing that.
"I'll see you after the game, okay?"

But rather than let me go, he grins and pulls me toward the
bleachers on the other side of the field. "Come with me."

The bleachers aren't full by any means, but there are enough
people that I won't be completely alone. There's a group of younger
kids wearing Gryffindor scarfs, others wearing Slytherin or Raven-
claw colors. A few people are brandishing wands.

Someone catches my eye. It's . . . Sage. And there's Frank
and—I have to lean forward to get a closer look—Huan is wearing
a huge lion hat like Luna Lovegood. I burst out laughing. And I
thought today couldn't get better.

"You made it!" Huan shouts when we get closer. "I was scared
you two would get caught up and forget to come."

I twist toward Dev. "You finally told them about Quidditch?"

"I felt bad denying them all these new ways to laugh at me."

"But now I don't have anything to blackmail you with."

"I'm sure you'll come up with something soon," he says, and
kisses me.

"Ellie, come over here with us!" Huan waves me up. He's like a giddy little kid still high from opening Christmas presents. "Are you ready for what we're about to witness? Dev playing *Quidditch*! He's freaking Indian Harry Potter!"

Dev laughs. "I don't play seeker."

"And he wouldn't be in Gryffindor," Sage adds.

Huan waves them off. "Doesn't matter, it's still the best thing in the world. The teams were just practicing down there. One of the players ran around trying to reach into another guy's shorts to get a tennis ball—" Huan's laughing too loud to finish.

"That was brilliant!" Frank adds. "And look how ridiculous Huan is!" He points at the lion hat. "Mate, you've got to sign it after the game. And we need pictures."

To my surprise, Dev doesn't look embarrassed. Well, not *that* embarrassed. In fact, he pulls me closer and poses for the camera.

After a few shots, Frank holds the phone out for me. "Do you mind?"

I nod and bite my lip. He seems to understand what I'm asking without words.

"No hard feelings," he replies quietly. "He'll always be one of my closest mates and I hate to see him down, but I think it's for the best. I talked to him this morning and he'll bounce back."

I nod, grateful, and take a photo of the boys together. Sage steps up next to me.

"You look happy. Are you feeling good?"

"Definitely." I look back at Dev, who is now pretending to fly for the camera. "I'm great. As long as you're okay with . . ."

"Of course. It was clear you two were going to get together.

It was only a matter of waiting for you both to stop being idiots."

That would be an insult from anyone else, but it only makes me want to hug Sage.

"You still owe me a scarf, you know," I tell her. "I haven't forgotten."

"I *may* have been working on something for you. But you'll have to wait until Christmas to see it."

I rub my hands together eagerly, already imagining exchanging presents back home with the group. Someone on the field blows a whistle and Dev is next to me in a second.

"For good luck," he says, and kisses me long enough that the guys start catcalling.

He runs down to the field, and my friends press around me, cheering and calling out made-up spells. I can't stop laughing. Dev was right. Life can be messy and difficult.

And really, *really* great.

acknowledgments

Even though I've been writing since elementary school, it took me a long time to believe my publication dream could become a reality. Now that it has, I have so many people to thank. First, thank you to my agent, Tara Gonzalez, who believed in this story from the beginning. I'm so grateful you took a chance on me. To my editor, Catherine Wallace, for being supportive, attentive, and giving me fabulous advice that made Ellie's story so much stronger. Thank you for making my childhood dream come true. And to everyone at HarperCollins who helped make this book a reality, including Caitlin Lonning, Kimberly Stella, Chris Kwon, Shannon Cox, and Mitchell Thorpe. A special shout-out to Jacqueline Li for illustrating the *best* possible cover!

I am blessed to have a big support system that helped me get here. There are many names but they all deserve a shout-out! Thank you to all my SCBWI friends who listened to updates about this book for years, and to the Highlights Foundation Whole Novel Workshop participants and faculty, including Sarah Aronson, Jennifer Jacobson, Amanda Jenkins, Melissa Wyatt, Rob Costello, and Nicole Valentine. A special round of applause goes to my mentor, Nancy Werlin, for seeing the first potential in this story *and* suggesting my book title. I am eternally grateful to the entire PitchWars community and especially my PitchWars mentors, Carrie Allen and Sabrina Lotfi. I wouldn't be writing these acknowledgments without you. I love you! #TeamGirlPower forever!

To all my early readers and critique partners who kept me going through revisions: the Highlighters, Laurence King, Stephanie Cardel, Holly Ruppel, Keely Parrack, Becky Gehrisch, and Diane Mungovan. I am so grateful to Debbi Michiko Florence for believing in me and cheering me on through the years. We did it, Debbi! And Kathryn Powers, our Chinese buffets, late-night pancakes, and unicorn GIFs got me through many rough days! I couldn't have done it without you!

To all my nonwriter friends, including Missy, Anna, Kristin, Courtney, Kristy, Beth, David, and Emmett, for keeping me grounded and celebrating the successes with me! Maggie Stevenson, what can I say?! We started writing (adorably bad) stories together as children and you've been with me every step of the way since then. Thank you for being such a passionate supporter of this book! I'm so grateful we're best friends.

To all my family for their support, most especially my parents. I'm thankful to have parents who always encourage my aspirations and dreams. I love you both. Dad, thanks for being my first reader.

Finally, I don't have the pages needed to express my love for Mike and Liam. Liam, you make every day brighter and happier. I love you and I can't wait for you to read these words. I told you I'd put you in the book!

Mike, thank you for *always* believing in me, for helping me prioritize my writing no matter what sacrifices you have to make, and for picking me up (sometimes literally) when I'm at my lowest. You're the reason I write YA romance. You taught me that high school sweethearts can last a lifetime.